Consumed

Cursed Magic Series: Book 4

Casey Odell

This is a work of fiction. Names, characters, places, and incidents either are the product of the author's imagination or are used fictiously, and any resemblance to actual persons, living or dead, business establishments, events, or locales is entirely coincidental.

Copyright © 2018 Casey Odell

Editing by Caitlin Carpenter

All rights reserved.
No part of this publication may be reproduced, distributed, or transmitted in any form or by any means, including photocopying, recording, or other electronic or mechanical methods, without the prior written permission of the publisher, except in the case of brief quotations embodied in critical reviews and certain other noncommercial uses permitted by copyright law.

To everyone who still believed in me.

1

Claire hit the ground hard.

It was the second time it had happened since she'd set out on her own. She'd fallen asleep while atop her horse, and well, her balance had never been the best. Bruises had already formed on her sides and she hadn't even seen any action yet—nothing notable, anyway. She was just so *tired*. The mark and its effects on her were getting stronger. The pendant seemed to barely keep her magic at bay anymore. Her time was running short.

It had already been weeks since she'd left the palace. She'd made a stop at the Haven to leave Farron's horse there, hoping that it would be the first place he would stop coming back to Derenan. To say that Maria and her daughter weren't exactly thrilled to see her instead of Farron was an understatement. It was definitely one of the more uncomfortable moments in recent memory. And she'd once faced two Beasts of Old… She'd made a hasty retreat from the Haven, not wanting to expose herself to their stares any longer than she had to, or them to Bahkar and the multitude of other people after her.

She'd crossed the Great Rift a few days before. Only this time, she'd admired the view—from a safe vantage point, of course. She may have gotten a little braver, but not about heights. She'd gawked at the enormity of it, the vastness. It was amazing that magic could cause such destruction and permanently alter the very earth. It had given her pause about her mission. Was restoring magic the right thing to do if all it had led to in the past was devastation and the oppression of humans? Would history repeat itself?

Though there might have been some selfishness in her reasoning, the land was dying and about to erupt in chaos once again without magic. At least with magic, everyone would have a fighting chance. Hopefully. She *had* to believe she was doing the right thing.

The days were cold now and they were only growing colder on her northern trek. She'd bundled up tightly in her jacket and a thick woolen cloak from the palace. Uru Baya was high in the Solinian Mountains and most likely freezing. But it was where she had to go for answers... and hope.

Claire slowly got up from the hard dirt road and dusted off her clothes. Her joints were stiff from the cold. She groaned as her body protested with pain. Why did things hurt more in the cold? Azra snorted, having stopped when she'd fallen. What a good horse. Claire stroked her forehead.

"Sorry girl," Claire said in a soft tone.

The sun was sinking toward the horizon. The day was almost over. She'd need to set up camp soon and start a fire, a task that was much easier these days with magic. She wondered what Farron and the other Star Children would say if they saw what she used her mighty magical powers for. But it was much handier than trying to use a flint or other means.

Claire smiled as she led Azra from the road into the trees. It had been a lonely few weeks. Her only companions lately seemed to be the scenarios she'd dreamed of in her mind, her memories, and a horse, though, she supposed it could be worse. She'd definitely had worse travel mates...

Consumed

After brushing down Azra and starting a fire, Claire sat before the warm flames, clutching her cloak tight around her. There was a small village just before reaching Uru Baya. She shouldn't be more than a few more days away from there. And then?

She sighed. She was putting a lot of her hopes in Uru Baya. But what if she didn't find any answers there? What would she do then? Just how would the mark consume her? It was a fate she was not looking forward to, that was for sure. She shook her head of the thoughts. She had to think more positively. She wouldn't be able to do any of this if she let herself sink down into the deep dark hole of despair.

Soon she found her eyelids growing heavy. She was too tired to even worry about her safety, sleeping alone under the stars in the woods. But sleep swallowed her up before she could do anything about it. Just like the night before and the one before that.

Samota was really more of a gathering of buildings than a village, a sort of hub for the local farms and other even smaller villages in the area. There was one inn that doubled as a tavern and stables. A market and a spattering of other buildings completed the village. Claire's breath escaped her like smoke, though her insides were anything but warm. The air was thinner here, making her feel a little lightheaded. Suspicious glances from the villagers were the first hint that they didn't get many visitors—especially a lone woman. Claire took a deep breath and proceeded to the inn, Azra in tow. She clutched the purse at her side. She had some gold thanks to Lianna's insistence, not that Claire had protested too much. She didn't have a lot to her name these days.

She found a boy napping in a bale of hay in the stables next to the inn, who'd seemed surprised to see a visitor. After she reluctantly left Azra with him, she entered the inn, stomping the dirt from her boots. Wary eyes settled on her, but her diminutive, innocent appearance worked in her favor at times, their suspicion turning into curiosity before returning to their drinks. The place was simple, reminding her of the inn she had stayed at back in Lendon, only much less rowdy and crowded. Heavy wooden beams supported the walls and crisscrossed the ceiling. A stone hearth took up most of the back wall, filling the room with a hazy smoke. And best of all, it was warm. She could feel her extremities slowly start to defrost.

Claire walked up to the bar and the old man behind the counter eyed her up and down as he wiped dry a wooden mug.

"A new face," he said, his voice gruff. His thick gray mustache was trim and tidy, matching his hair. "Not many of those around here."

She didn't know what to say to that. She figured the less anyone knew, the better. His eyes drifted down to her neck where the mark peeked above the cloak. Curiosity was there, but Claire distracted him, saying, "I would like a room if you have any available." And she hoped that they did, or else she'd be joining the stable boy in the hay. Claire brushed her cloak aside to show her purse.

The man glanced down and nodded, not asking any questions, much to her relief. He slid a key across the bar. "Two gold," he said.

Claire's jaw dropped. "That's absurd!" she nearly shouted, drawing attention to her once more. "One at most." Even that was exorbitant. Highway robbery is what it was.

"Where else you gonna sleep?" he shot back, a grin forming.

Claire contemplated the stables, even if it was to prove a point. She started to turn away, lamenting her stubbornness, when the man sighed.

Consumed

"Fine," he said. "One gold."

She had to stifle the smile on her face before turning back to him. Though really, she was just relieved. The stables smelled. She dug in her purse and set the gold piece on the counter—even if it was still too high for such simple lodgings.

"You weren't really gonna sleep out there, were ya?" The man gave her a skeptical look.

"You weren't really going to charge two gold for this, were you?" She motioned around her. The man's smug look faltered. "A hot meal and bath better be included."

The man snorted, amused. "Yeah yeah, off with ya then."

Claire took the key and headed for the stairs in the back, lugging her heavy pack, filled with what little she did own. The number two was engraved on the brass key. Claire found her room at the end of the short hall on the second floor. It was small and dark and definitely not worth the price, but it would have to do. A window above the bed revealed the gray skies outside and a surprisingly pretty view of the mountains beyond, white tipped and imposing.

After she set her pack at the end of the bed, she sprawled out across it. Its lumps dug into her, but she was too tired to care. The hike up the mountain had been exhausting, even though Azra did most of the work. Her eyes were just drifting closed when a knock came at the door.

With a sigh, Claire hoisted herself off the bed and answered it, preparing for the crotchety owner, but was surprised to find the stable boy doing double duty as other help. Guess it was hard to come by in such a place.

He held up a flint and some logs.

She opened the door wider to let him in. She hadn't even noticed the small fireplace on the right wall. He silently lit the fire, making the task look way too easy. He gave her a slight smile on the way out in a bashful manner. After he was gone, Claire sat on the edge of the bed and took out her purse. She counted the coins she had left. Even though Lianna had been generous, she would have to be more careful and make it last.

Her stomach growled thinking of the hot meal the owner might or might not provide. There was only one way to find out.

After a rather unsatisfying meal of bland stew, Claire journeyed back out into the cold. She shouldn't have expected much, she supposed, but at least it was warm and filling. Still, it was a departure from her usual fare these days. Across the street, a few stalls were set up for farmers and other tradesmen to sell their wares. She needed to restock her supplies. Who knew where the journey ahead would lead?

After buying some cheese and a loaf of bread, Claire was browsing the rest of the sparse market when a hand grabbed her by the wrist. Instinctively, her free hand went to the dagger at her side, the food falling into the dirt. Her heart racing, she faced the accoster. Then froze. Relief washed over her instantly. The stature of the man was tall and menacing, but Claire knew better.

"Fare," she whispered, her breath escaping in a sigh.

He lowered the hood of his thick black cloak. His usual shock of white hair was dyed to match the rest of his somber attire—which only made the blue of his eyes stand out more.

Before she could say anything more, he swept her up in a tight hug, her feet hanging helplessly above the ground.

"I see you received my message," she managed to squeeze out. She could hardly breathe. Before she could faint from air deprivation, he set her back on the ground and cupped her face in his hands.

"You're all right?" He brushed her hair from the right side of her neck and eyed the mark.

Consumed

She nodded. There was no use hiding the fact that the mark had spread even more since she'd last seen him, crawling higher up her neck and down her shoulder to start overtaking her back. "As much as I can be, I suppose. Are you?"

"I am now." He pressed his lips on her forehead, then the bridge of her nose, finally landing on her lips. The kiss was soft at first, but quickly grew with a burning passion.

The sensation of prying eyes made Claire draw back. She took a deep breath to gather herself, straightening her cloak around her again. She looked about, feeling a little embarrassed, and confirmed her suspicions. The elderly stall owner a few paces away averted her gaze suddenly, blushing herself.

"Although I'm glad you're in one piece, perhaps we should go somewhere a little warmer…" She bent to pick up her fallen wares and brushed off the dirt. They were still good.

She led the way to the inn, Farron and his horse in tow. The same boy from before rushed into the stable, out of breath. Claire almost felt bad for him, having to work so hard, when she remembered how she first came across him, napping buried in the hay. Perhaps he wasn't as overworked as she thought. His eyes went wide when he saw Farron. He'd probably never seen an elf before, especially one that looked as intimidating as Farron. He took Farron's horse without a word.

As they were entering the inn Claire said, "I don't know if your new hair color makes you more or less menacing."

Farron chuckled. "I was hoping for inconspicuous."

The tavern part of the inn was more crowded than before as people took off for the day to enjoy a pint or two. Or three. Several heads turned in their direction, a few with obvious shock as they spied the strange elf. But they all quickly went back to their drink, most likely thanks to a glare from said elf.

The fire was bright and crackling when she entered her room again, making it warm and cozy. Claire stripped off her cloak and went to the hearth to thaw her hands. She heard the clinking of Farron's weaponry being set on the wood floor.

"You got here faster than I thought," she said, gazing into the flames. "Honestly, I wasn't sure if you would get my message at all." She turned to face him. "I'm glad you did—"

He grabbed her then as he sat on the edge of the bed, pulling her onto his lap. After she recovered from the shock of it, she sat up, straddling him. He buried his face in her neck, his lips tracing along her skin, his breath warm.

Claire shivered slightly, losing her train of thought.

"When I came back, you were gone," he said softly. "I didn't know where you went, who took you…"

She stroked his hair in a calming manner. That *would* be frightening, to have someone you loved just taken from you.

"But there's not many people that could leave no trail." A hint of anger crept into his voice. "So I rode, I walked, night and day, until I reached the Haven and my suspicions were confirmed. Next time I see that Council Dog, it won't be a happy meeting."

"Were they ever?" Claire mused.

A short laugh rumbled his chest. "I suppose not."

"Your ears are cold," she said as her hands brushed against them. They were like icicles. She guessed he meant what he said about riding day and night, even in the cold. He must have been exhausted.

"Hmm." His lips moved up to her jaw as his hands slipped off her jacket. Goosebumps raced down her skin. "You'll just have to warm them up then." He pulled her down on top of him on the bed and Claire happily obliged, losing herself in him once again.

Consumed

Moonlight shone in a sliver between the curtains. The fire had died down to a few glowing embers. She would have been freezing if she weren't snuggled under the blankets and furs with an elf. Her head rested on his shoulder as she traced circles absentmindedly on his chest.

"All the Star Children are gathered," she said. "All except for… that madman." She avoided saying his name, fearing it would somehow summon him. The thought seemed silly, but she never knew with the things she had seen. "I'm still not sure it was the right thing to do. I freed them from one prison and delivered them to another."

"You just did what you thought was right, Claire. You didn't know you were being used."

His words were only slightly reassuring. If she found a way to restore magic to the land, would they be free? There was no telling what would happen if she did. One step at a time. She was at least confident they were in the right hands with Lianna and Razi, now that he had seen the Council's true nature.

"Do you think we'll find anything?" she asked. If they didn't find answers in Uru Baya, then where would they?

"I don't know," he said, his voice solemn with truth. "There's only one way to find out. And if we don't, we'll look somewhere else, and we'll keep looking." He gave her shoulder a squeeze before moving out from under her. He reached down and dug around in his pack.

Claire sat up, the cold air dulled by her curiosity.

Silver glinted in the low light as Farron produced the familiar contraption. Shackles. She was both happy and sad to see the magical device once again. The memories associated with it were definitely not good ones. But it was a necessary evil. One that may help keep her powers at bay. And maybe even the madman. She touched the cold metal, the craftsmanship simple and surprisingly elegant for such a device.

"Are you sure you want to wear this, Claire?"

"I don't *want* to," she said, letting her hand fall away from it. "But I think I have to. Not here though. The others may sense me—or rather they suddenly won't. If they're alarmed, they may come running."

Farron nodded and laid back, holding the contraption up to examine it. "Such powerful magic in such a small thing."

Claire snuggled against him again, pulling the covers up around her. "Are you talking of me or it?"

Her eyes drifted closed as she listened to the soft rumble of laughter in his chest. Soon they would find answers, she hoped.

The world was covered in white the next morning. A blanket of fresh snow had fallen overnight. They'd left the horses back in the village, with some gold and threats from Farron, as the trail up to Uru Baya was not suited for them according to the locals. The path wasn't as maintained as the one up to Samota. Many of the villagers had looked at them suspiciously as they'd left. No one visited Uru Baya. No one came from Uru Baya. The place was as much a mystery to its neighbors as the rest of the world.

It was midday and Claire's legs and feet were tired already from the relentless uphill hike. The snow seemed to muffle everything and the pine forest that lined the trail was eerie. Beautiful, but too quiet. The only sound came from the crunch of her boots beneath her. The sun was hidden behind overcast clouds, the wind biting. Her fingers and toes, pretty much her entire body, were numb, but somehow still in pain.

Consumed

Her foot caught on a rock for the twentieth time since they'd started out and Claire hit the ground once again, a sharp yelp escaping her. She just laid in the snow for a few moments, savoring the brief break. How did she manage to find all the rocks? She'd been following along in Farron's path carefully.

She felt his shadow looming over her. She rolled over and just looked up at him. As usual, he seemed barely winded. How was he not exhausted already? Claire blamed the mark. As for being clumsy, well, she'd always been that.

Farron offered a hand and Claire just looked at it for a few moments. She didn't want to move again, not yet. But the impatient expression on his face spurred her into action. She hesitantly took his hand and he pulled her up with ease.

"They said it was at least a two-day hike to Uru," he said. "We shouldn't waste any more time than necessary."

There was a seriousness and coldness in his voice and demeanor she hadn't seen since he'd been the Ice Prince. What was with that? Claire nodded and he turned and continued on his way. Claire brushed the snow from her, shaking out her cloak as well. Her joints ached with each movement, her bruises adding to the pain.

Claire watched Farron. Surely he had a lot on his mind. He was tense, lost in his own world, barely having said a word to her in hours. But she had a remedy for that.

She bent and picked up a handful of snow, shaping it into a ball with her gloved hands, and, with her best effort, threw it at the elf, hitting him on the shoulder. Not exactly her target, but it would have to do. He stopped and slowly turned toward her.

Claire covered her smile with her hands. She had poked a sleeping bear, but it *was* funny. She'd caught him off guard finally. She thought for sure he'd dodge it.

"Did you just throw a snowball at me?" he asked, eyes glaring with a menace reserved for his enemies.

A slight thrill ran through Claire, bringing with it much needed warmth.

An evil grin flashed across his face, breaking the tension immediately. "I believe that was a grave mistake, my lady." He set his pack on the ground and knelt, gathering snow up to form his own ball.

Like a girl half her age, Claire dropped to the ground and hurriedly started to gather more snow, giggling, feeling energized. Farron threw his before she could stand again, hitting her on the arm. She yelled, lurched to her feet and threw hers. He ducked swiftly, gathering another one as she did the same.

Soon they were both laughing, out of breath, covered in snow. But in those moments, their troubles were forgotten and they were allowed to be normal—if a little immature. Claire collapsed back into the snow, the exhaustion catching back up to her. Farron sat next to her, leaning back, finally winded himself.

"Sorry," Claire said. She looked up at him and smiled. "You just looked a little tense."

"Don't be," he said, a smile forming on his face. "I was." He leaned over her, placing a soft kiss on her forehead. "I'm just worried, is all. Lost in my thoughts."

Claire grabbed him and kissed him, long and deep to banish those thoughts. At the very least, it helped warm them both.

When he finally drew back he raised his eyebrows. "Well, that certainly helps." He stood then, pulling her up beside him. "Come," he said simply, keeping his hold on her hand. Claire obliged, feeling invigorated.

Before the sun set, they found a rather dismal area to camp under a rocky overhang. Remnants of an old fire told them they

Consumed

weren't the only ones that had stopped on their way up the mountain. How old it was, she couldn't tell. They settled in for the night, Farron having to start a fire with his powers much to Claire's amusement. So she wasn't the only one then? Mighty powers, mundane uses.

Uru Baya was a sharp contrast to Samota. Where the previous village had been a small group of unassuming buildings, the one that stood before them was a veritable fortress. High weathered walls of granite surrounded the front half, the mountain guarding the back. Thick doors blocked their entry.

Everything was quiet, still. Clouds shrouded the late day sun once again, threatening another snowfall.

Farron pushed on the doors, but they wouldn't budge. Then he pounded a fist on them three times and stepped back to wait for a reply of some sort.

Claire shivered. She hoped they wouldn't be stuck out in the cold. Surely they'd freeze.

A few minutes had gone by when a man finally appeared on the top of the wall to the side of the gate.

"What's your business here?" he shouted down to them. He gave them both once-overs, but he particularly focused on Farron.

"We've just come for answers," Farron replied.

"To what?"

Sensing the guard's hesitance, Claire revealed her arm, pushing up the sleeve of her jacket to show the mark. The man eyed it then nodded, disappearing once again.

A moment later a series of loud clicks sounded from the doors before they slowly opened, creaking and groaning.

Inside was much less intimidating and looked like almost any other small village. There were perhaps ten buildings in total, none bigger than her home back in Stockton. Made of stone and wood, they were half buried with thick roofs, some with multiple chimneys producing steady streams of smoke. They had to be in the right place. If not, then why the security?

The doors closed with a resounding thud behind her as if to illustrate her last point. The guard approached them, huddled under a thick cloak and furs. "This way." He led them to the largest building of the bunch and then entered.

Claire glanced at Farron and he just shrugged before following the man.

Inside was dim and smoky. And plain. Exposed stone made up the wall of the large circular room, and a fireplace stood at one end behind a line of cushions. The only decoration was the swirl-patterned rug underfoot that took up half the wooden floor.

They waited in the room as the guard disappeared again. Claire warmed herself by the fire, the feeling slowly returning to her fingers. She was glad that they had been let in. Whether or not they would be allowed to stay remained to be seen.

The door clicked open and the guard entered again followed by an older man—no, not a man, an elf. Claire kept her surprise contained. Was he an *elder*? He certainly looked ancient. Perhaps the forest elves had been on the right path. He used a staff to shuffle over to the largest cushion in front of Claire, looking her and Farron over with his faded blue eyes. Gray hair was shorn close to his head, different than most of the elves she'd crossed paths with in the past, who'd worn their hair longer. He stood, slightly hunched over, for a minute, taking Claire in. The guard stayed back by the door, his hand on a sword at his side.

"I suppose it was only a matter of time before one of you showed up here," the old elf said, his voice brittle but still deep. He turned his back to her and sat slowly on the cushion, groaning on the way down.

Claire came around to face him, unsure of what to say. Where would she even begin?

But Farron broke the silence first. "You know what she is?"

The elder nodded solemnly.

"Then we need your help."

Straight to the point, that one. Claire examined the old elf. He wore plain clothes, dark gray and monotone, thick and warm, matching the utilitarian design of the rest of the place.

The Elder looked Farron up and down. "And who sent you? Which king?"

Farron's eyebrows scrunched slightly, not looking pleased with the question.

"Don't be surprised. That dark hair of yours isn't fooling anyone. Just because we are at the top of the world doesn't mean we don't get news. It's my business to know these things." He settled his staff across his lap. "I know who you are, Farron, bastard son of King Earnehard, half-brother of King Líadan. Who used to serve in the court of King Ryaenon. I have eyes everywhere, connections like a web. Who do you serve? Who are you loyal to?"

"Her," he said plainly, nodding toward Claire.

The Elder raised his eyebrows. Claire could feel her cheeks grow hot, a little embarrassed.

The old elf looked at her. "Is that true?"

"I—" Claire hesitated, then glanced at Farron. After everything they'd been through, she knew it was true, it was just awkward hearing him say it out loud. "Yes." She turned back to the Elder.

The Elder chuckled. "Well, that is unexpected. Still, I do not know if you speak the truth. Not with your... colorful past."

She could see Farron shift slightly. His cold mask slipped into place, emotionless. She knew it stung him, that his past was still haunting him.

"I can't trust you, and if I don't trust you, I won't help you." The Elder held Farron's gaze, matching his iciness.

Claire swore the temperature dropped a couple degrees in the room.

"So that's it?" Farron asked. "All this way for nothing?"

"Understand, my knowledge can change the world. *Has* changed the world. There are walls around this place for a reason. I don't, I haven't, and I will not give my knowledge to anyone that just asks."

Farron clenched his fist, anger flashing in his eyes.

"Fare," Claire said and reached out to touch him. The sting of the Elder's words had hit her as well. Was there really no way? She had to think of a way to convince him.

Farron turned, pulling away, then stormed out the door, the guard smartly avoiding him.

Claire followed, hesitating at the door to glance back at the Elder. He looked after her, his eyes sad. The sky had grown gloomier, hiding the sun behind thick clouds. Farron stood in the middle of the courtyard, his face tilted up, eyes closed.

"I thought I would be able to escape it," he said when she drew near. "My past. I'm sorry, Claire." He turned to her, his expression matching the weather, dreary and full of regret. "It's because of me he won't talk."

Consumed

"We'll find a way," she said, reaching out to him again, only this time he didn't pull away. "We're so close. That this place exists, that *he* exists, means we still have hope." She squeezed his arm and gave him a slight smile. She didn't tell him that her hope was hanging on by a thread itself. That her panic was just as high, or higher than his.

"I can always *make* him talk," he said in a lowered voice. "I have ways, you know."

Claire hoped he was joking. "I think that is the type of thing he spoke of when he mentioned your colorful past."

Farron shrugged. "One way or another, we are not leaving here empty-handed."

He had made the statement seem lighthearted, but Claire knew better. She knew what desperation could drive men, and elves, to.

"Miss Tanith," the guard called from the doorway to the building.

Claire turned to face him. Hearing her name come from him was a little strange since she'd never given it to him. At least the Elder hadn't been lying when he said he had eyes and ears everywhere.

The guard stepped aside and motioned for her to come. She glanced at Farron, but the guard said, "Alone."

Farron crossed his arms, not happy, but he didn't protest either. The first light flutters of snow started to fall and he looked back up at the sky.

With a deep breath, Claire went back into the room with the Elder. When she did, the guard stepped out into the cold and closed the door behind him, leaving Claire to fend for herself. The old elf remained sitting cross-legged on the cushion in front of the blazing, crackling fire.

"Come, sit," he said, gesturing with a hand in front of him.

Claire did as told, sinking slowly to the floor, unsure what he wanted.

"I may be old, but I can still sense magic," he said, his expression solemn. "And by the feeling I get from you, there is probably more than one reason you came to seek me out."

Claire nodded, gulping.

"Let's see it then."

Slowly, Claire began taking off her layers, growing colder with each one shed. She was shivering by the time the mark was exposed. She tilted her head to the side to show how it went up her neck and over her shoulder.

"I see," the Elder said. He sighed and it was long and mournful. "An unforeseen consequence," he mumbled, more to himself than Claire, it seemed. "I am sorry, child," he said to her this time. "There are many things we didn't foresee, *couldn't* foresee. What's happening to you, the land… we never planned for any of it."

Claire looked at him, trying to process what he was saying. "Do you mean—? Were you there? The Great War?"

The Elder nodded, his eyes clouding over with memories of ages past. "It was a dark time. If we hadn't done anything…" His eyes cleared as he looked at her. "I was there when it happened. I was one of the ones that helped seal away magic."

Her jaw dropped a little. It seemed he was more important than she, or probably anyone, knew. Not only was he there for the Great War, but if what he said was true, he was one of the reasons magic had disappeared from the land.

"We only did what we thought was right," he said, his eyes pleading like he was seeking her forgiveness. "The war was going on and on. And it worked, for a bit, what we did. What happened to you and whoever else got cursed with those marks, we are sorry. The sacrifice of a few for the good of all was what we believed."

"Who was *we*?" she asked, curious.

Consumed

The Elder shook his head, somewhat surprised at her question. A thoughtful look came over his face as he recalled the past. "*We were a coalition of men and elves who wanted peace between our races. We were small, and secretive because we had to be, a precursor to the Ophiuchus Syndicate, though nowhere near as insidious. Hume Sylnias*, they called us—human sympathizers. Back then the term was used like any curse word today. The movement grew, on both sides, until it was quashed and we had to retreat to the shadows."

Claire listened to him talk with rapt attention. "Then what happened?" It wasn't every day she heard history from so long ago, from someone who lived it.

"We escaped to the mountains in Derenan. King Earnehard was also a sympathizer, and it was one of the few safe places for us. We needed time to formulate a plan. A plan Rialla had researched for years. No one thought it would work, but we had to try. Seven humans volunteered. A knife in the back of elves." A short laugh escaped his lips, followed by a raspy cough. "Old magic, it was. That the spell even existed meant that the balance of power had been off long before elves ruled, though, they—the ones who'd crafted the spell—had never been foolish enough to use it. We sealed the magic away in the humans and hid them away, and thus changed the course of the war and history. The Ophiuchus Syndicate was born to protect the Star Children, only we couldn't control who the mark would be passed to. The spell had taken on a life of its own; such power, how could it not? And peace was known for the first time in years. My brothers and sisters were forced to pay for their evils and go into hiding. The age of humans. No one ever thought that would come to pass."

"What happened to them, the others that helped you?"

"They passed in their own time. I am the only one left, burdened with the weight of what we have done. We bought peace for a while, but the winds of war are stirring once again. There is unrest in the earth itself. I have felt it. Heard the stories of the Beasts of Old, once tamed and sealed by my brethren, ravaging the land once again. I fear what we have done has only set the stage for something much worse. Only now we have lost the knowledge of magic and spells. What was once our undoing may now be our only hope." He looked at the mark climbing up her arm. "However, that may not be true for you."

Claire shivered and slipped her jacket and cloak back on. "That's why I came to see you. To find out if there is a way to restore it all."

"You wish to restore magic?" His eyebrows shot up in genuine surprise.

She nodded.

"I thought for sure someone had sent you, to find out how to use you. That Líadan… he has the others, does he not?"

"He does, but his goal and mine are the same. He knows what is happening to his people, his land. Though my reasons may be a little more selfish."

"I see." He retreated into his own world for a few moments of thought. He held his hand out to her then, his fingers long and frail looking. "May I?"

She gave him a questioning look.

"I need to know if you speak the truth."

Did he know how to dive into her mind like Razi? The thought of having yet another person rattle around in her head was unpleasant, but if it was the only way to get him to trust her, she'd just have to do it.

Hesitantly, she put her hand in his. His flesh was cold to the touch and seemed as thin and delicate as paper. And then she was lost, sucked back into her memories. She saw flashes of her childhood, her mother, and the tavern, the peaceful times, followed by that blazing fateful night, a great ball filled with dancing and reverie, red eyes in the dark, the Haven, the palace. It all went by so fast. She felt like she lived a lifetime in mere moments. The real world was a shock when she finally came back to it. She gasped for breath as if she'd been holding it the entire time. Her pulse quickened and she could feel her hands shake.

The Elder looked winded as well, his slight frame heaving. Sweat beaded on his brow. "The trials you have suffered… I am sorry."

"You couldn't have known."

He nodded, but he didn't look reassured. She could see the guilt clear on his face. "There is a way," he said. "To restore it."

She stopped breathing for a moment, her body stilling. So there was hope.

"Like you, I believe that it is time to return magic to the land, for the good of all. But," he said, a stern hint of warning in his voice, "I want you to understand the consequences of your choice, unlike we did so long ago."

Claire swallowed hard and nodded ever so slightly.

"The balance of power will most likely shift back to the elves. They may try to take back what once was theirs. The land may flourish, but humans may not."

"If I don't, then no one will have a chance."

"I agree, I am just trying to warn you. As for a solution to keep history from repeating itself, I do not have one I'm afraid. I am but an old relic from a different time."

Claire let his words sink in. Could restoring magic lead to another Great War? Was she betraying humans with her decision? Was she letting her selfishness rule her thinking?

"And as far as your problem, beware," he said, his voice growing soft. "The mark has entwined itself so deeply within you, there is no telling what would happen if it were released. If it spreads too far, there may not be enough of you left. It could kill you just the same."

The blood drained from her face. "Oh…" was all she could manage to say. Even after everything, there may not be hope for her after all. She took a long shaky breath and let it out slowly. Was she doomed either way?

"I sense hesitance in you, child. If you are to do this, you cannot falter. The task is too great to waver before it is done. Your fate is not set in stone yet. There may be a chance to cure you, but there may not be. Either way, you know your fate if you do nothing."

He had a point. If she did nothing, she would succumb to the mark and go mad before the end. At least if she restored magic to the land she'd be able to do some good before her demise. Either way, it was a lot to take in. The weight of it all already crushed down upon her. She took another deep breath to keep calm.

"I'll do it." The words tumbled out of her mouth before she could really think about what it would entail. Before consulting Farron. It was selfish of her, but no matter what she decided, he would follow. Would he still help her if he knew? She didn't want to risk it. Not yet.

"Good." She could see relief flood the old elf.

His burden had now become hers. If she lived, would spend the rest of her days in a place like this, filled with guilt over her decisions?

"The spell used was old magic, so old magic is needed to break it. An incantation to be exact. Words and their meaning lost to time."

Claire looked at him expectantly, hoping he would know them.

"Of course I don't know them. Only Rialla did."

Claire's shoulders sank. Of course, it wouldn't have been that easy.

"But she didn't leave us without any hope. The words exist but they are hidden. She had them set in stone before she passed and hid them across the land. Only the power of a Star Child can reveal them."

Consumed

Claire thought instantly of the stone fragment she'd found in the palace. Old language set in stone that she had felt drawn to. It definitely fit the description. She scrambled to her pack and dug the fragment out from the bottom, sending her belongings sprawling across the floor in her haste. She knelt in front of the old elf once again, showing him the fragment.

"My child," he said, breathless. "You keep surprising me! Yes, this is part of it. Wherever did you find it?"

"In the palace, King Líadan had it stored away in his library. He's been hunting for anything that is connected to the Star Children."

"Well, then. I think you are already well on your way. Perhaps it has been your fate all along."

Claire didn't know about that, but the way some events had played out, she wasn't so sure anymore.

"I will have Will take you to the cave tomorrow," he said as he started to rise. "It grows late. More will be explained to you in the morning."

Claire offered him a hand, but looked at him questioningly. There was still so much she didn't know. Was that it?

The old elf chuckled when he saw the distressed look on her face. "Do not worry, child. There will be enough of that in the coming days. There is much to do and much to think upon. I have lived long enough to see magic disappear from the land, but I never thought I'd see it return. I have faith in you. Take the night to rest. I will have Ophelia bring you some blankets and food. I'm afraid this will have to do. We are not equipped for visitors."

"Anywhere is fine as long as it's not out in the cold." Speaking of, she had forgotten about Farron. He was surely an icicle by now.

She escorted the Elder to the door. He turned to her when they reached it. "Apologize to your friend for me," he said, patting her hand kindly. "I had misjudged him. It is my job to be cautious."

"I understand. I will."

The Elder knocked on the door with his staff twice and the guard from earlier opened it. He shivered and rubbed his hands together. Claire was shocked at his dedication. He must have been freezing. Without complaint, he escorted the old elf across the small clearing to another low-roofed building, walking by Farron. As the elder passed, he gave the younger elf a nod that Farron returned, looking both relieved and confused.

Snow fell harder in the dim light after the setting sun. Farron stood as a grim, dark counter to the surrounding white. He looked at her, questioning, then came with a slight jog in his step. He shook the snow off his cloak and stomped his boots before entering. He eyed her overturned pack.

Claire ushered him in and quickly shut the door. After stuffing her things back in her bag she went back to the fire to warm up again, Farron trailing closely behind. She could almost feel the impatience emanating off of him.

"Well?" he finally asked. White flecks dotted his darkened hair.

"I'm going to do it," she said. "I'm going to restore magic to the land. He said that there is a way. There's hope, Fare."

He swept her up into his embrace, her feet hanging helplessly as he swung her around in a circle. When he finally released her she sank back to the floor to sit in front of the warm flames. He followed suit, warming his hands, taking his gloves off. She told him almost everything the Elder had told her, leaving out the bit about her not surviving either way. It was a big omission, one that she felt guilty keeping from him, but in a way, she felt that if she didn't acknowledge it, perhaps it wouldn't come true.

Ophelia came with the blankets and hot stew shortly after Claire had finished her retelling of events. Farron had just as many questions as she had, maybe even more. He was just as astounded to learn that the unassuming old elf they'd met had a hand in changing the course of the war, and the world, so long ago. It was a lot to take in. They examined the stone fragment even closer, trying to figure out the secrets it held, but it was no use. It was just as mysterious now as when she'd first found it back in the palace.

"He also said he was sorry," Claire told him. "That he misjudged you."

Farron smiled in a sad way, though she had a feeling that it relieved him a little to hear it. Not much, but maybe a little. To know that maybe he *could*, if not escape his past, at least overcome it.

Although she was grateful not to have slept out in the cold, the hard floors hadn't done her already sore body any favors. She was stiff and her joints and muscles ached. Even Farron seemed to have suffered, his movements more stilted than usual.

Will turned out to be the guard from the night before. He came to get them just as the sun was peeking up over the far mountain. He escorted them to the back of the village, where the mountain loomed above them. There, the Elder already waited for them in front of a pair of carved granite doors. They were overgrown, though the vines had turned brown and brittle.

"This hasn't been opened since Rialla sealed it years ago," the Elder said, his eyes misting over once again.

"What is it?" Claire asked. She couldn't be the only one curious about what it was. Did Will know? How much did the other residents know of the old elf and his past? How many other residents *were* there?

"This will show you the way," he said, using his staff to clear some of the vines. He looked at her with a sort of amused expression. "You didn't think those walls were built just to protect little old me, did you?" He chuckled and returned to clearing the vines.

Will and Farron jumped in, clearing the way quickly. Upon closer inspection, a scene was carved into the stone of a battle and far above in the sky a great shining star.

"They will only open with magic," the old elf said. "Go on, give it a try." He pointed with his staff.

Claire approached the door, unsure, but curious. She reached out with her right hand and placed it on the granite. She could feel the cold seeping through her glove. She pushed but they didn't budge. She took a step back and looked at the doors again. Was there some sort of trick? She removed the glove from her right hand and placed it on the doors again, this time closing her eyes. She concentrated on pushing her magic into the stone. The doors grew warm under her touch and a low rumble sounded, followed by a vibration. Slowly, the doors creaked open on their own. Dust fell away, clouding up a dark corridor beyond that led into the mountain.

Shocked, Claire just stood there, frozen for a few moments. It had actually worked. She looked into the inky blackness of the tunnel with apprehension. Was she really ready to take on this responsibility? She took a deep calming breath and turned to the old man. He just nodded and gestured for her to enter.

She stepped into the cave, Farron close behind. The old man and Will stayed near the entrance. Wide stairs led them downward, but the rest of the corridor looked roughly hewn from the rock with sharp, uneven edges. It was cold but warmer than outside. A dim light shone at the end of the tunnel. Claire couldn't help but think back to the last time she'd been underground and the unpleasant memories associated with it. A shiver ran through her. Hopefully, a Beast of Old didn't lie in wait for them.

Much to her relief, a room greeted them, free of any beasts. Round and with much more attention to craft and detail than the tunnel, the room was simple, with a natural skylight that let a ray of sunshine fall at an angle in the center of the floor. The walls were blank and smooth. The floor, however, was not. Small channels spread out in a web from a central altar where water flowed in a continuous clear stream. A bowl sat on the edge of the altar. Everything was coated in a thick layer of dust, looking untouched for years.

"Well," Claire said, unsure of what to do. The Elder said she would find answers inside, but where? The room was pretty sparse. She took a step onto the channeled floor, and that's when she felt it. Magic. It slithered across her skin, raising goosebumps. "Do you feel it?" she asked Farron. It was strong here. A heady feeling took over her mind like back in the ruined Haven. She could easily lose herself here. Her own magic stirred inside of her.

"Yes," Farron replied simply. He walked the edges of the room, examining the wall, looking for any clues.

Claire approached the altar, drawn to the crystal-like water. Made of white marble, faded from the ages, it was shaped like a pedestal with a deep depression in the middle. The water flowed over the edges all around it to fill the channels. From there, she didn't know where the water went. Along the rim was an elegant script. Elvish, most likely. She meant to ask Farron what it said, but she couldn't get her mouth to form the words. She reached out with her right hand and skimmed the cool liquid with her fingertips. A thrill rushed through her, a slight sting starting along the scar, followed by the blue glow of the mark.

"Claire," Farron said, but his voice sounded far away.

Without thought, following some deep compulsion, she picked up the bowl and dipped it into the water before bringing it up to her lips. The memory of Farron warning her not to drink the water at the ruined Haven played in the back of her mind, causing her to hesitate.

"Claire, don't!" Farron's shout echoed through her mind, but it was too late.

She tipped the bowl up and drank, the iciness slid down her throat, and then she was gone. Swallowed up by a hazy darkness.

When she awoke, she was no longer in the small room, but she was in another cavern. Only this one was bigger. Much bigger. The sky was visible through a large hole in the ceiling, and it was filled with stars. Greenery surrounded her, moss and ferns and vines covering some ancient looking ruins in the center of the cave. Orange firelight from multiple torches gave off an ominous flickering. She wasn't alone. Dark, cloaked figures stood gathered in a circle before her, chanting in an unknown language. A woman led the chant—not just any woman, an elf. Her hood was drawn back, revealing her ethereal looks. A mixture of elves and humans made up the rest of them. Slowly, Claire made her way toward the group, careful not to make a sound, but something told her it didn't matter. This wasn't real. It was only a dream. A memory. Was this from that fateful night? From when they sealed magic away?

She peered in between two tall figures and saw humans knelt down in the center. Seven of them. This was it. This was how they did it. Claire didn't have to squeeze through the figures, she just passed through them until she was in the center. She walked around the kneeling people. Half-dressed, their skin was marked with the same scrolling designs that made up the Star Children's marks, only theirs were accompanied by the same elegant letters that were carved on the stone she'd found in the palace. Old magic. The people remained still, calm, eyes closed as the chant went on.

Then the marks and script started to glow, taking on a life of their own, twisting and writhing across their skin. A pained look took over their faces, and some cried out. The elves of the group closed in, each taking a human and placing a hand on their heads. The chant grew louder as they repeated the same line over and over again. Soon the glow from the marks rivaled the torchlight. Magic filled the area, so much that it was suffocating. The elves looked pained themselves, a sadness touched their faces, perhaps over what they were giving up. Magic built up more and more until finally, the humans collapsed, writhing in pain on the floor. A gust of wind blew out the torches, the only light coming from the marks. The elves fell to their knees, winded from their efforts.

A single torch was lit again. The female elf from before held it aloft, looking around. "Did it work?" Her voice was smooth but strained.

"Yes, Lady Rialla," an elf replied.

Rialla closed her eyes as if mourning a great loss, tears falling quietly. "So it has…" She opened her eyes again and it was as if she looked right at Claire. They were bright blue and full of sorrow. "I'm sorry," she said, and the scene started to fade.

Claire woke with a start, gasping.

"Claire!" Farron cradled her on the floor.

She blinked a few times to clear her vision, trying to digest what she just witnessed. "I saw it," she said, breathless. "How they did it. Locked away the magic." She sat up slowly, her head clouded. She shivered. Had Rialla really seen her? "It was like the Elder said…"

Claire rose to her feet, steadied by Farron's helping hand. She looked around the room again, just as lost as before. "It was a memory, a message, but it didn't say what we had to do next. I think she, Rialla, was just trying to show me, or whoever came here, what had happened."

"This room was built so that only a Star Child could use it," Farron said. "What do your instincts tell you?"

Claire shrugged. Perhaps the wrong Star Child had come to this place. The compulsions she had felt before had faded, leaving her to fend for herself. "I probably shouldn't drink that again." She motioned to the fountain.

Farron gave a short snort of laughter.

"But, what if I don't need to drink it?" She looked down around her. "There are channels here for a reason."

"You think...?" He looked at her, his eyebrows scrunched with concern.

"Something may need to go in. What do I have that no one else has?" She drew her dagger and stood in front of the altar.

Farron came to stand next to her. "Are you sure?"

"Well, there's only one way to find out." She rolled up her left sleeve and drew the blade across her forearm. Blood welled in the cut and she held it over the fountain. Red droplets fell into the water, dissipating and flowing down over the edges.

A bright white glow began to emit from the channels, spreading outward toward the wall. Claire whirled, watching as the room came to life. Images started to appear on the wall. Gradually they formed into lines and edges, drawing mountains and plains and towns and seas. It was a map. Farron approached the wall, touching it.

"Incredible." He walked along it, examining it closely.

Indeed it was. Claire turned slowly to take it all in. Everything was there, from Derenan to Stockton. Even the seas and a faraway land. Small pinpricks of light started to shine on four points on the map.

"Look," Claire pointed.

Farron stepped back to examine them. Two formed on the western part of the map, with the other two forming on the eastern.

"It's showing us where the other pieces of the spell are at," Claire said.

Farron pointed at the top left one. It was located on a small island off the coast of northern Derenan. "Atalan Island," he said. "Seat of Council member Bolin..." he trailed off, his voice a little concerned. He then pointed to the one lower. It was inland more, in the middle of a desert region. "Zaqar." He walked over and motioned to the one further east. He gave a short laugh. "This looks like one of your favorite places." He glanced back at her with a grin.

She raised her eyebrows, waiting for his answer.

"That field you were so curious about has more secrets than I thought. Clever." He turned back to the map and motioned to the last one. "Now this is the most troubling one."

Before he could say any more, Claire looked closer at it and agreed. It was just north of Stockton, right in the middle of the Forbidden Forest. "It seems the Forest King may have more knowledge than he let on."

"Indeed." He turned back to her. "If these are pieces meant to be gathered, then it won't be easy."

"I think that was the point."

Farron took a deep breath and joined her again to look over the map. "Are you sure you are up to this?"

She wasn't, but what choice did she have? "Are you?" she countered.

"Sounds like an adventure." He grinned sideways at her. "A dangerous one. I expect there will be resistance."

Claire nodded. There were definitely parties that didn't want magic to return. If they learned what she was up to, she was sure they wouldn't hesitate to kill her to stop it. "I have always dreamt of adventure." She countered his grin with an unsure one of her own. "Have you memorized it?"

"Yes," he said, his eyes sweeping over the map again.

The map and the points started to fade. "We should—"

Farron whirled and faced the entrance suddenly and Claire followed suit, only she didn't see anything. She listened, but Farron's ears heard things hers didn't.

Her pulse picked up. Had they been followed? They weren't the only ones to know of Uru Baya, after all.

"Come," Farron said, racing back up the corridor.

Claire gasped as they reached the opening. Fire engulfed the roofs of the buildings. Will lay slumped against the entrance, unmoving. Farron drew a dagger and carefully led the way into the village. He stopped when he reached the courtyard. In the center lay the elder and the woman, Ophelia, stood over him, a dagger clutched in her right hand. Blood dripped off the end.

The woman spun to face them, a wild look in her eyes.

"What did you do?" Claire yelled, her hand going to her own blade.

"I won't let you!" Ophelia replied. She held her dagger up in front of her, her hand shaking. "I can't let you betray your own kind!"

Farron started to advance, but the woman turned and ran through the opened gate.

"Fare," Claire gasped as she went to the elder. She knelt next to him and Farron scanned the village. The old elf still breathed but didn't look good. Blood soaked through his robes around his stomach. Too much blood. Too much red. Tears escaped from her eyes. How much more destruction and death would be caused because of her?

The elder looked up at her with half-unfocused eyes. "You must succeed," he said, his voice weak. Blood dripped from his lips. "I only wish…" He coughed up more blood. "… I could have seen it." He fell slack and his eyes looked up to the sky before losing the spark of life.

She started to sob but stopped short. There was no time for that. She took a few deep breaths to calm herself, fighting against resurging memories. "The packs!" she yelled out, suddenly remembering. She stood and whirled toward the burning building they'd spent the night in. The shard was still buried in the bottom of her bag.

Farron ran toward the door, Claire close behind. "Wait here," he said, before disappearing into the smoke-filled room.

Claire stood back, antsy, waiting for Farron to reemerge. She turned to take in the town again. Sorrow filled her, and then anger. This act that was meant to stop or dissuade her only made her desire to succeed stronger. She wouldn't let the elder die in vain.

A few moments later, Farron burst out of the building with both of their packs, coughing. He set the bags on the ground and doubled over to catch his breath.

"Are you all right?" Claire asked as she rushed to him.

He nodded and stood upright. "We should leave."

Claire agreed, shouldering her pack, and they left, Uru Baya burning behind them.

Claire was in too much shock to say anything on the hike back down the mountain. They were both on edge, anticipating an attack from—well, there seemed to be too many people after them to settle on just one group.

"Do you think she was working for someone?" she broke the silence after what seemed like hours. The sky had turned overcast again, making the surrounding forest seem even more ominous.

"She could have been a double agent." He shrugged. "But in the end, it doesn't matter. The deed is done."

"Still, all that time she'd been there… I wonder if she was waiting for someone like me to show up, or if it was a sudden act of desperation." She sighed, running scenarios through her head. To betray someone like that… Claire's trust was shaken. She was even more grateful for the elf in front of her then. Loyal to her until the end.

"As unfortunate as it is already, there is another problem." He looked back at her but didn't slow his gait. "He was one of the few that could still read the old language. The only others I know…"

"… are in the forest," Claire finished, the problem dawning on her. Would the forest king work with them after Farron had betrayed him? They may not have much of a choice.

The hike down was easier than on the way up. They grew tired as the sun sunk to the horizon, but they didn't stop. They couldn't risk it. So they walked on into the night as snow started to fall from the sky.

Samota was untouched and as unharmed as when they'd left it. Their horses were still in the stables, much to their relief. Claire didn't think she could handle it if this town had suffered the same fate of Uru Baya and too many other towns in her wake.

It was late when they returned. Exhaustion racked her body. All she wanted to do was collapse where she stood and sleep. But Farron wouldn't let her.

"We need to keep moving," he said.

Though dismayed, there was a part of her that agreed. It was too dangerous to stay here. She dragged herself to the stables as Farron collected their horses. The boy from before helped saddle them. Farron slipped him some coins and the boy went back inside, yawning, his eyes already half closed.

Instead of handing the reins of her horse to her, Farron tied them to the saddle of his. "You'll ride with me," he said, the tone of his voice not leaving any room for protest.

Consumed

Not that she had the energy to. She could see the exhaustion on him as well, but he hid it as best he could. Was this what he was like when he was trying to get back to her?

Without saying anything, Claire mounted his horse and he got up behind her. His warmth was welcome. She relaxed back against him as he spurred the horse on. Her eyes grew heavy and she slowly drifted off. At least now she wouldn't be falling off, and for that she was grateful.

4

Rays of the rising sun woke her. She still swayed atop the horse, enveloped in Farron's cloak. She could feel his deep, slow breaths against her back.

"Fare," she breathed.

He stirred, shifting in the saddle.

"You need to rest." Had he been up all night?

"Not yet," he said, his voice strained. He was pushing himself too far.

"Yes," she said, sitting up straighter. "Just for a little while. I'll keep watch. Don't be stubborn. Besides, we need to figure out our next move."

Without another word, surprisingly, he guided his horse off the road into the trees. They found a spot far enough away to stay hidden from passersby.

Claire stretched, still feeling fatigued. But it was probably nothing compared to how Farron felt. After tying up the horses, he settled back against a tree and reached out to her. He pulled her down next to him, leaned his head back against the rough bark and closed his eyes, his hand gripping hers.

"It's not your fault," he said quietly.

"It doesn't feel that way." Guilt weighed on her heavily. If she had never showed up, Uru Baya would still be standing and the old elf would still be guarding his secrets.

He squeezed her hand hard. "If you keep taking the blame for everything, the guilt will swallow you up before the mark can." He cracked his eyes open and looked over at her. "If it wasn't you, then it would have been another Star Child. It's not you, Claire, it's what you are, and that's not something you can control." He leaned his head back again. "Besides, he was slipping if he had a traitor in his midst."

A little bit of the Ice Prince seeped out with Farron's last comment. She wondered if she would be seeing him more as the road grew tougher.

He slipped into sleep and Claire kept watch, ruminating on her thoughts. She managed to pry herself away and paced the area. If she stayed still, she'd end up falling asleep as well. The horses pawed at the thin layer of snow for something to nibble on. Her own stomach growled, her fatigue making her even hungrier. But their resources were limited until they could reach another town.

After a few hours, feeling antsy, she dug into his pack to find the silver magic contraption. She felt a little guilty for going through his things. It was then that a much more familiar bracelet tumbled out of his bag. Her mother's snake bracelet that she'd given him way back before he'd left her in the palace. Its ruby eyes glinted in the light, the silver tarnished. With everything that had happened, she'd forgotten about it and couldn't believe he'd managed to hold onto it this whole time. She looked up at him and jumped slightly, startled when she saw he was awake and watching her. Her cheeks grew red with embarrassment.

"I'm sorry, I…" She tried to come up with an excuse, but couldn't.

He raised an eyebrow.

"I was just looking for this." She held the contraption up in her left hand, her mother's bracelet in her right. Two pieces of jewelry with sordid histories. "I shouldn't have…" She drifted off, feeling guilty all over again.

"It's fine," he said, yawning. He looked somewhat refreshed, though she knew what little sleep he'd gotten wasn't enough. He stood, stretching, and came to kneel in front of her.

"I can't believe you kept this all this time." She held her mother's bracelet up, looking over its familiar shape.

He smiled. "I *did* promise to return it."

But she wasn't sure if she really wanted it back. Not after her experience with the Syndicate. Not yet. "You hold on to it," she said. "For a little while longer." She put the bracelet back in his pack.

"Are you sure you want to wear that?" he asked again. It seemed like *he* was the one who was unsure about it.

Claire nodded. "Hopefully it will keep at least one party at bay." She was thinking of the madman, mostly.

Farron dug around in his pack until he produced the key on a silver chain. "We should be ready to go," he said, standing.

"Did you get enough rest?" Claire asked.

"As much as I'm going to get without thieves rifling through my things." He gave her a sly look.

Claire rolled her eyes. He wasn't going to let this go easily, was he? She helped him pack up the horses again. When all was set, she brushed her cloak to the side and took her jacket off. The air was cold against her skin. But it was nothing compared to the iciness of the metal bands as Farron slipped them onto her arm and wrist. He looked at her as he turned her arm upwards, the key in his other hand. She took a deep breath, then nodded.

With three small clicks, the contraption sealed her magic. He slipped the key over her neck and led the way back to the horses. He untied her horse from his and handed her the reins. And then they rode, fast and far, with one less worry on their shoulders. For now.

5

An ocean of ochre sand stretched out before Claire. She stood in the shade of a spindly tree while Azra and Farron's horse nibbled on a sparse patch of greenery nearby. The desert of Zaqar. It had its own sort of beauty, even if it was hot. And bright. The sun was merciless as it beat down on them. She'd long ago shed her layers as they neared the region, her arms and mark bared for all the world to see. Except, there was no one. They hadn't seen a soul in at least a week.

It had taken them almost a month to reach Zaqar after they'd left the mountains. They'd avoided the capital and any large towns on their way, only stopping in remote villages for supplies or a much-needed bed and bath, at Claire's insistence. Crossing the great Rift again proved troublesome, but nothing some threats hadn't solved. Whether or not the guards had recognized Farron remained to be seen.

The elf in question stood at the edge of the last remaining shade before the sea of sand, scanning the horizon, squinting at the brightness.

"It won't be easy," he said, then looked over at her. He'd shed his layers as well, along with a few weapons, and only one silver hilt stuck up over his right shoulder.

Claire nodded. "I suppose that was the point," she said, referring to the plan to hide the artifacts. "Have you ever been in the desert before?"

He shook his head. "I never had the need, nor desire, to."

"I could call for Razi," she said, a smile forming, though she was somewhat serious. He *was* from Zaqar, after all.

Farron frowned at her.

That was a no then. She did have her own apprehensions about Razi still. He may have gotten wise to the Council's scheming, but he wasn't free from them. Not when they still held his family. So, the hard way it would be.

She sighed, already tired from the prospect of crossing the desert. The silver contraption had held her mark back so far, but she still felt the fatigue, like her life force was slowly draining away.

"We will travel in the evening," he said. "We should rest until then."

Claire nodded. It was as good a plan as any. As to where they were headed and what they were looking for, she had no idea. The map back in the cave gave no clues other than the dots of light. They were just heading in the general direction. And then? She didn't know. She'd tried searching for hints of magic, like the kinds she'd felt in the Haven and the cave, the way she had been drawn to the water. But the contraption made it nearly impossible.

Sleep came easy after their relentless trek, despite the sun burning bright above.

Consumed

It felt like she'd only been asleep for a few minutes when Farron stirred her awake again. But when she cracked open her eyes, the sun hung low on the horizon. He knelt beside her, his gaze concentrating on something far away. Claire followed his focus to find a cloud of dust rising in the northeast.

A caravan soon came into view. Wagons covered in colorful cloth made up the bulk, surrounded by men on horses and a few people walking on foot. The men on the horses were armed with long spears and curved swords at their sides. Claire stood up next to Farron, unsure what to do. They didn't look harmful, but she couldn't be sure these days. A chill swept over her and she noticed that the temperature had dropped considerably since earlier. She went to Azra, dug her jacket back out, and put it on. It would help hide most of her mark from view and at least now it wouldn't seem so strange for her to be wearing it.

The caravan slowed as it approached them. A few of the men on horses rode ahead. Farron tensed, but his hands remained at his sides. The men shouted to them in another language and Claire and Farron just shook their heads to show they didn't understand. The men circled them twice before coming to a stop, the tips of their spears trained on them. Azra and Farron's horse stirred nervously. Farron held his hands up in surrender and Claire followed suit.

"Who are you?" asked the man in front of them, his accent thick. He had the same dark features as Razi, with a closely trimmed beard and hair tied back into a bun. His clothes, as well as the others', were colorful. A saffron, long-sleeved top hung loose on his frame atop dark blue pants. A deep red sash similar to Razi's encircled his waist.

"Just travelers," Farron replied carefully. He eyed the man and the ones surrounding them. "We're looking for passage across the desert. We can pay you if you'll allow us to accompany you."

The man raised his eyebrows, considering Farron's offer. He looked him and Claire over and then lowered his spear. He said a few words to his men and they lowered theirs as well. "Which way are you heading, stranger?"

"West," Farron answered.

"Very well then," the man said, a smile breaking across his face. "A man with gold is a friend to me."

Farron lowered his hands and went to his horse. When he returned he tossed a few gold coins to the man.

The man caught them and bit each of them, testing them with his teeth. When he was satisfied, he smiled broadly at them. "My name is Toriz. I will be your shepherd." With that, he turned and rode back to the caravan, followed by the others.

"Well, that solves that problem," Claire said, turning to gather her things and Azra. "Now let's just hope gold is enough to keep them from asking too many questions."

They traveled well into the night by the light of the moon. Millions of stars dotted the expansive sky. Nothing surrounded them but sand. Claire felt exposed, not used to such... openness. The Zaqari welcomed them warmly. They'd asked questions, but nothing too probing, so far.

Just when Claire didn't think she could stay awake any longer, they stopped to make camp. With the wagons in a circle, the men and women started a massive fire in the middle, singing in their foreign tongue as they cooked and set up tents. Before she could protest, the women pulled her away from Farron and set her to a task of cutting vegetables for a stew. Farron just shrugged when she looked after him, and joined the men in setting up the rest of the tents. The women

Consumed

talked and laughed around her. And even though she didn't understand a word they were saying, their jubilance seeped into her, making her smile and putting her at ease. She didn't know how much she had missed the hustle and bustle of people until now.

"They wonder," said an older woman next to her. An orange scarf held her dark hair back. "If he is your lover?"

Heat rushed to Claire's cheeks. She could feel the other women's attention on her as they waited for an answer. "I—" Claire stuttered. She didn't know why she was so embarrassed. It was the truth after all. But she had never had to admit to it out loud. To complete strangers, none the less. "I suppose so."

The surrounding women giggled as she confirmed their suspicions, making her embarrassment even greater.

After supper and another round of singing, Claire was exhausted, her eyes barely able to stay open. But when it came time to finally retire, the women commandeered her again, shuffling her off to a separate tent. Farron looked after her helplessly, his mouth open, ready to protest, but he held his silence.

"You may be lovers," said the older woman from before, "but in Zaqar, we don't share tents unless we are married."

It was Claire's turn to shrug as Farron looked after her. A little distance would make the heart grow fonder. Or drive them both mad.

6

It felt like she was inside an oven with how hot and dry it was. The sun beat down mercilessly, so intense she could barely see. Claire and Farron both ended up using their cloaks as makeshift headscarves to help provide some protection from the baking heat. Though the caravan traveled mostly by night, there were a few stretches too treacherous to pass by moonlight, so they had to brave the daylight hours. Water flasks were running low and sand was getting everywhere, making the experience just that much more unpleasant.

"Where is it that you are heading, my friend?" said a slight man walking next to Farron.

The elf walked a couple paces in front of her, almost every inch of his fair skin hidden from the waning sun, making him seem even more intimidating, which she hadn't known was even possible. Claire just felt silly in her getup. Farron tilted his head, looking at the man. Then he glanced back at her.

"We haven't decided, quite yet." He left it at that, being purposefully elusive.

Not that she could blame him. They would be foolish to trust these people, even if they had taken them into their caravan.

It also helped that it was sort of the truth. The wall had only pointed to a vague area in the desert. She supposed it was up to her to pinpoint the actual location using her magic. But with the silver bands on her, it was proving to be more difficult than she had thought. And she didn't know if it was worth the risk to take them off. But they might not have much of a choice if they wanted to actually find the place. What would they discover when they did locate it? Would it be just as simple as finding the piece of spell? Or were there more trials in wait?

She was hoping for the former but knew that it probably wouldn't be that easy.

Farron slowed his pace to wait for her, and the man walked ahead without them, getting the hint.

"Anything yet?" he asked, his voice low.

She shook her head. He was growing eager to leave the caravan, for more than one reason. Tension vibrated through him, the Ice Prince mask appearing more and more over the last few days. And she couldn't blame him. She had been keeping her distance from him, sleeping in separate tents, not touching much after the first night in the caravan. It would do no good to offend the people giving them safe passage through the desert. But that didn't mean she had to enjoy it. Though, it was sort of gratifying seeing how it affected Farron. She'd seen the effects, of course, in the past, when she'd broken things off with him. The lingering looks, the longing, the tension, but it seemed so much more amplified now, knowing that they both wanted each other, but not being able to do anything about it. It was thrilling in its own right.

Farron just sighed, a low sound escaping him, almost a growl. Yes, very frustrated.

A smile tugged at her lips and she reached for his hand. But as soon as their skin touched, he pulled away.

Consumed

He looked at her out of the corner of his eye. "That's probably not a good idea." He grinned. "For more than one reason."

Heat rose to her cheeks, making them redder than they already were. "I hope we find the place soon, then."

He gave a short laugh and continued ahead of her.

Daydreams occupied her mind for the rest of the day, as the sun gave way to night and relieved them of the scorching heat, of sneaking out after everyone had gone to sleep for a midnight tryst with the elf. Or maybe running off together, or—well, there were too many scenarios involving him and she wondered if she were slowly going mad. She remembered a time when she had wanted to run away from him, not with him. She smiled. Perhaps she had gone mad already.

They traveled well into the night. Claire pulled her cloak down around her, feeling the chill of the dark. The temperature extremes were too drastic for her to ever get used to. It was almost routine by now, when they stopped, she would help the women with the cooking and setting up, Farron with the men, doing manly things. Then they slept in groups in the tents on itchy rugs. She didn't get much rest, not with the snoring and the whispering between the other girls. They asked her questions about the elf, about the world, about what they were doing in the desert. Claire tried to be as vague as Farron, but she found herself slipping occasionally, giving away more than she'd intended. Nothing too important, however. They asked about the mark, and Claire fell back on her original lie, that it was a custom in her homeland. She thought about adding the rest on, about being engaged, just for fun, but she figured that would bring more trouble with this group than it was worth.

Another two days passed. Claire tossed and turned during the night, morning just a few short hours away. Exasperated, she got up and walked around the camp. She didn't like the desert and she just wanted it to be done with. How did Razi stand it out here?

The only redeeming quality was the massive, star-filled sky. She stood on the edge of camp, the fire dimmed down to embers, and tilted her head back to take it all in. It made her feel small and insignificant in the grand scheme of things. She took in a deep breath, closing her eyes to revel in the coolness before the sun rose again. She let her body relax, her guard down and opened up herself to magic, searching for any hint of it out there in the vast sand dunes. The silver bands grew warm, as they did whenever her magic stirred inside of her, extinguishing it just as fast. She let it, waiting for it to quell inside of her completely, then pictured a door in her mind and pushing it, slowly, easing it wider, opening her senses up, disregarding everything else. It was only her and the magic. Somewhere out there.

She turned slowly, searching, waiting for a spark, anything. It hadn't worked before when she'd tried, and perhaps it wouldn't work at all, not with the silver contraption on her. She thought about unlocking it, maybe just one band—would that work? Or would it be too risky? They couldn't wander the desert forever.

Her hand was reaching for the key on the chain around her neck when she felt it. It was small, but it was something. She froze, concentrating on the sensation. A faint tingling feeling played along the edge of her mind, pulling, like the water in the Haven and the stone fragment. Her eyes flew open.

"There!" she exclaimed in a whisper, hoping she didn't wake anyone. Though she was tempted to wake Farron, she didn't think it would look good if they just left without saying a word. No, she should wait, see if he felt anything too. But it was a start. A beacon of hope.

Consumed

"Do you feel it?" she asked, impatience making her feet dance slightly in the sand.

Farron stood with his eyes closed, the sun burning high above. The camp was slowly coming to life around them, rising later in the day than usual, preferring to sleep as much as they could through the heat. A few men gave them curious looks but went about their business.

He frowned. "I don't," he said. "But I might not be able to feel it regardless."

Claire nodded. That would make sense. It wouldn't be much of a secret if anyone could sense the magic coming from it.

"You need to be sure, Claire." He opened his eyes and leveled them at her. "We can't afford to be wrong, not out here."

She chewed the inside of her lip, her anxiety growing within her. He was right. They didn't have enough supplies to last them for too long out in the desert. Once they left the caravan, they were on their own. But there was no mistaking the feeling of it—the pulling—the captivating draw of magic. It had grown a little stronger since she'd first sensed it like it had locked onto her, a fish caught on the hook.

"It's there," she whispered.

"All right." Farron glanced around, then settled his gaze back on her, the beginnings of a grin touching his lips. "I think we've overstayed our welcome here, no?"

"And here I was just getting used to it," she teased.

His smile faded a little, a spark flaring in his eyes. He leaned closer to her, his body almost brushing against hers, just close enough for her to feel the vibrating tension. Her breath caught. She wanted to reach out to him, touch him, but forced herself not to. She swallowed hard, trying to dampen her desire. The effort must have shown on her face.

"That's what I thought," he whispered, and it slithered over her body.

He had called her bluff a little too easily. As always. "What are we going to tell them?" She nodded to the men taking down the tents, the women passing out breakfast.

Farron shrugged. "We don't have to tell them anything."

Blunt, of course. She opened her mouth to protest but stopped. Perhaps he had a point? Whatever they decided to tell them, the nomads would suspect something regardless. They already did. It wasn't every day that an elf and a woman with a strange mark on her arm showed up in the desert.

"All right," she said. "We'll try it your way." He had been doing things like this for much longer than she had, after all.

He gave her a skeptical look. It wasn't like her to just give in to him without putting up some sort of fight.

She simply didn't have it in her to be stubborn over every little thing anymore. Or was she just learning to trust him more? The thought struck her hard. But it was the truth. "I trust you."

The uncertain look melted into a smile and he nodded. "The heat must be getting to you."

Another possibility. She playfully nudged him as she walked passed to go get some breakfast. They had a lot of preparations to do if they were going to leave the safety of the caravan. Worry stirred with excitement within her, along with a growing anticipation. What would they discover out there in the sand? Would they be all right all by themselves? How long would they last before pouncing on each other?

❊

After breakfast, they lounged beneath the tents with the rest of the people, listening to stories, answering questions with vague responses. Neither of them told the caravan that they were leaving. Not yet. Claire was hoping Farron would be the one to handle that task. He was a much better liar than her by far.

They exchanged glances throughout the day, a fire slowly building between them, the anticipation growing. Almost so much so her body became jittery, and she was finding it harder and harder to concentrate on anything else. Never before had she felt like this, the wanting, lusting—not for the General, nor her betrothed. It was entirely new, but she didn't hate it. Far from it.

When the sun was on its descent, Farron came to her. "Make sure you have everything ready," he said. "We'll leave at dusk." There was a strained edge to his voice, his movements tense.

Claire's mouth ran dry and she could only nod. She might be the one doing the pouncing after all.

Time passed too slowly for her liking. The sun seemed to be stuck in the sky. She made sure she had everything, filled the flasks and took some extra provisions. The women looked at her with curious eyes, and Claire gave one of the elder women a few coins for the supplies and for giving them shelter, thanking her. Before the woman could ask her, Claire shuffled away.

She was checking the tack and saddles on the horses when Farron approached her, his bag in tow. The blue in the sky was darkening and the first stars shone like pinpricks.

"Ready?" he asked, but his voice was loaded with anticipation and darker things.

A shiver ran through her. She nodded.

He led the way out into the desert, toward the direction she'd indicated earlier. Claire glanced behind her to see the confused faces of the people of the caravan. A man shook his head slowly, frowning. Surely he thought they were riding out to their deaths. Perhaps they were. But Claire had to think more positively than that.

It seemed to take forever for them to get out of sight of the caravan. Even when they finally did so, Farron continued to walk ahead of her, his pace unwavering. The tension rose sharply with each minute that passed. Was he teasing her? Seeing who would break first?

Growing frustrated, she hurried her pace to catch up to him. Fine, she would just be the loser of that game. She dropped the reins of her horse and grabbed his arm, pulling him around.

He looked down at her, surprise on his face, a sly grin slipping into place. "I was wondering how long it would take."

"Shut up," she said, digging her hand into his cloak to draw him down to her.

He dropped the reins to his horse and then he was on her, his kiss smothering, his presence hot and buzzing along her body.

She pulled him back away from the horses, stripping off articles of clothing, leaving a trail in the sand. He somehow maneuvered his cloak off and behind her, letting it fall to the ground before pushing her down onto it.

What a gentleman. But the rest of his actions proved otherwise.

The horizon was just showing the first sunlight when the rock outcroppings seemed to rise from the sand. And they were in the direction that the magical pull was drawing them toward. It had grown stronger and stronger as the night wore on. As much as they would have liked to linger, entangled in each other under the stars, they knew they couldn't.

"Let's hope there's some shelter there." Farron motioned toward the rocks.

Claire nodded. They wouldn't be able to reach it before the sun rose fully and she wasn't looking forward to it. "Do you still not feel anything?" she asked, curious.

"No," he said, shaking his head.

By the time they reached the rocks, it was almost midday. Claire was trying to preserve her flask, ration it out, but it was a losing battle. She was just so thirsty, her body tired from trekking all night through loose sand—and other activities. The draw was so strong now that her body buzzed with the sensation, the bands warm on her arm as her magic continually stirred and quelled inside her, like a pulsing storm just waiting to explode out and swallow her whole. Sweat drenched her body. If there was one thing that she knew for certain, it was that she hated the desert. She would take an endless sea of water over one of sand any day.

They found an overhang that provided some shade and drew the horses underneath it, cupping their hands so the animals could drink from their meager water reserves.

"Sorry, girl." Claire stroked Azra's head. It was a wonder how well they had kept up, and she hoped that the journey wouldn't prove to be too much for them.

"We should rest here for a little bit. Cool off." Farron was stroking his horse.

She definitely wouldn't argue with that. After making sure the horses were fed and watered, they settled down on their laid out cloaks and fell asleep quickly.

7

Farron was already awake when she opened her eyes again. The sun was still up but lower in the sky. How long had she been asleep? By the way she felt, not long enough. She stretched and looked over at the elf.

"It's too hot to sleep." He frowned, the dark circles under his eyes proof enough. "Let's find this thing and get out of here as soon as we can." He looked at her. "There's a reason I have always avoided the desert."

"I know how you feel." She sat up. "I don't know how anyone could live out here."

"We're near, yes?"

She could hear the impatience in his voice.

She closed her eyes and let the magical lure wash over her. "Yes."

"Good," he said, standing. He scanned the horizon quickly before turning to her. "Let's see what's in store for us, shall we?" He offered her a hand up.

Claire took it but wasn't as thrilled as he seemed. Her anxiety had grown along with the pull of the magic.

They left the horses in the shade to get more rest as they ventured out. The place didn't feel too far. The landscape gave way to more rocky outcroppings with some sparse plants here and there. It was eerie how still and calm everything seemed. The area felt so secluded from the rest of the world. An excellent place to hide something so important, she supposed.

Claire followed the magic for what seemed like an hour before she finally stopped in front of a small, unassuming cave in the largest outcropping in the center of them all.

"Here," she said.

Farron stepped up to the mouth of it, examining every inch. "It's strange, I still don't feel anything at all. There must be some strong warding used."

Claire took a deep breath and released it. She didn't really want to go in there. It gave her an ominous feeling. But it would at least provide some relief from the heat.

She followed Farron into the dark depths, not pleased to be going underground once again. Nothing good ever seemed to come from it.

The cave was rough, lacking any sort of man-made structures, and seemed to lead down at a very slight decline. She wouldn't have believed that they were in the right place if it hadn't been for the intensifying feel of magic the deeper they went. The light faded and she was soon unable to see clearly. She reached out to Farron, grabbing ahold of his cloak so he could lead the way. A moment later he came to a stop in front of her. She was about to ask him why when he snapped his fingers and flames illuminated the area, hovering over his hand.

A door hewn from the rock stood before them, crudely carved, lacking the refinement of the doors in Uru Baya. Two lines of plain script decorated the stone.

Consumed

"What does it say?" she asked Farron.

He shrugged his shoulders. "I don't know."

Claire stepped up closer to the door and reached out to touch it.

"It must be in the old language." He stepped closer as well, examining it. "Maybe it's the warding that has kept the magic sealed away from the outside world, from us." There was a wistful quality to his voice.

Her fingers brushed the dusty surface. Were they the first ones to come to this place since it had been made all those years ago? She swallowed hard. "Let's hope this works."

She closed her eyes and opened herself up to the magic of the place. Her own responded, a sudden intense flash inside of her, before being snuffed out by the bands. The door trembled, dust and pebbles falling around them, then calmed.

"It won't work, not with these in place." She held her right arm up. The silver glinted in the firelight.

Farron crossed his arms, his brow gathering in concentration. He was quiet for a moment as they both searched for an alternative.

"What if we cheat it?" he said.

"What do you mean?"

"It needs you, obviously, to open it, but what if we use my magic?" He looked at her, an eyebrow raised inquisitively.

Claire thought it over quickly. It was worth a try. "Might as well." She laid her hand on the door again, closing her eyes, opening herself up again. Her magic flared and then died once more. Then she felt the slight sensation of his magic being pushed into the stone.

Everything was still for a moment. Then the rumbling started again, only this time it didn't die down; it became more intense. The door shook and they both jumped back as it started to slide into the ground. Inch by inch the door disappeared, revealing the bowels of the cave beyond. Farron's flame only illuminated far enough for her to see carved walls and a flat tiled floor, both the same ochre stone as the rest of the cave.

When the door was finally level with the ground, she looked at Farron. "I can't believe that worked."

He looked at her, letting out a breath.

They waited for a moment for something to happen. When it didn't, they looked at each other again and he shrugged.

"Be careful," he said, taking the first step.

She nodded, her nerves on edge. She followed after him, keeping close, examining the corridor. More utilitarian than anything, it seemed like it had been made in a hurry, but considering the circumstances, it probably had been. Had Rialla done all of this herself? Claire wished that she had had more time with the old elf in Uru Baya. There were so many questions still unanswered. And it was possible they always would be.

Farron's pace slowed, drawing her attention back to the present. The corridor opened up several paces ahead into a massive space, dimly lit by streams of sunlight. He tilted his head, first looking to the side then up, and then finally down to his feet. Claire followed his gaze to what had piqued his interest. The same script from the door was scrawled in multiple places all over the walls, floor, and ceiling, in an eerie, haphazard way.

"Different words," Farron said. "Another spell?"

"For what?" she asked. Was it another ward? Or something else? "There's only one way to find out, I suppose."

"I'm starting to get a bad feeling about this place."

"You and me both." Claire stepped up next to him, looking at the carved letters in the stone, wishing that she knew what they said. She took a breath and held it, then stepped over the script. When nothing happened, she released it and looked back at Farron. They remained still for a few moments, listening, waiting for something, anything, to happen. "I guess it doesn't—"

But as soon as Farron stepped over the spell, the script burst to life, emitting a bright white light. A low rumbling started deep in the earth and spread rapidly to the surface, engulfing the whole cavern in tremors. Dust fell from the ceiling, the rock groaning and crackling.

"Go!" Farron shouted, pushing her further into the cave to the opening.

Flames erupted in sconces lining the walls, following in their tracks. They reached the immense open area and skidded to a stop. Farron grabbed her arm and pulled her back toward him, away from the ledge. The floor ended in a platform high above a vast darkness. Her shoulders heaving from their sprint, Claire's eyes adjusted to the room. Massive almost seemed like an understatement. A rocky ceiling formed a dome over the space, so vast that she could barely see the other side in the dim light. The torches lit all around the room in sequence, but their meager light did nothing to illuminate the darkness. The rumbling eased a bit and a large bowl blazed to life in the center of the room atop a circular pillar. But the most horrifying part was the narrow bridge that led out to it, no more than a foot wide.

She was so lost in the enormity of it all that she nearly missed what Farron said.

"Look."

She followed the finger he pointed out to the platform. A thin pedestal stood in front of the flames, and on top of that a square fragment of stone. She could feel the pull of it, strong and steady.

Claire gulped and looked up at Farron. "I don't know if I can cross that." She nodded to the bridge.

"Well, I can try," Farron said, his tone doubtful. "But if there's any more of those spells, you'll have to be the one to get it, unfortunately. Who knows what I just triggered?"

He looked up at the room around them. It seemed to be holding so far.

Farron inched up to the bridge and peered down into the darkness.

"Do you see anything?" Claire asked, hanging back. Her pulse remained a little too fast.

"Just... sand."

The rumbling and shaking stopped then, plunging the room into a sudden silence. Claire froze for a second, waiting for the next thing to happen. Farron did as well and then stepped out onto the bridge, testing it before he put his full weight onto it.

"Be careful!" Claire called after him, her words echoing strangely.

One foot after another, Farron eased his way across the too narrow bridge, causing a nervous sweat to break out across her skin just watching him.

When he was halfway across, a deafening, birdlike shriek pierced the air.

Claire's blood ran cold. Farron stopped and crouched down low, steadying himself into a ready stance. It couldn't be, could it?

The room seemed to shudder and then the noise of shifting sand followed. The second shrill cry all but solidified her fear. They had just awakened a Beast of Old.

Nothing good ever happened underground.

Claire watched in horror as a massive shadow emerged from the sand below, slow and lethargic, just like the Maelin she and Lianna had faced in the tiny mountain town, like the feline-like beast she had fought at Lord Byron's estate. Her worst fear had come true. Of course, if it were any other Star Child, they could simply defeat the creature. It was another safeguard in place to protect the stone. Clever of Rialla, but bad for Claire and Farron. She wondered for a split second just how the woman had trapped a Beast of Old in the first place.

Like a wet dog, the creature shook its body to free itself of the sand. It was far enough away that she didn't think it had noticed that they were there. Yet. She and the elf remained frozen in place, afraid to make a move and catch its attention. They watched in silence as the beast ambled awkwardly across the sand toward the far side of the room.

Farron took the opportunity to carefully take another step. Claire held her breath, afraid even that would give them away. He took another step, but as he was putting his foot down on the bridge, a loose piece cracked and fell off into the abyss down below. Farron stilled and Claire's heart leaped up into her throat.

Then the beast's cry filled the cavernous room, echoing, deafening, terrifying. Farron stood, keeping his knees bent and ready, and drew one of his daggers. The air seemed to quiver when the creature flapped its wings. It took a few tries for it to become airborne.

"Farron!" Claire cried out. He wasn't planning on fighting that thing, was he?

He gave her a sharp look. One that told her that that was exactly what he meant to do.

And there was nothing she could do about it.

And that meant if he was going after the creature, then she was going to have to cross the bridge. Suddenly she didn't know who had the easier job. The avian beast circled high above them, crying out once more. Farron turned on the bridge to follow its movements. Claire was amazed at how sure-footed he was.

"Don't you dare die on me!" she shouted. "You hear me?"

He glanced at her, a grin forming on his face.

Claire sighed. He had a foolish lust for excitement just like Lianna. No wonder they had once been drawn to each other.

The beast was coming around again, its path descending, closing in for the attack. Farron crouched lower and drew his hand along the back of his dagger. Lightning-like sparks engulfed his blade, crackling. The creature swooped down and grabbed the elf with its talons, and flew up in the air once more, hauling him into the darkness.

Claire remained in place as she stared after him, hoping he knew what he was doing, that he would be all right. It was all she could do now. No—she had to go get the stone, or else all this would have been for naught.

It took her a few tries to get her body to move toward the bridge. When she neared the edge of the platform she looked down into the void. It was too far down. Way too far down for her comfort. If she fell…

But she couldn't think of that now. She had a job to do. Sweat already drenched her, her pulse hammering in her chest. She eased a foot out onto the narrow path. It had held for the elf, so she assumed it was safe in that regard. But even after all of her training, she was never, and never would be as sure-footed as the elf. After taking a deep breath, Claire swung her other foot out and in front of the other. She held her arms out to help steady herself. Just one foot after another, she kept repeating in her head.

She let her mind get absorbed in the task, shutting out the surrounding world, trying her best to ignore the ground too far down below. But an ear-piercing cry shattered her concentration. Her head snapped up toward the beast. It tumbled through the air, free falling for a few moments before righting itself once again. Claire swayed slightly and snapped her attention back to the bridge.

Hours seemed to pass by the time the platform came into view. She was almost there. The creature still circled around the room, occasionally tumbling and dipping under the bridge before flying up high again. Claire didn't dare stare for too long. She couldn't risk it. Just two more steps.

On the last step, she lurched forward onto the platform. She took a long shuddering breath, her body shaking. But she was only halfway done. There was no time to relax now. She rushed up to the pedestal. The piece of stone just sat on top of it, a layer of dust obscuring the script carved into it. But there was no mistaking that it was a part of the same piece that her stone had come from. Claire examined the pedestal, looking for any more of the strange letters, for another ward or spell that would be triggered. Not finding any, she touched the fragment, her magic reacting to it. The silver bands grew uncomfortably hot on her arm.

Another cry of the beast spurred her on. She grasped the stone and carefully lifted it, pausing only for a moment to see if anything else would happen. When it didn't, she turned to begin the long journey back over the bridge. She held the fragment tightly under one arm, close to her body, and stepped onto the thin path once again. One foot after another, she repeated again, over and over.

When she was a little more than halfway across the bridge, the beast let out a more guttural cry. Claire turned her head to look up. The creature jerked back and forth, dropping before catching itself a few times. She saw that Farron had somehow gotten onto its back. He drew back an arm, the sparking dagger in hand, and plunged it into the beast's back. It let out a miserable cry as it spiraled into a free fall.

"Farron!" Claire shouted.

He jumped as the creature passed over the platform ahead of her, rolling as he landed. The beast circled the room once more, its path dropping lower and lower, coming right for a collision course with the bridge she still stood on.

"Fare!" she yelped.

He got to his feet and rushed to the edge of the platform, his hand outstretched.

"Come on!"

She was too far to make that jump. Her feet moved faster than she thought possible, her balance faltering as her body swayed from side to side. Panic took over, making her knees weak, her stomach drop to the floor. She was still several steps away from the platform when the beast collided with the bridge. The rock underneath her feet shook, throwing her balance off. She stumbled and only managed to push off in the direction of Farron's outstretched hand before falling out into the abyss. A scream tore out of her throat. She reached out to him, but he seemed too far to grab her. Butterflies filled her insides as she fell, weightless, and she thought all was lost, but then Farron's strong grip encircled her wrist, jerking her to a stop. Her breath came in small, short gasps as she waited for her mind to catch up to the present.

"I've got you, Claire." His voice sounded strained but sure.

Relief washed through her even as her feet dangled helplessly in the air.

A muffled thud shook the room as the creature finally crashed into the sand below. And then all was quiet and still once again. The only things she could hear was her own heart beating inside of her, her ragged breaths, and the cracking of the bridge as pieces fell off of it.

Farron grunted as he slowly started pulling her up and onto safe ground. Claire collapsed on the solid foundation below her. Farron did the same next to her. They both stared up at the ceiling while they caught their breath.

"That was not fun," she said, still shaking.

Consumed

"Oh, I don't know, I found it rather thrilling." She could hear the grin in his voice. He raised onto his elbow and looked down at her, said grin in place. "I told you I owed you a Beast of Old, didn't I?"

A short laugh escaped her. She had never thought he would actually do it. It took her a few more moments to be able to move again. She sat up and held the stone piece out to look at it.

"Is that it?" Farron looked at it, unimpressed.

"All that trouble for this." She blew the dust off the script. The letters matched the markings on the piece she had and the ones used in the wards and spells throughout the cavern. Other than that, it was fairly unremarkable. Could this thing really be the key to restoring magic? Whatever her doubts, it was her only hope.

"Let's get out of here, shall we?" He rose to his feet and pulled her up along with him.

She swayed a little, her knees still weak. She couldn't wait.

8

Claire had never thought she would be so happy to be cold again in her life. She even almost welcomed the shivers that racked her body.

After their ordeal in the desert, they'd headed north and then west to Atalan Island, seat of Council member Bolin. According to Farron, he was a moderate who would swing whatever way the coin flowed. And he had a rather peculiar interest in antiques. It was as good a guess as any that the piece of stone may have resided in his private collection. As to how the man might have gotten ahold of it, that was a mystery to them both. Especially after what they'd been through. Did he know the importance of what he had? Or was it just another artifact to add to his collection?

Clouds shrouded the skies, the dampness chilling her to the bone. They arrived in the small seaside town in the late afternoon. Mud already caked her boots and the hem of her cloak. Farron had kept his hood drawn up over his head for the past several hours, ever since the town had first risen up on the horizon.

"Have you been here before?" she'd asked him.

"Yes," he had said, though by the tone of his voice, it wasn't a happy memory.

She had decided not to push the subject. Not only was she too tired to, but even though she was curious about his past, she wasn't sure she wanted to know all the grisly details.

A few curious eyes spied them as they walked down the main street leading into the town. Shops and inns lined the road, houses, a tavern or two. Not as colorful as Linesbrough, the atmosphere of the place seemed less grim, despite the dreary weather. It was almost quaint.

They continued on down the road that led towards the water. A small port sat in the center of the town. The docks weren't as bustling as the ones she'd come across previously in her journey.

Farron stopped and nodded out over the water. "That's Atalan Island."

Claire followed his gaze. An island rose from the middle of the bay. Scattered buildings sat along the water's edge under the imposing manor atop a hill. "I'm guessing that's Bolin's estate?"

He was silent, some past memory hazing his eyes.

She looked at the island again. Although she doubted they were going to run into another Beast of Old, she knew it wasn't going to be easy. She could feel the slight pull of magic coming from that direction. The stone was definitely somewhere on it. It was a different sort of challenge, one that Farron would be perfect for. She was curious to see the side of him he tried to keep hidden, locked in his past, and wondered if she would see some of the *Sin de Reine* reemerge. She'd seen flashes of it in the past and it was chilling, to say the least.

"Come," he said, and turned to continue down the street.

They rented a room at a little inn with a window that looked out over the bay and island.

Claire warmed her hands by the fire. Farron had been quieter than usual since he'd seen the island, feeling distant once again. Only this time she had no snowballs to lob at him.

She turned to face him. "Fare–"

"I'm all right," he said, cutting her off. His voice was soft but held a hint of gloom. He tried to force a smile, but it wasn't very convincing.

Claire took his hand in hers and rubbed it, trying to warm it up. "I'm here," she said, "No running away."

The smile he gave then was small but genuine.

"In fact, your special skills are exactly what we need for this one."

"I knew they'd come in handy someday." The amusement faded from his face.

"Do you have a plan?"

"A few," he said. He looked down at her. "It depends on whether or not I can convince you to stay back."

"Not a chance," she said. Even though the mission made her nervous, she couldn't let him risk himself for her while not doing anything to help. "Besides, I can sense the stone. How would you know where to go?"

"It wouldn't be my first visit to his manor," he said, his voice grim.

"Well, in any case, I won't let you go alone. Not for my sake."

"If there's no convincing you…" He sighed. "Then we go in after dark and infiltrate the main house. We have to be stealthy." He gave her a pointed look.

"I can be sneaky."

He raised an eyebrow.

"I can," she said, crossing her arms. "Not everyone has exceptional hearing like you do."

"And you have to do what I say," he said. "No arguing."

"Yes, sir." She straightened her back like a soldier taking orders. She had to stop herself from saluting him. He probably wouldn't think it was as funny as she did.

"All right," he said, opening his pack to dig out supplies. "I know you must be tired, but let's get this over with before my presence here is discovered. Too many people here know my face, even with my hair changed."

Claire didn't like the prospect of going straight into it. She was exhausted. But he had a point. She would just have to endure it.

Farron looked out the window. The sun was setting already.

"We should go. The row over will take a while."

Claire gulped, already regretting her decision. There was rowing involved? Nothing good ever came from that either, especially with him in the boat.

※

Her cloak was sopping wet by the time they touched shore on the island. They'd rented a rowboat from a man by the docks for a few too many coins. The man had given them a curious look, but an extra coin was added to his fee for his silence.

Farron had insisted on doing the rowing, making a jest about her skills in the past.

She didn't mind—though she felt a bit guilty about it—and she took the opportunity to close her eyes for a little while.

Darkness took over the sky completely by the time they went ashore, the only illumination coming from the stars. The moon wasn't out, providing extra cover. A boon for them.

Farron had rowed out and around to the side of the island where no buildings stood, and had landed on a tiny beach under a rocky cliff. The crashing of the waves and swaying of the boat had woken her up. She perked up just as he jumped into the surf to pull the boat up onto the sand. When it was safe, she jumped out onto solid ground, her body shivering from the damp cold. She stripped the cloak off and tossed it into the boat. Farron did the same.

He strapped his daggers on, a hilt sticking up behind each shoulder, but she was sure they were far from the only weapons he had on him. Claire made sure her own was in place. She was hoping that they weren't going to have to use them, but it was better to be safe than sorry.

She looked up at the imposing cliff face. This journey was testing her to the fullest, that was for sure.

Farron gave her a concerned look. "You can still stay back, Claire."

Why was he so eager to leave her behind? Was she that much of a hindrance? Or was there another reason? "No, I'll be all right." Though her insides told otherwise. They were twisted up into knots already.

He took a rope out of the boat and tied one end around her waist. "Just follow in my path," he said, tying the other end around himself.

She nodded and followed him over to the cliff. It didn't look extremely high, but it was enough to make her anxious. She watched as he mounted the rock and started climbing, a little too swiftly and easily. He'd done this before. She wondered how many times. She shook her head at the thought. This wasn't the time to be dwelling on such a thing.

She started to climb up after him, regretting her decision not to take her gloves along. They were back at the inn along with the rest of their things. They'd hidden their packs as best they could and hoped that no one would want to raid the curious travelers' room.

The rock was rough and porous, scratching up her hands. Her boots made getting a good foothold a challenge. Her reach wasn't the same as the tall elf's and she was lagging behind him. The slack in the rope was almost pulled taut. He had glanced back at her a couple of times but hadn't said anything.

They were already halfway up the cliff when her boot slipped and she plummeted a foot or two before gripping the stone again, stopping her fall. She shrieked, her heart beating furiously inside of her. The rope pulled at Farron and she could hear him grunting with effort.

"Are you all right?" he asked, trying to keep his voice low.

"Yes," she replied in between quickened breaths. She regained her footing and took a moment to steady herself before continuing on. The sooner they got this over with, the better.

By the time they reached the top, her arms and legs were sore and shaking from the effort. Claire doubled over to catch her breath and to calm her nerves. She peered back over the edge and her vision spun. She looked away quickly. That wasn't going to be any more fun on the way back down.

Farron untied the rope from them and set it aside underneath a nearby bush. The fact that he looked barely affected by the climb irked her, though she supposed she should have been used to it by now.

"Stick close to me." He crouched a little and slipped into the dark forest.

Claire followed after him, trying her best to do so. He didn't seem happy that she was still coming along, but that was just too bad. He wouldn't be on this mission if it weren't for her. This was just as much, or even more so, her responsibility than his.

It was hard to see him in the darkness of the forest, but she was sure he was able to see her. He was like a shadow come to life, darting

Consumed

in between trees, disappearing completely at times, his footsteps unnervingly silent. Claire tried her best to keep quiet but occasionally stepped on a twig or dried leaves, making a loud cracking or crunching noise. She was like a drunkard next to him. His past words bubbled up from her memory. He'd been right all along, but she wouldn't give him the satisfaction of admitting it.

It seemed like an hour had passed before they spotted the glow of the house lights through the dense forest trees. Farron slowed his pace, waiting for her to catch up.

He dipped behind a bush and ducked down low behind it. Claire followed suit.

He poked his head up and studied the manor for a moment.

A metal fence surrounded a vast manicured garden full of fountains and statues. The main house was an imposing two-storied stone building with long wings that stretched out to either side. The place was huge.

Farron ducked back down and turned to her. "Where to?"

Claire closed her eyes and opened herself up to the pull of the magic. It came easier to her this time, now that she knew what to do. "There," she whispered, pointing to the left side of the manor where the windows remained darkened. That could be a good sign, right?

He slid off back into the darkness and Claire followed after him as they circled around the fence. She wondered how he planned on getting over it. The spiked ends wouldn't be easy to climb around. He stopped at the edge of the tree line before the fence. He remained still, crouching next to a tree in its shadow, his eyes studying the house and gardens. Claire followed his gaze, kneeling behind him. The grounds seemed quiet. No one patrolled. In fact, she saw no life at all, but she would trust his instincts on that before her own.

After several moments, he moved forward towards the fence and knelt in front of it. He pressed his hands to the ground and she could feel the surge of magic that he pushed into the earth beneath them. It shuddered a little as rock shot up to form a crude set of steps that led up to the top of the fence. But only on one side. Farron climbed them quickly and dropped gracefully onto the grass on the other side. He turned and motioned for her to come. Claire scampered up them, pausing at the top, looking down at him. He held his hands up to her, impatience in his eyes. With breath held, she jumped and he caught her, then lowered her down before kneeling once more. He touched the ground again to get rid of the stairs.

He snuck up to the house, slipping between expertly trimmed topiary. He pressed his back up against the stone and peeked around the corner. Claire did the same, following his motions as best as she could, trying not to be a hindrance. It was a challenge, but she had to admit it was sort of thrilling to be sneaking around. Not something she ever wanted to do again, though.

Farron turned to her with a finger up to his lips. Her heartbeat picked up again. He held a hand up in a signal for her to stay. She nodded and he slipped around the corner.

After a moment she slid up to the edge and slowly peeked around it. A guard patrolled near the backside of the house, strolling languidly into the garden. Farron hid behind a hedge, waiting.

When the man came near Farron sprung into action, like a wild cat, silent and lethal. He snuck up behind the man and slipped an arm around his neck, the other over his mouth, before pulling him back onto the ground, disappearing from Claire's sight, the whole movement took only a few seconds. She started to worry when he still hadn't shown after what seemed like forever, her worry making time stretch. When he finally did, he motioned for her to come.

Claire stooped down and hurried to join him. She looked at the unmoving man. Farron had pulled him back behind a shrub so that he wasn't visible from the house.

Consumed

She gulped and looked up at Farron. A spark of fear must have shown on her face because his own fell slightly, the icy mask slipping into place. She said she wasn't going to run and she meant it, but she reminded herself to never make an enemy of the elf.

Without a word, he crept up to the manor again to the side of a set of glass-paned doors. Claire pressed herself against the wall behind him as he peered in. No light came from within. After a moment of watching, waiting, he knelt by the handles, pulling some thin metal tools from his boot. He stuck the ends into the lock and a few moments later there was a soft click. He put the tools away and opened the doors. Claire followed him into the dark room.

Her nerves stood on edge when she crossed the threshold. She wasn't sure why they rose so sharply. Perhaps it was because now she was inside a stranger's home, their territory, uninvited, intruders in the night. They were the burglars, the bad ones this time. The forbidden aspect sent a thrill through her.

Moving swiftly, Farron crossed the room to check the hallway through an opening.

Claire waited by the door, closing them carefully behind her. The room was big, exquisite and a little too opulently decorated for her tastes. Another set of matching doors sat on the same wall further down. Somewhere a clock ticked away the minutes. She wondered how late it was.

Movement caught her attention as Farron waved to her, a frown on his face. She'd messed up, letting herself get lost in her thoughts instead of focusing on the task at hand. She mouthed an apology to him as she joined him.

"Where?" he mouthed the word.

She closed her eyes briefly and searched again. The magic lured her to the left. She pointed in the direction and he dipped out into the hall, and she followed. He stopped at every open doorway and corner to listen before moving on to the next. The pull of the magic became stronger the deeper they went. A good sign. They hadn't encountered any more guards so far. Another good sign. Maybe. She didn't want to let her guard down too soon. Not until they had the stone in their hands and they were safe and warm back at the inn. Or better yet, far away from this place entirely.

They took a hidden servants' stairway up to the second floor and had crept deep into the bowels of the house when they finally came across the room where the magic pull was strongest. Farron stopped outside the wooden double doors and waited for a moment, listening, before trying the handle. It was locked. Curious. Who was Bolin trying to keep out inside his own house? Maybe he was just overly cautious. It only took Farron a few moments to pick the lock. He pushed open the door carefully.

The room was dark. Farron snapped his fingers and the flame appeared above his hand. The dim, flickering glow made the shadows dance. Antiques and artifacts littered the room, some organized and on display, others stacked and gathered haphazardly about. From furniture to jewels and gold to books and scrolls, there was a little of everything. Claire paused by a suit of metal armor. It was towering, taller than even the elf. She wondered who had worn it. Whoever it was must have been impressive. A couple of other things caught her eye, a golden beetle encrusted with emeralds, painted wooden masks, weapons of all sorts. She could spend hours in here just rummaging through it all, exploring, but they didn't have the time, much to her dismay.

Claire followed the lure of the magic to the other end of the room. The fragment sat on a desk, an unrolled scroll underneath it. The surface of it was cleaned, the script easy to make out compared to the last piece. When she reached for it, she noticed that the scroll underneath had some of the same script written on it, the ink faded, the paper old, yellowed and brittle. She ran her fingers along a line of words, wondering what it said.

"Leave it," Farron whispered close behind her.

She jumped ever so slightly. She'd never get used to that. But he was right. As much as she wanted to take the scroll, it just wasn't practical to do so. The water would destroy it and all the knowledge within. She grabbed the stone, her magic responding, the bands growing warm as they stomped it back down again. A shiver went through her. It wasn't a pleasant feeling.

Claire gripped the fragment close to her body and turned to Farron.

He gave her a curious look. "Are you all right?" he whispered.

She nodded.

Then he froze, his body growing tense. He tilted his head as he listened, to what she didn't know, but she was sure it wasn't good.

"We have to go," he said, turning back toward the door.

He rushed out into the hallway, extinguishing the flame, but instead of going the way they had come, he turned to the opposite direction. Claire followed, closing the doors behind her. They rushed to the end, Farron pausing only momentarily at the corner before moving on. She held the stone close to her chest securely in her arms.

Farron suddenly stopped in front of a closed door. After listening for a moment he opened it and slipped in. He snapped again and the flame appeared as she closed the door. It was a small, simple room with no windows and no other way out. Why had he taken her in here?

"Wait here, Claire," he said quietly as he lit the oil lamp by the bed. He inched up to the door again and slipped out before she could protest.

She sighed, looking around her at the room once more. She had to trust that he knew what he was doing. And in fact, she probably didn't want to know what he was doing. Although she doubted that he had seriously harmed the guard out in the garden, she couldn't be sure. With each passing minute, her unease only grew. Did Bolin know they were there? Had they been found out? What exactly was he doing with the stone fragment? He'd been onto something, based on the scroll, but how much had he figured out? She doubted that he would answer her if she asked.

Several minutes had passed and there was still no sign of the elf. She held her breath and closed her eyes to listen, but the manor was quiet. Should she go and look for him? She would be defying his orders, but if something had happened to him… Claire was reaching for the door handle when it opened suddenly. She jumped back, not sure who to expect, only breathing a sigh of relief when she saw it was Farron.

"What took you so long?" she whispered, trying not to show her annoyance.

He gave her a sharp look. "There are more guards than I thought. Bolin is either more cautious than I remember or he is expecting trouble."

That didn't help to ease her worries.

"I took care of a few of them, but it won't be long before the others find that they are missing."

Claire nodded.

"Be ready, Claire," he said, "and stay close."

She wasn't going to argue about that. He slunk out the door again, Claire on his heels. He turned right and then crossed over to another servants' stairs that took them down into the kitchen. A fire burned in the hearth, a thick stew still simmering over it. The hearty smell stirred her stomach, making it growl. Farron glanced back at her.

Consumed

"Sorry!" she whispered. She really couldn't help it. All the action was making her hungry. Would they notice if a roll was missing? A fresh stack sat atop the counter and the temptation was almost too much. But she held back at the risk of Farron's wrath.

He rushed to a door that led to the outside and pushed, but it wouldn't budge. He tried again, putting his weight into it, but still, it wouldn't give way.

"It's blocked," he said. "I have a feeling they don't want us to leave."

He came around the kitchen and went to the open archway that led deeper into the house and waited, listening. When he was met with silence he slipped out into the hall and she followed after him.

Worry gnawed at her. She didn't like where this was heading.

"Claire," Farron said as he grabbed her arm and started to pull her along at a more frantic pace.

He turned and ran down the twisting hallways, pausing at every intersection, seeming to change his mind as if he had heard something she hadn't. Panic started to brew inside of her. This wasn't good. Were they being led somewhere? It just felt like what the centaurs had done in the ill-fated town before. But at least this time their enemy wasn't so frightening. As far as she knew.

Farron's pace slowed as they passed through a set of massive carved wooden doors into a dimly lit hall. Chandeliers hung from a soaring ceiling and oil lamps lined the walls at intervals. The hall was currently set up for a banquet of some sort, long tables running parallel to the red rug that ran deeper into the room where the head table was set up, a chair that rivaled any throne in the middle. An elderly man sat calmly in it. He stared at them, challenge and annoyance flashing fiercely in his gaze.

Farron slowed to a stop, his shoulders tensing. "Lord Bolin," Farron said, calmer than she thought would have been possible. "It's been a while."

Claire peered around the elf at the Councilman. She didn't recognize his face, but she knew he probably did hers. Fine clothing draped his frail frame, dark red with gold trim and more jewelry than was tasteful. Firelight gleamed off of his bald head.

"I should have known that you'd come for me eventually," Lord Bolin said. His voice held a deep authority that echoed in Claire's memory. "The infamous *Sin de Reine*." He rose from the chair and began to walk slowly around the long table. "But you should know, that since you declared your fealty to the Council, this is treason."

Farron took a few steps toward the man, the tension leaving his body.

Claire hesitantly followed. She eyed the second-floor mezzanine that circled the back of the room. It was empty, for now. She doubted that the lord of the manor would expose himself so freely without some sort of protection.

"Unfortunately, I haven't come to kill you, Lord Bolin." Farron tried to make the comment seem light, but there was a hint of malice. "Though I do believe that you and the Council have been wanting to rid of me for a while now, regardless of loyalties."

Lord Bolin laughed. "Is that right?" His eyes settled on Claire. "But you have come all this way to steal from me?"

Claire shifted, uncomfortable as the center of his attention. Guilt surged through her. He *was* right.

"Is this the king's doing?" Lord Bolin came around the edge of the table, his hands behind his back. "Has his highness stooped so low as to send you to do his dirty work? What a waste of your talents."

Farron glanced at her, then back to the old man.

Consumed

Her mouth grew dry. Why did the Council inspire such fear in her? He was just a man, not a centaur or a Beast of Old. Not that she knew what to say anyway. The wrong words here could spark trouble down the road.

"Or is an agent of the king and his brother acting of their own accord?" Lord Bolin finally came to a stop and leaned back against the table, crossing his arms in front of himself. "If that's the case, then I would be glad to rid the crown of two traitors."

He nodded his head and men poured out onto the second-floor mezzanine and through the door at their back and two doors at the sides of the room. They were surrounded. Claire spun around, gauging how bad it was. She edged up closer to Farron. How did they always seem to end up in these situations? Anticipation radiated from the elf.

"It is curious, though," Lord Bolin continued. "Of all the treasures, why that one? If you were willing to risk your lives for it, perhaps it is much more important than I thought it was. Which begs the question, if you aren't working for either the king or Council, what could you be up to?"

Claire didn't want to tell him that she was on a mission for the king. She knew that he wouldn't believe her. Not many humans would. Not that she could blame them. Sometimes she felt like a traitor to her own race for what she was trying to achieve, and maybe she was, but if she didn't do this, who knew what kind of fate lay ahead? Besides, if she did tell him, a war would surely erupt to oust the elven king from his throne. There was still a chance to salvage things, somewhat. If the Council believed they were acting on their own, maybe a civil war could be avoided. Maybe.

She finally found her voice and hoped that it didn't waver. "Why Farron, I do believe we've been found out." She shifted the stone under her left arm and rested her right on the dagger at her waist.

The jacket she wore hid the silver bands from view, but Bolin and his men didn't know about it and its effects. As far as they knew, she was a powerful threat. "Anyone will go rogue for enough gold; isn't that right, Bolin?" Claire turned to eye the old man, faking a sly grin. She hoped her ruse would be believable and that Farron would catch on.

"Something you're quite familiar with, isn't that right, Lord Bolin?" Farron added.

Claire's back brushed up against his. She was glad that he'd caught on. He had always been quick-witted.

Lord Bolin's face twitched slightly and he tried to cover it up with a frown.

"Don't worry, my Lord," Claire said, "I'm sure you aren't the only one that's been in the *dark*." She emphasized the last word hoping Farron would get the hint. It was a reach, but it was worth a shot.

"We should have killed you the second you showed your face in Derenan again," Lord Bolin said, ire clear in his voice and on his face. "I'll be glad to finally put the Council Dog down."

Lord Bolin raised a hand to signal his men, but before they could act, Farron raised his own and all the flames from the chandeliers and lamps streamed toward his hand.

The men and Lord Bolin paused, fear and awe stark on their faces. Claire wasn't sure what he had planned, but she crouched just in case, drawing her dagger for show, though she didn't intend to use it. Heat from the large fireball now hovering over Farron warmed her head and back, the undulating light casting ominous shadows across the hall. The edges of the room dimmed and she lost sight of half of the men.

"Until next time, Bolin," Farron said and then he raised his hand higher. The fireball shot out in a circular blade of flames towards the

Consumed

men. Farron ducked quickly as the room plunged into darkness. Shouts of the men filled the air, Lord Bolin's lost among them. Farron's hand found Claire's and he pulled her back toward the main door that they'd entered. She felt him shift and then a moment later heard a man grunt, and then a thud as he fell to the floor. A few more were dispatched with relative ease as they fought their way out. A hand grabbed at Claire, but she was able to fend it off. The shouts only grew in intensity and anger, replacing the fear and confusion from before.

Cool fresh air touched Claire's face. They were almost out, just a little further. Farron paused, then let go of her hand as he fought a man—or was it two, or more? She couldn't tell. Unable to see anything, she froze in place, afraid to move or make a sound. She listened to the scuffling and the thuds and grunts of fighting, hoping that the elf was successful. He was capable, she knew, but there were a lot of guards. The noises stopped abruptly and there was a brief moment of silence between the shouting. Claire didn't dare call out for him for fear she would give her position away to the others. But she knew how to get his attention and started to walk as normally as she could, straight ahead.

His hand found her wrist and pulled her along again. Moments later they burst out into the front courtyard and ran toward the metal gate. Two guards stood at attention by it and perked up when they saw the elf and Claire running full speed right for them. They lowered their spears in a hurry, caught by surprise. Perhaps they'd thought that the many guards inside would have stopped the intruders. But they didn't know who they faced.

Several paces from the gate Farron let go of her hand. "Go!" he shouted as he dropped to a knee.

Claire continued running. He would catch up, even be able to surpass her again, so she wasn't worried. She felt the buzz of his magic at the back of her mind and a column of rock shot up underneath the gate, bending and twisting the metal until it broke. The rock slid into the earth again and the gate fell open, useless.

The guards jumped to the side, dropping their weapons, holding their hands up in surrender. Claire's pace still didn't relent as she hopped over the mangled metal. She only slowed briefly to look back at Farron. He still knelt, but his back was now toward her. Great earthen spikes shot up in a half-circle around him, blocking the way out. Not a bad idea, but it would only delay them for so long.

"Farron!" she shouted, and turned to continue her escape. She didn't know where she was going without him. She was following a gravel path that led down into the forest and presumably to the buildings that lined the shore.

A minute later he was passing her with his long strides and he took her wrist again, pulling her into a faster pace that she could barely keep up with. Then he dipped into the trees. Claire yelped as a bush caught her leg and stumbled. Only Farron's hold on her kept her from falling. It took her a few strides until she could get her bearings again. The way he weaved in between the trees so quickly in the dark boggled her.

The sound of waves crashing reached her ears, along with the strong taste of salt on the cool air. They were close to the shore. Distant shouts rang out behind them. The men were combing the forest. With the numbers they had, it was only a matter of time before they were found. At their frantic pace, Farron wasn't trying to be as quiet as before, and it was almost impossible for her to be. Their position was no secret to their pursuers.

And as fast as they moved in the dark, the shouts of the men drew ever nearer. Claire's breath ran ragged down her throat, her sides beginning to hurt from the furious pace. She wouldn't be able to keep it up for much longer before her body quit on her.

Consumed

Just when she felt like she was about to collapse, they burst out of the forest before the edge of the rocky cliff. Farron dropped her wrist and she doubled over for a moment to catch her breath. His shoulders heaved as he scooped up the rope and tied one end around her.

The shouts of the men were close, their fumbling footsteps closing in around Claire and the elf. Farron led her to the edge as he looked over his shoulder. She noticed that he didn't tie the other end around himself, and was about to protest when he suddenly pushed her over the edge.

"Go!" he shouted.

Claire flailed, a shrill scream ripping from her lungs. It was all she could do to hold on to the stone fragment. The rope around her waist stopped her fall, knocking the wind out of her. Her feet found purchase on the rock, but her pace was still too fast. The ground rushed up too quickly and she fell hard onto the sand, the rope piling up around her.

She rolled onto her back to look up at the top of the cliff. There was no sign of the elf.

"Farron!" she shouted, but the strong breeze dulled it.

There was a flash of lightning, followed by the clang of metal. Claire rushed to her feet and backed away from the cliff, hoping to catch a glimpse of him, but it was no use. They'd disappeared back into the forest. A few dark shadows appeared up on the ledge and she barely had time to react as one of them drew an arrow and loosed it at her. The arrow dug into the sand behind her as she ran toward the boat. The tide had come in since they landed and the back end already bobbed in the surf.

Claire had a decision to make. Should she wait for Farron? Or do what she was told and go ahead without him? Worry gnawed at her insides. She didn't like the idea of leaving him behind—loathed the thought, actually—but what choice did she have? She was useless in a fight without her magic. Besides, it would take her too long to scale the cliff again. He was drawing them away so she could escape unharmed. She had to trust that he knew what he was doing, that he could survive, that she would see him again.

Another arrow dug into the sand and then, a few moments later, another thunked into the wood of the boat. Claire ducked behind the far side of it as she began to push it back out into the water. When the water was waist high, she crawled into the rowboat, keeping as low as she could to avoid the arrows. The breeze worked in her favor, blowing toward the mainland. She watched as the shadowed man drew another arrow and loosed it, but the wind carried it away and it dropped harmlessly into the water.

With trembling hands, Claire wrapped the stone up in her cloak and stowed it under the bench, then settled herself on the seat and took up the oars. She'd watched Farron do it earlier. It didn't look so hard. But she probably wouldn't be saying that an hour from now when her arms would feel like they were about to fall off.

She dipped the oars into the water and pulled, her gaze never leaving the island, hoping to catch a glimpse of a foolish, silver-haired elf. Her guilt grew with each stroke. If he made it out alive, he would get that beating she owed him, that was for sure.

9

Day was breaking by the time she docked the small boat. Her arms had never been more sore in her entire life, not even after the many training sessions with any of her past mentors. It took her way too long to climb out of the boat and onto the dock, and when she finally did she collapsed onto the dirty planks on her back, the cloak-wrapped stone clutched in her hands, and just stared up at the sky, watching the clouds roll in off the bay. Raindrops started to fall in a light sprinkle.

Footsteps further down the dock made her stir again. She didn't have time to dawdle. She had to get back to the inn and prepare to leave. And even though her body protested, the fatigue bearing down on her, they couldn't stay. Not after last night. Had Farron made it out all right? She hadn't been able to see anything during her row back and that concerned her.

Claire sat up and the man, an older fisherman by the look of him, gave her a curious glance, then put his head down and hurried to his boat. Claire reached down and grabbed Farron's cloak from the rowboat and made sure it was tied securely to the dock before leaving. Her feet moved at a quick pace, but not so much as to draw attention from the waking townspeople. It only took her a few minutes to reach the inn and her room on the second floor. She had to hop up to reach the key that Farron had stashed on top of the frame. Her heart skipped a beat. So, he hadn't made it back before her. She unlocked the door, still hoping to find the elf within, but the room was empty. She hurried inside and closed the door behind her, locking it again. The room was cold, the fire having gone out hours ago.

Without pausing, Claire rushed to where they'd hidden their packs between the bed and the far wall and dug them out, preparing as much as she could for when the elf returned. She wouldn't let her mind go down the *if* path. He would return. When all was as ready as it would get, she found herself pacing back and forth, unable to stay still for too long. Each hour that passed, her worry only grew, until she felt she would go mad.

So many questions and scenarios raced through her mind. Had he been captured? Or worse, killed? Her worst fear could have come true, the thing she'd been wanting to avoid. He had put himself in danger for her for the hundredth time. He was a fool. A stupid fool. Was this even worth it if she lost everything she cared about? What would she do if she did lose him?

No, she couldn't start to think like that. Her mind couldn't take it.

Loud thumping footsteps out in the hall caught her attention. She froze, her hand going to her dagger at her side. Had they found where she was? It would only be a matter of time, especially in a town this small. The footsteps stomped closer, slow and stumbling. Then they stopped outside her door. Her pulse raced, her limbs trembling with anticipation. The doorknob jiggled and turned.

"Claire..." The whisper was ragged and breathy.

Consumed

But she recognized it instantly. She raced to the door and unlocked it before pulling it open wide, revealing the elf that stood slumped against the frame.

"Fare!" Claire gasped when she saw that he was gripping his side. He was soaked from head to toe and looked exhausted. But worst of all was the arrow that protruded from his side underneath his ribs and the red that was spreading across the cloth of his shirt. She had to smother a sob, her throat tightening. He was alive, but not well.

She pulled him into the room, supporting him the best she could. What should she do? He was in no condition to ride. And they couldn't stay here. She kicked the door closed with her foot and helped set him down on the bed. He moaned with the motion. Claire watched him as he tried to lean back, his face scrunched up in pain. Sweat glistened on his paler-than-usual skin.

"What happened?" She knelt before him to look at the wound.

He had broken the shaft of the arrow off so that only a little bit still protruded from him. It stuck in his side, toward his back at an awkward angle. She wondered why he hadn't just pulled it out.

When she didn't get an answer, she looked back up at him. His eyes were drifting closed and he slumped further onto the bed.

"No, no, no, no!" she exclaimed. "You can't fall asleep, not now, Farron!"

Claire looked around the room, feeling helpless. He was too big for her to move all by herself. She didn't want to ask the inn workers or anyone else to help her. It was too risky. She stood and looked down at him, her heart sinking. Her hand went to the silver chain around her neck. There was a way…

Without pause, she dug the key out from her shirt and slipped the chain off her neck. She'd only done it once before, and she hadn't even been in control when she did it, didn't even know if she could now, but she had to. For him. As quick as she could she undid the locks on the silver bands. With each one removed, her magic surged more within her, rising to the surface a little too eagerly after being locked away for so long. She stuffed the bands into her pack and slipped the chain back around her neck.

Shouts sounded from out on the street. She edged up next to the window and peeked out between the curtains. Armored guards spread out along the street, searching alleys and going into buildings. The door below their room slammed open. She didn't have long. With shaking hands, she gathered up the packs and stirred Farron awake.

"Come on, Fare," she whispered. "You have to get up."

He murmured something, but she couldn't discern what it was.

"You can do it," she said, putting more urgency in her voice. "I ask a lot, I know." She pulled his arm out and wrapped it around her shoulders. "But you have to do this. I won't let them have you." With all her might she heaved him to his feet. The momentum almost pushed her to the floor, but she was able to steady them both.

He was heavier than she'd thought he was and his weight threatened to overcome her fatigued strength. She was only upright out of sheer force of will. Footsteps pounded up the stairs, the men shouting, and then there was a loud crash as they kicked in the door down the hall. Claire's heart threatened to burst out from her chest. She clamped her eyes closed, flinching as they kicked in another door. She let her magic rise to the forefront, trying to remember the feeling she had when she had last flown, and then concentrated on a destination. There was only one place she could think to take him.

Wind started to swirl around her, her pulse picking up even more. She didn't like the thought of doing this, but she would do anything to keep him from dying.

The door next to their room was kicked in, the patrons inside yelling out. They were out of time. She pushed her magic even more, the sting starting in her arm, the pendant growing hot against her chest. She was using too much of her own magic, but her mind was too frantic to concentrate. The footsteps were getting closer—they were almost to their door. The wind was whipping her hair. She peeked her eyes open and the room was starting to blur. The footsteps stopped and the first kick shook the door. She clamped her eyes shut again and pushed all she had into it. The door burst open just as they disappeared from the room.

She couldn't tell if the screams were from the men or from herself.

10

When the world came into focus again, she saw that they had landed on the great terrace at the rear of the Haven's main building. Claire collapsed to her knees, taking Farron with her. A sob escaped her, and tears fell freely down her cheeks. She dropped the packs onto the ground.

It took her a few times to find her voice, to swallow the lump in her throat enough to speak. "H-help!" she shouted, and it came out weak and raspy. She hoped someone had been able to hear her.

The skies were grim and cloudy here as well, matching their predicament perfectly.

"Someone, help!" she rasped again, louder this time.

The glass-paned door opened then, and Maria came rushing out in her white robes.

"What in the—" She stopped as she took in the situation. "How did you get here?"

"Please help, he's hurt," Claire pleaded. There was no time for questions.

"Sarah, come quick!" Maria shouted.

The young woman hurried out, her cheeks flushing when she spied Claire and especially Farron.

It took all three of them to move the elf into a room and onto a bed. Farron stirred, moaning with each movement, but he was too out of it to know what was going on.

Claire collapsed into a chair by the bed. She'd never seen him like this before. Usually, he was so strong and resilient. It broke something deep within her to see him like that. So… helpless. She had done that. It was because he was protecting her that this had happened. The guilt weighed heavily on her shoulders and the tears flowed thicker.

When she came back to the present, she noticed that Sarah had wheeled in a cart full of supplies and Maria was already at work, cutting away his shirt to reveal his wound.

Claire leaned over to get a better view. "How bad is it?" she choked out.

"I don't know yet, dear," Maria said, her voice tense, but calm. "But I've seen him in worse shape."

That reassured her a bit. Only a little. He had been hurt badly before, judging by the numerous scars on his body, so he was tough. But she still didn't like to see him suffer. Perhaps it looked worse than it actually was. But she didn't want to make any assumptions before she knew for sure that he was going to be all right.

Sarah handed her mother supplies, both working in skilled unison. Their speed and adeptness amazed Claire, how they were able to look so calm and collected in the face of tragedy. But she supposed that they saw things like this often. There was no way she could ever thank them enough for all that they had done for her and Farron.

"Young lady," Maria said, and it took Claire a moment to realize she meant her. "I'll need your help to keep him still while I get this blasted thing out."

Claire nodded and jumped to her feet, going to the head of the bed. She helped the other two roll him up onto his side so that they could get a better angle. Farron groaned with the movement and she stroked his head, trying her best to soothe him, her other hand clamping down on his shoulder.

"This will only hurt for a moment." Maria gripped the wooden shaft of the arrow.

Claire knew that was a lie from experience. She pushed down harder to steady him.

After a deep breath, Maria pulled the arrow from his side.

Farron jerked, a weak cry coming from his mouth, then he grew still once more.

Maria covered the wound with a cloth, dropping the arrow onto the cart. Red soaked through the bandage a little too fast, and when it was saturated she replaced it with another one.

"Here, press down on this," she told Claire.

Claire did as told. "You're going to be fine, Fare, do you hear me?" she whispered.

She thought she heard him groan a response, but she couldn't be sure.

Maria replaced the cloth one more time with one covered in a sour-smelling poultice. She pressed the bandage over the wound as Sarah wrapped a strip around him to hold it in place.

The older woman wiped her forearm across her sweaty brow and breathed a deep sigh of relief. "I think the worst is over with, for now." She looked at Claire and it wasn't exactly happy. "Now I think you've got some explaining to do, Miss Claire."

An hour later the room was finally quiet. Maria and her daughter had left after making Farron drink a dark liquid, an antidote of sorts in case Farron had been poisoned. If he had been there was no telling with what.

Claire sat in the chair next to his bedside. Her own body was starting to crash now that the worst seemed to be over with, and it was a struggle to keep her eyes open. Only her nagging anxiety kept her awake. Farron rested peacefully in a deep sleep, occasionally muttering something softly that she wasn't able to make out. He didn't usually talk in his sleep, so she wondered what he was dreaming about. Was it good? Most likely it wasn't.

She sighed and took his hand in hers, stroking her thumb across the back of it. His skin was warmer than usual, his palms a little clammy. Tears started to form in her eyes once again. Seeing him like this, she couldn't help it. She knew he chose this path, to stay with her, protect her, but she still didn't like it. The thought of losing him and the fact that she nearly had shaken her to her core. She loved him. There was no doubt about that now. And as much as she wanted to be with him, she wanted him to be safe even more. That's what you did when you loved somebody. Sacrificed for the ones you loved. Her mother did it for her, giving her up to live a better life, and then Marion, setting her free even if she never saw her again. Perhaps it was time to do the same for him?

The tears escaped her eyes and flowed freely down her cheeks. She had tried that in the past, tried breaking it off with him to save him, but had she really even *tried*? She had been selfish then, wanting to keep him close. But he was stubborn. He wouldn't just let her leave, not if he could help it. Claire had to make a choice. Keep him and risk losing him forever, or leave now and maybe he stood a chance of living a long life. He would try to follow her, search for her, but now she knew how to fly. She could stay ahead of him, play the mouse to his cat indefinitely until her time came. She had half of the stones already, she only needed two more.

Consumed

She lifted his hand and brushed her lips across his knuckles, which were reddened and starting to bruise. It was for his own good, she kept telling herself. Leave him to keep him safe—this time for good.

Letting go of his hand, Claire struggled to rise out of the chair. Her body was near its breaking point, but if she was going to leave she had to do it while he still slept. She needed the head start and she didn't think she could stand to face him, see the heartbreak on his face yet again. She'd done that enough to him already. It was cowardly, she knew, but she had never been that brave to begin with.

She was fumbling with her pack when a soft knock sounded on the door.

"Come in," she said.

The door opened a crack and Sarah peeked her head in. "I was just check—" Her eyes narrowed when she saw what Claire was up to and she opened the door wider, ire on her face. "What do you think you're doing?" she said in a hushed tone.

"I can't let him get hurt anymore," Claire said, annoyed. "I won't." The tears had thankfully stopped.

"So you're just going to leave?" Sarah placed her hands on her hips, her voice rising in pitch with each word. Soon she would be shouting. "Without waiting to say goodbye?"

Claire sighed and put her pack down to look at the young woman. She appeared exactly the same as when Claire had left the last time, innocent and angry. She knew that Sarah had never liked her, and was sure that this wouldn't help her case.

"I would think you would be happy to see me out of the way," Claire said, letting the malice show.

Sarah's cheeks grew satisfyingly red and she looked away briefly. She flexed her hands by her side a few times, taking deep breaths before facing Claire again. "As much as I would love to see you out of his life forever, I know that it would destroy him when he woke up to find you gone." Her expression softened a little. "I've seen him get hurt too much over the years. He may be tough on the outside, but you and I both know how fragile his heart really is."

Claire's shoulders slumped, her resolve faltering. "I know," she said, struggling to stifle a sob. "But you don't understand…" She glanced at Farron, still asleep, so peaceful. Safe.

"Don't I?" Sarah's voice was barely above a whisper, sorrow dripping from it like a rainstorm.

Claire looked at her and saw the heartbreak plain on her face. Of course, she understood. She'd understood it for years.

"He's made his choice, Claire." Sarah turned to her, fire in her eyes once again. "And as much as I detest it, there's nothing I can do about it. You might think it's selfish to keep him near you, that you are doing the right thing, but I think it's selfish not to consider his wishes, what he wants."

Claire took a deep, shaky breath and released it slowly. Now she was more confused than ever. The girl had a good point. Farron had chosen to remain by her side, chose to risk his life, had ridden day and night to find her again. She wanted to leave to keep him safe—that was what *she* wanted. She'd made the choice for him. How was that not selfish?

"I hope you make the right choice, Miss Claire," Sarah said, turning toward the door. "No matter how painful it may be."

With that, the young woman left, closing the door softly behind her, leaving Claire standing in silence as a whirlwind of emotions raged inside of her, not sure what she should do.

<hr />

She was awoken by a hand on her head.

"Claire…" said a soft voice.

Consumed

Her eyes cracked open, still sleep-heavy. Pain rushed in from all over her body as the last couple of days finally caught up to her. Stirring, she stretched her stiff joints.

"Fare," she said, looking down at the elf, relief flooding in. He was all right. In fact, he looked much better than—well, she wasn't sure how long she'd been out. After Sarah had left, she had made the decision to stay, though the choice didn't come easy. She still had her reservations about it, but in the end, it *was* his decision to make. She had fallen asleep in the chair next to the bed, resting her head on her arms in the soft covers by his side, putting her body in an awkward position. A painful one, at that.

Some color had returned to his face, the sheen of sweat gone. His eyes still looked a little hazy, tired, but he was coherent.

"How do you feel?" she asked, examining him.

"I've been better," he said, his voice strained. "But I've been worse, as well."

Claire took his hand again and kissed his palm lightly.

"I had a dream that you left me here."

She froze, her face falling. Had he heard her earlier somehow?

A snort of laughter escaped him followed by a few coughs, though it didn't sound happy. He closed his eyes for a few moments. "So, it wasn't a dream after all."

"Fare, I…" Her voice faltered. She didn't know what to say.

His hand gripped hers. "I'm glad you stayed, Claire." He opened his eyes again and rested them on her. "Besides," he tried to make his voice light, carefree, but it was still strained, "this is nothing."

It was her turn to laugh, but it was short-lived as tears started to fall. He wiped one away with his thumb.

"Come here, Claire." He pulled her gently onto the bed next to him.

She let him without protest and buried her face in the crook of his neck. He stroked her hair, his body warm and comforting against hers, his heartbeat strong and sure in her ear. "I thought I was going to lose you, Fare," she whispered.

"Now you know how I feel on a regular basis." He wrapped her tight in his embrace.

"It's not the best feeling in the world."

His chest rumbled with a laugh. "No, it isn't, is it?"

Claire squeezed him back, careful not to do it too tight, afraid she would hurt him.

"I can't believe you actually flew for me," he said. "You must really like me."

Never mind. She pinched his arm and he laughed. He couldn't be too hurt if he was already teasing her. "The horses!" she said, perking up, raising up to her arms above him. Why had that just occurred to her now? She'd been so worried over Farron that she had forgotten that they'd been left behind at the inn.

Farron let out a deep breath. "Perhaps Maria can arrange something," he said. "If not, then they're now the new property of Lord Bolin."

"And his evidence," she said, growing grim. "He could use them to start trouble with the king."

"There's nothing we can do about it now," he said, fatigue showing in his voice.

She shouldn't be bothering him with this now. But her mind surely wouldn't let her forget about it. It was just another problem to add to the growing pile.

"I'll send word to my brother tomorrow," he said. "Then after, how would you like to join me for a little swim?" His condition didn't stop him from grinning.

Consumed

Heat rose up to her cheeks as she remembered their little tryst. "I don't know…" she teased, "nothing good ever came from being in the water with you."

He smiled and pulled her down for a kiss and she surrendered to it freely, losing herself in him. Nope, nothing good at all.

11

Claire tossed a pebble and watched as it disappeared into the field, the ripples spreading out like waves in water. She'd never thought that she would see this place again, the cursed field. It had changed slightly from the last time, the illusion shifting with the season. How clever. But now that she knew what to expect, there was something about it that seemed off. A cold breeze stirred the trees to their back; otherwise, it was calm, quiet. She had forgotten how eerily serene it was here.

After sending word to the king, followed by a too-steamy swim in the spring, they had left the Haven, borrowing two horses. Maria had said that she would deal with the horses that they'd left behind. She just hoped that Azra and Farron's horse would be all right and that they wouldn't be used to cause trouble that the country couldn't afford at the moment. Claire and Farron being discovered had done enough damage already.

Farron stood next to her on top of the rocky outcropping above the field, his ice blue eyes scanning, analyzing. His wound had healed, leaving only a small scar in its wake to join his growing collection. According to him, he'd fought off the guards on the island successfully, only for one to get a lucky shot in while he faced off against four men at once. The nonchalant way that he had told the story annoyed Claire, how he seemed to just dismiss the condition that he had been in. She knew that he was cocky, that he always would be, but she didn't want him to brush things off to try to prove a point to her, to make her feel better. After he had gotten hit with the arrow, he made his escape, diving into the cold waters to swim back to the mainland, a fishing boat picking him up when he was halfway across. He claimed that his condition was because he had overdone it, both physically and magically, and that there must have been poison on the arrow. He had been able to fight off the worst of the effects of the poison because of his built-up immunity to it.

Maria, Sarah, and Claire had listened to his story with worried, rapt attention, all three of them with disapproving frowns on their faces, But Claire knew for a fact that Maria and Sarah's scowls were half reserved for her. It was her mission, after all. The fact that they would leave only a few days later on yet another dangerous quest only deepened their frowns. Not that Claire could blame them. She was actually rather glad to be away from that place. It wasn't as soothing for her as it was for Farron. So much for being a Haven…

It took them weeks to reach the field again. Farron had brought her to the same place that he had the first time around, to the landslide where it was easier to scale. The memory had played in her mind as she climbed, and she'd smiled. How times had changed.

Farron threw a stone into the field and watched as it skipped a few times before disappearing. His hair was still darkened, but the dye was starting to fade, the ends turning a dark gray. His shirt had had to be replaced, the last one ruined when Maria had to cut it off of him. Much to Claire's dismay, he'd only replaced it with a similar one in the same inky black, keeping up the gloomy, intimidating visage.

"I'm going," he said.

Consumed

"No," she said, tying one end of a long rope around her waist, "You're not." The silver bands were back on her arm. She'd used too much of her own magic when she'd flown Farron to the Haven and the mark had expanded even more, the tendrils snaking up her neck and even further down her back. Her own magic had become this looming presence inside her body, like a dark storm just on the verge of releasing its rage upon her. It was like it yearned to be free and she was the prison cell keeping it locked up. It took its toll on her mind and body, the nightmares returning once in a while even with the enchanted contraption. She needed to complete her mission soon.

"I can't let you go in alone, Claire." Farron turned to her, his hands on his hips, disapproval clear on his face. "You don't know what's in there."

"That's right, I don't," she said, pulling the knot tight and checking again, and then once more just in case. "But you remember what happened in the cave. It was you that set off the trap. If I go in alone, then maybe this can go smoothly for once."

Apprehension filled her already. She didn't like the idea any more than he did, but the trials were meant to be for her, for the Star Children. And she really didn't feel like facing off against yet another Beast of Old. She'd had enough of them to last a lifetime.

"Besides," she said, trying her best at a convincing smile, "I need you up here to pull me out again."

She handed the other end of the rope to him, ignoring the very unhappy look he wore.

"If you're not out in half an hour, I'm coming in after you, you hear me?"

Claire raised her chin, her stubbornness rising to the surface. "At least give me an hour."

He sighed. "Fine."

"Remember, if I pull two times, pull me out."

He nodded. "Be careful, Claire." He pulled her close and kissed her, a hard press of the lips, before reluctantly letting her go again.

Claire faced the edge of the cliff, took a deep breath to help calm herself, and then began the slow descent down into the enchanted field.

The illusion shifted strangely the lower she got, fading into a gray fog until that was all she was surrounded by. It was so thick she could only see a couple of feet in any direction. The temperature of the air dropped by several degrees and she was glad that she was wearing her jacket then, though she could have used her cloak. She shivered. The magic of the place slithered across her skin, but it wasn't soothing like the water at the Haven or in Uru Baya—it was dark, disturbing, much like the madman, Bahkar's, and like her own. The feeling of this place, she didn't like it one bit. It was full of pain and despair.

Wanting to get this over with as quick as possible, Claire closed her eyes to seek out the stone fragment. A flood of depressing emotions engulfed her when she opened herself up: sadness, hate, hopelessness. She had to fight against them to find the slight lure of the stone. It lay ahead, not too far away.

With slow and steady steps, Claire made her way through the dense fog, her hands stretched out in front of her. The further she went, the colder it got. Goosebumps sprang up across her skin. The sound of her footsteps and breath were dampened. Her heart beat wildly inside of her, anticipation building. There had to be more than this, she just wasn't sure what to expect. This was different than anything she'd ever experienced before.

After a few more steps the fog started to thin a little. And then the moans started, drifting in the air, giving her pause. There were hundreds of them, all in pain, crying out every now and then for people long gone to the ravages of time. An explosion shook the ground several paces to her right. Claire crouched as dirt rained down on top of her—only it passed right through her, ghostlike. This was another vision like the one she'd had back in the cave in Uru Baya. Was Rialla trying to show her something again?

The earth shook again and bright purple magic streaked across a darkened sky.

She knew where she was—or rather, when she was. The Great War. Was this the Battle of the Stars? No, it was probably the battle that took place here all those years ago, the one that the humans had lost so bitterly. The first soldier materialized an apparition that chilled her to the bone. He was young, probably even younger than herself, and he lay on the ground writhing, covered in too much red. Claire stepped around him, not able to take her eyes off of him. Her feet passed through another young man and she yelped, stumbling, almost falling into another soldier. They were everywhere. The fog cleared a little more, but still obscured most of the field. She could only see several paces in front of her. She wasn't sure she even wanted to be able to see further.

It was like a nightmare come to life. Clanging metal sounded in the distance, the crash of lightning, the rumbling of moving earth, the roar of fire, but even more chilling were the screams of hurt and dying people. A lump formed in her throat, her mouth going dry. A cold sweat spread over her body. Why show her this? Was this a warning to any future Star Children of the consequences of returning magic to the land? Was this a preview of the future?

Guilt froze her in her tracks. Was this what she would be unleashing on the world? This is what magic returning could lead to. More wars, more death, more destruction. Could she really go through with it? Be responsible for all of this? The groans and cries of the soldiers echoed in her mind, threatening to drag her down into their dark anguish.

Claire covered her ears and let out a wordless yell, trying to block it all out. No, she couldn't stop, not now. She had to believe she was doing the right thing, that this time it could be different. If the land died, then so did everything else, elf and human.

Her legs trembling, Claire continued on, repeating the song her mother had sung to her all throughout her childhood to calm her down. It worked, a little. The sounds of battle drew nearer and a soldier stumbled by, clutching at his stomach. Claire paused as he passed. She knew that he wouldn't be able to affect her, but it felt disrespectful to just walk through him. A silly notion, perhaps, but one she had nonetheless. A few others passed her, some injured, some rushing nobly to battle, to their deaths with ragged battle cries. Her stomach churned. She was not built for war, for fighting. As someone had once said to her, the magic and all the power it gave her was truly wasted on her.

A lone figure appeared up ahead, obscured by fog, marching slowly toward her, its calm stride ominous and intimidating. Claire paused, unsure if it was another ghost or real. But her fears were quickly extinguished when he came into view. An elf in elaborate silver toned armor raised his arm, a blue orb forming in his hand, and then launched it at a target she couldn't see. His beautiful face was an icy mask, much like the one Farron had perfected. He held a lordly posture, tall and straight, proud, edging on arrogant. Claire stepped out of his way, eying him with morbid curiosity, the way he struck fear and awe in her, beautiful but deadly. Noble but cruel. A giant snuffing out an ant. The world belonged to him and his kind. He disappeared back into the fog and Claire let out a breath she didn't know she'd been holding. No wonder humans had had such a hard battle. She couldn't imagine a whole army made up of elves like that, or worse, like Farron. Now there was a truly terrifying thought.

Consumed

Fighting another shudder, Claire moved on, feeling the lure of the stone stronger now. How long had she been in the illusion? She didn't see any sign of Farron, so she assumed it hadn't been too long, but still, it felt like eons in the war-ravaged fog.

A quiet sobbing caught her ears before the soldier came into view. A young man sat hunched over atop a wooden chest, his left arm bandaged with bloody rags. Cautiously, Claire approached him, the pull of the stone radiating from where he sat. She looked around but could see no trace of the fragment. Was it in the box? If so, how was she going to get it out? He wasn't real, of course, but that seemed too simple.

Claire circled around the apparition. His shoulders heaved with his muffled cries, and he cradled his right arm close to his chest. Dark brown leather armor covered his body. An empty sheath sat at his waist. His hair and skin were smeared with dirt and grime, mixing with blood, but she wasn't sure if all of it belonged to him or not. Misery and hopelessness radiated from him like he held all the pain of the world within him. Claire had to fight against the overwhelming waves of emotions. She couldn't lose herself in them, couldn't let them affect her and drag her down into their frozen dark depths. She stopped in front of the soldier. He was young as well, his face too innocent still to experience the horrors of war.

After watching him for a moment, Claire moved to the side of him and crouched down to examine the chest. The stone was definitely in there. She could feel it. She glanced at the young man again to make sure that he didn't notice her. She felt silly. They were years and worlds apart, but he just looked too real for comfort.

With breath held, she reached out and touched the lid of the chest, then carefully undid the brass latch. The lid lifted without any resistance, passing through the young soldier as she swung it open. She paused for a few moments as she waited for something to happen, but when nothing did, she breathed a sigh of relief. Then, still on her knees, she peered into the chest. The stone fragment lay at the bottom atop a nest of cloth scraps. Nothing fancy, but considering the surroundings, anything more would seem out of place.

Claire touched the stone, her fingers sliding over the script, then picked it up and carefully lifted it out of the chest. Her magic reacted, the silver bands stamping it out again. She was just standing up again when the soldier reached out suddenly—only his hand didn't pass through her. It gripped her left forearm, real and hard, and so very cold, like ice. He looked up at her, fear in his green eyes, his lips trembling. Claire's heart leaped up into her throat, blocking the scream that bubbled up within her.

"Beware the wrath you unleash upon the world," he said, his voice wispy, ragged.

Were those his words or Rialla's?

Her skin began to burn where his hand touched even through the material of the jacket. She tried to pull her arm out of his grasp, but he was strong. His eyes pleaded with her, the desperation and sadness almost unbearable.

"Is this what you really want?" he cried. "Death, destruction, subjugation, to be their slaves once again?"

Claire had to stifle her own sob as she struggled to tear away from him. She couldn't take it anymore. She had to get out of here.

"Let go!" she shouted, her own desperation making it sound shrill. With a final tug, she tore her arm away and stumbled to the ground.

The soldier sank down onto his hands and knees and started to crawl after her. "Please," he begged. "Don't let history repeat itself. For our sake. For yours."

Claire scrambled to her feet and ran, using the rope as her guide. She felt like she couldn't breathe. She needed to get out of there. The

Consumed

sounds of battle and the sad cries of the soldier faded away behind her, then the rest of it as the fog became thicker, the illusion disappearing. She pulled the rope twice and the slack grew taut and soon she was being lifted up and out of the nightmare, the bright rays of the sun chasing away the gloom that seemed to cling to her.

When she reached the top, she collapsed to the ground, letting her sobs out freely.

Farron kneeled in front of her. "Are you all right?" he asked, a little frantic. "What happened in there? Are you hurt?" He looked her over quickly, his face screwed into worry and then confusion.

She leaned forward on her hands, her breaths coming in short shallow bursts, her body starting to tremble. "I don't know if I can do this," she said between sobs. She ripped off her jacket when the sting on her left arm didn't go away. A dark handprint wrapped around her forearm where the soldier had gripped her. She rubbed her hand over it, back and forth, trying to scrub it off, but no matter how hard she tried it remained just as dark and immovable as the magical mark that now covered almost half her body. Would it fade with time? Or would it remain as a reminder of all the humans that had lost their lives, of the people that may lose their lives in the future? A warning, and another burden to weigh her down with guilt.

Farron grabbed her face and turned it toward his. "Claire, look at me."

The stern tone in his voice made her listen, calmed her. She peered up at him, her tears blurring his visage, and she took a deep breath.

He brushed the tears from her cheeks. "You can," he said, his voice soft but sure. "And I'll be right here, next to you."

The frantic fear that had consumed her was slowly seeping away. He was her anchor. How could she have ever thought that she could do this without him? "Promise?"

"Promise." The corners of his mouth lifted into a reassuring smile and then he leaned in and kissed her on the forehead.

"I'm sorry," she said, feeling much calmer. "What I saw in there..." She looked up at him, memories of the soldier racing through her mind. "Made me question things."

"What did you see?"

"A battle from the Great War. It was a nightmare," she said, trying to stand on her shaky legs.

Farron helped her, his hands steadying her. He was her anchor in more ways than one. "A warning?"

"I think so." She nodded.

His expression softened as he studied her. "And have you? Changed your mind?"

She looked up at him, considering. The visions that she had seen would be enough to sway anyone, but amazingly, her resolve came through intact. "If we do nothing, then things could possibly be worse. I just sometimes question if I'm strong enough to pull this off."

"Well," Farron said, touching her chin, "considering that we've collected three pieces so far, I think you've proven that you can, Claire."

"But not without you." She took his hand in hers. "I'm sorry for trying to leave you back at the Haven."

"You've already apologized three times." He smiled and shrugged. "But another couldn't hurt."

Claire poked him in the side causing him to jerk away. "I worry about you, Fare."

"It's nice to know you care."

"You know I do," she said, a grin forming on her lips. "Most of the time, anyway."

Consumed

"Are you feeling better now?" he asked, putting a hand on his hip.

She nodded.

"Good," he said. "Then we should leave before the spirits follow you out of there."

Claire's eyes widened. "Do you think they could do that?" She would have dismissed his comment as just a tease, but after the soldier had grabbed her and had started to crawl after her, she wasn't so sure. He would certainly make his way into her nightmares, however, and the mark he had left on her arm made sure that his memory clung to her no matter where she went.

Farron only chuckled as he gathered up the packs and headed to the other side of the outcropping to start the descent back down.

Claire looked at the stone fragment gripped hard in her hand. She hoped she was doing the right thing. Because even if she was somehow saved from her mark, she didn't think she could live with herself knowing that she was the cause of the next Great War.

12

The world around her was dark, only this time she was actually awake. She swayed slightly in her saddle, not knowing where she was going.

"How much longer?" she asked a little too loudly.

Even though she appreciated the secrecy—she had even asked for it—the blindfold was itchy, and not being able to see anything for the better part of two days was really starting to wear on her. After the last fragment, she had asked Farron to take her to her mother. She had to see her, at least one more time in case… well, she was *trying* to keep a more positive outlook on things. It was the only way to keep herself motivated, and to keep from being overwhelmed by fear and unease. But just in case, she wanted to see Marion. Their last encounter had been too brief.

And so, to keep her safe from the madman, she donned the itchy scrap of fabric as Farron led her horse behind his. Since he had never been one for idle conversation, her days passed by too slowly, with no trees to count, stuck in her own mind. She sympathized with her birth mother. To go for years not being able to see anything… Claire couldn't imagine it. She understood why her mother had made the decision to let Marion raise her.

Claire sighed, exasperated. She didn't want to spiral down that road again. She'd already dwelled over it too much the past few days, weeks, months, years.

"It won't be too much longer," Farron said from up ahead, the annoyance showing in his own voice.

Not that she could blame him. She must have asked the same question about a hundred times already. Even she would get short with her.

"That's what you keep saying." Claire felt like they were stuck in a never-ending loop and knew that she was becoming irritable, and bored. Her curiosity was driving her mad. She knew that she should not know where Marion was, to keep her safe, but that didn't stop her mind from trying to work out and guess where they were going. It was her nature.

Farron was silent, but she knew his patience was wearing thin.

"I'm sorry," she said, immediately feeling regretful. He'd put up with enough from her.

"Well, this time I mean it," he said. His horse's hooves slowed their steady rhythm on the dirt road. "As much fun as this has been," he said next to her now, amusement in his voice.

Claire would have rolled her eyes if he could've seen it. Despite his growing frustration, he'd had his fun with the whole situation, sneaking up on her even more than usual—though he had never had any problems with that without the blindfold. Then there were the things that made her blush even thinking about…

"We should be there by nightfall, hopefully."

She turned her head in his direction, frowning. Although some light peeked in around the edges of the blindfold, she still had no sense of time beyond light and dark, and slightly lighter and slightly darker and—well, she had had too much time to think about that too.

Consumed

"It won't be too much longer, I promise," he repeated when her frown didn't disappear.

Claire released a long sigh. She supposed that was the best she was going to get.

"Do you know what you're going to say to her?" he asked, changing the subject.

With all the time that she'd had, she should've had it all perfectly planned out, but she was still at a loss. There was so much to tell her. Where would she even begin?

"Are you going to tell her about…?" Farron didn't need to say it, she knew what he meant.

"I don't know," she said, "but I'm leaning toward no."

Farron remained quiet. He hadn't said much about the subject, but she knew that he didn't approve based on the expressions he wore every time it came up. If only he knew the secret she still kept from him. Guilt seemed to be her constant companion, and it only deepened when the topic came up. But her reasoning was the same for both her mother and him.

"I don't want her to worry," she said.

Another long silence from the elf, but she could feel the tension vibrating off of him.

"What?" she asked, letting the annoyance back into her voice.

"It's just…"

"What?" she repeated, prodding him on.

"You don't think she deserves to know what's happening to her own daughter?" A touch of sadness edged his own exasperation.

"What would it change?" she asked. They'd been over this already. "There's nothing she can do to help. It would only make her feel worse."

"I just think you do all of these things to try to protect people, by pushing them away—"

"I apologized for that already," she said, ripping off the blindfold. She squinted in the light of the declining sun. She pulled her horse to a stop, forcing Farron to do the same.

"Yet you still do it." He met her look with a challenging one of his own.

"What am I supposed to do?" Claire said, her frustration rising. "Tell her that I'm being consumed and there's nothing that she can do about it? She would insist on doing something, anything, and I don't want to put her in that kind of danger. I can't, Farron. I couldn't bear it if something happened to her. She may be strong, but she's not like you, or even me. And you, you're too stubborn to admit that you would be safer without me."

"I would be safer," he said, "but to keep something like that from a person that loves you, it's not fair."

"That's rich coming from you." She'd had enough of this conversation. Her mind was already made up.

He gave her a sharp look before nudging his horse on and pulling hers after.

Her shoulders slumped and she put the blindfold back on. He may have had a point, but she just didn't want to put her mother through that kind of worry again. It was cowardly, she knew, protecting herself as much as her mother. But it was better this way. Ignorance could be bliss at times. Something she knew all too well.

❖

The sounds of the town came to her in waves, first the distant hum of commotion, then the individual noises—the shouts, hooves on stone, the murmur of the crowd—until she was surrounded by it all. She could feel the eyes on her. Not that she could blame them. She'd look at the strange lady in a blindfold, too.

Consumed

"May I—"

"No," Farron said sharply.

He was still mad at her.

She slumped in the saddle a little further, embarrassment extinguishing her curiosity. Was this punishment, or was he being extra cautious? Probably a little bit of both.

About half an hour later, by her estimation, they finally came to a stop. Claire shifted in the saddle, sore from the endless riding. Although she was grateful to have a horse, the one she'd been riding was no substitute for the gentle Azra, more skittish and jerky in her movements. She had never realized that horses could have such varied personalities. And it only made her miss her old companion even more. She hoped dearly that the horses had made it out all right.

Farron's hand touched her left arm softly, letting her know he was there before gently tugging it. "Easy," he said when she swung her leg over to dismount. He helped her down and led her a few steps away. "Wait here," he said, firmly.

Claire nodded. She didn't want to push it too far with him in one day, so she did as told, but it was a struggle not to lift up the edge of the cloth to take a peek at her surroundings. The urge was so strong, she was about to lose the battle when a hand clamped down on her upper arm.

"Farron?" she asked, uncertain, her pulse hitching.

"Is that your lover, little lady?" came a slurring voice.

The stench of the man reached her nostrils, making her jerk back as he leaned over her.

"Yes, it is," Farron said sharply from behind her.

The man shrank away, muttering something under his breath as he walked down the street.

"It seems more people are after you than I'd thought," Farron said. "You don't think I really smell like that, do you?"

"Well, when is the last time you bathed?" she asked, trying to lighten the mood a little.

"The same time you did."

He had gotten her there. One of the first things she wanted to do was soak in a nice warm bath, soothe the aches, wash away the grime and other unsavory things. Perhaps do more unsavory things with the elf. If he wasn't too mad still.

Farron pulled her with a gentle hand into the—she assumed—inn. The commotion of the town was muffled once behind closed doors.

Impatience buzzed through her. "Now?" she asked.

He was quiet for a moment then said, "Fine."

Claire ripped the blindfold off with enthusiasm and tossed it aside in her exuberance. Then picked it up a moment later. She would need it again, after all. It was such a relief to have it off that she barely noticed the strange look the innkeeper gave her.

It was a modest inn, nothing too fancy, but after the last long stretch in the woods, it was as welcome as the palace. Farron got the key from the older man behind the counter and motioned for her to follow him down a dark hallway. Reluctantly, she did. Now that the blindfold was off, she had to look at his disappointed face instead of just imagining it.

Like the rest of the inn, the room was simple, a bed, chair and side table the only furniture. A window let in the dim twilight, but the view was less than spectacular, only revealing the building next door's bland wall. Farron set down his pack and took off his daggers, still quiet. Claire stood awkwardly for a moment, wondering if she should say anything before shrugging out of her jacket.

"I'll send for a bath," he said, turning to the door again. "I'll be back a little later."

"You don't want to join me?" She tried to make it sound as enticing as she could, but uncertainty laced her voice.

Consumed

A slight smile tugged the corner of his lips. "As much as I want to, there are some things I have to do."

Claire nodded, trying not to let her disappointment show.

Farron opened the door and paused when he was halfway through. "I may not agree with you," he said, "but I won't tell her." Then he left, shutting the door quietly behind him.

She stood in the middle of the room, letting the silence consume her. Why did this bother him so much? Sure, she'd done it to him in the past, kept things from him, pushed him away—was still doing it—but it wasn't like he had been the most forthcoming with his own secrets. He had even played with the idea of sending her back to the palace for her protection without him. Even though she was disappointed that she would be bathing alone, perhaps a little bit of time apart would do them some good.

Meanwhile, she had to prepare to face Marion for perhaps the last time.

❦

His kiss awoke her. The hint of alcohol lingered on his breath. The room was dark save for the slash of silvery moonlight streaming in through the window, leaving his face in shadow.

"Fare?" she whispered, still groggy. What time was it?

"I'm sorry, Claire," he said, his voice heavy with sadness, guilt. He leaned his forehead on hers. The warmth of his body hovered above hers as he bent over her from where he sat on the edge of the bed.

She ran her fingertips down the side of his face. But she didn't know what to say.

"I know what it's like to be pushed away." He leaned back enough to look down at her.

She was just able to make out the somber expression he wore.

"And if there are things that you won't even tell your mother, then what hope do I have?"

"Fare…" she said, her voice cracking slightly. She stroked his cheek.

He took her hand and kissed her fingers in a light brush of lips.

She thought about telling him everything right then—let it all out, ease his worries—but would he try to stop her then? They were running out of time and options. If she didn't complete her mission then it would all be for nothing.

Instead, she just drew him down for a kiss, pulling him down to join her completely on the bed. She would rather ease his worries than add to them.

13

Claire had donned the blindfold once again the next evening as the elf led her through the crowded streets. This time she was glad that she couldn't see the stares that she was surely getting.

But the embarrassment was overshadowed by the pounding of her heart. The blend of nerves and excitement made her hands shake. Why was she so anxious to see her own mother? Was it because she had learned of Marion's past? Or the simple fact that she knew her mother and how tough she could be with her own daughter?

The commotion of the town was suddenly muted as the door closed behind her. Farron's warm buzzing presence was at her back and he untied the piece of cloth. Claire blinked a couple times to get used to the dim surroundings. They stood in a hallway, the walls painted deep red with dark wooden floors and accents, all richly decorated with paintings and rugs and knick-knacks. Simple oil lamp sconces lined the wall, illuminating islands of light in the darkness.

She glanced at Farron, but his face remained blank. Per her wishes, he refused to give her any sort of detail of where they were. It still drove her mad.

Farron held up an arm to motion for her to go forward. She took a deep breath and walked down the hall, following it into the depths of the building, all the way to the back where a door stood open, leading into a private garden surrounded by high walls. A stone path led through trimmed hedges, around a pond filled with orange fish, little lanterns lighting the way. It was beautiful, calm, an oasis.

And then Claire saw her.

Sitting on a bench at the rear of the garden was Marion.

"Mother," she whispered before rushing to her.

Her mother barely had time to stand before Claire wrapped her arms around her.

"Claire," Marion said softly. She hugged Claire tight. After several moments she pulled back to look her daughter over. "You look well. Are you well?"

Farron's words played through her mind, but she nodded. She still didn't want to tell her mother. Not now, not ever if she could help it. Marion had enough to worry about.

Claire looked her mother over. She wore a plain off-white dress, her wild hair tamed into a messy updo. The bags that had been there the last time she'd seen Marion had lessened, although the gray strands peppered into her red waves seemed to have multiplied. Still, they didn't detract from her beauty. "How about you?" she asked. "Are you well?"

"I'm well when you're well." She brushed a strand of hair from Claire's face, her fingers lingering. Her eyes held a smile that Claire hadn't seen in far too long. "Though, I am a bit tired of hiding out here," she said, her eyes filling with the fire Claire had admired all her life. "He told me it was for my safety." She nodded her head behind Claire.

Consumed

Claire followed her gaze to the elf standing at the edge of the pond several paces away. His back was to them, giving them some privacy.

"It is," Claire said. "It's a long story."

"Well then," Marion said, "you better get started."

The look on her mother's face told her that she was going to get a story out of her daughter no matter what. So, Claire relented and sat on the bench next to her mother and let it all out, starting with that fateful night in Stockton to the elves and the journey, the places she'd seen, the General, Derenan, meeting the king—more than one actually—all the way to when she'd met her in Linesbrough. She was careful with the details so she didn't give anything away that she didn't want to. As for her current mission, well, she was vague there, as well. What would Marion think about her daughter returning magic to the world? Would she think of her as a traitor? She'd been in the Syndicate, after all. It had been her duty to prevent her from doing just what Claire had set out to do.

Marion was quiet for a long stretch when Claire finished, her face almost as unreadable as the elf's. "Well…" she said, letting out a breath. "You've always dreamed of an adventure."

Claire smiled, grateful for the levity. Telling her story had drudged up some memories that she liked to keep locked up deep in the back of her mind.

"Oh, Claire." Marion took Claire's hands into hers, her eyes traveling up her hand, hesitating at the long scar the General had carved into her skin, the silver chains and bands. "All that you've been through. It was the last thing that I wanted for you. I hope you know that."

Claire nodded.

"I only sent you away from me that night to protect you."

"I know," Claire said softly, "it's all right. I'm fine, really." She squeezed her mother's hands.

"But you're not. You've been caught up in the web that I was supposed to keep you out of," she said, sadness in her eyes. "I've not only failed as an agent of the Syndicate, but also as a mother."

"No," Claire said. "Far from it."

A smile touched the corner of her mother's lips.

"I've had a taste of the Syndicate's hospitality. Now I know why you sent me away into a dark forest, it's much more preferable."

"They've always been a dour lot." Marion frowned.

Claire could think of much stronger words to describe them.

"So, Deliah's…" Marion muttered.

Claire nodded. "The madman, the one I'm trying to protect you from, he destroyed the whole fort. There was nothing I could do." A lump formed in her throat, tears stinging her eyes. "Did you know her well?"

"I did," Marion said, her eyes hazed over with the past. "Years ago. She used to be a good woman before the Syndicate got their fangs deeper into her. And the boy? The others?"

"They're safe," Claire said. "Lianna and Razi are looking after them in Derenan."

Marion gave a short snort of laughter. "Now, there's a woman. That Lianna gave even me a good run for it."

Claire smiled. Somehow she knew Marion and Lianna would hit it off. "I think she liked you as well."

"Although it gave me pleasure to raid those Syndicate hideouts, I have to know, Claire, that it was all for good. I did it to help you, to set them free from their prison, not deliver them to a new one."

Her sentiments exactly. But it was unfortunately what she had ended up doing. But hopefully for not much longer. "It is," she said, trying to reassure her mother. "It will be."

Consumed

"And this mission that you're on now," she said, giving Claire a sharp, studious look. "I feel like you're hiding things from me."

Claire swallowed, the lump returning.

"Out with it."

"I don't want you to be disappointed in me," she said, her voice falling along with her gaze, "to hate me."

"I could never do that, Claire." She touched Claire's chin and tilted her face back up to face hers.

"Well," Claire said, hesitantly, "I'm going to try to restore the magic back to the land." Her pulse picked up as the words left her mouth. She watched her mother carefully. Waited for the disappointment, the anger, but it didn't come.

Marion opened her mouth, then closed it. Claire had never seen her mother speechless before. She had always had something to say, regardless of the situation.

"Is that possible?" she finally said.

"I don't know, not for sure. But I have to try."

"But why you?" She ran her fingers down Claire's cheek. "My innocent Claire taking on such a mission."

Claire hesitated. She could see Farron shift from the corner of her eye. "Why not me?"

"It's just such a big task…"

"I can do it, Mother. You did raise me, after all."

"Well, I'm glad to see your confidence has finally grown. After all that you've been through, how could it not?" She smiled, a proud look on her face. "Although, I suspect he might have something to do with it as well." She nodded toward Farron. "You say he's your lover? He's a long way off from the sweet little farm boy you last brought home." A sly grin tilted her lips.

Claire could feel the heat creep up her cheeks.

"Does he treat you right?" Marion continued, her face growing serious. "I've heard stories of his past. He's quite notorious, I believe."

"He does," she said, "A little too well, at times. I wouldn't be where I am now without him."

"Can you trust him?"

"More than myself."

Her mother narrowed her eyes, studying her, then glanced at Farron. Her trust was hard won, and rightfully so.

Claire leaned close and lowered her voice, but she was almost certain he would hear her anyway. "Believe me," she said, "it surprises me still."

Marion laughed, a rich hearty sound. "Well, I suppose love can be found in the strangest of places, in the people you least expect. Or elf." She gave Claire a considering look. "Perhaps I need an elf lover myself. Human men are a hopeless cause."

Claire laughed. She knew that all too well after years of experience. She was young enough to still dream of knights in shining armor and hadn't grown as jaded as her mother. Yet.

"Trust me," Claire whispered, "it's not all it's made out to be."

Farron shifted again but remained quiet. Served him right for listening in.

"Well, I will trust your judgment," Marion said. "The last one wasn't bad either, the farm boy I mean." A spark flashed in her eyes. "I have half a mind to hunt down that General and carve him up with an ax."

"I'll get you the ax," Claire said, not sure whether or not Marion would actually do it, or if she cared if her mother really *did*.

Marion's face softened. "I really wanted you to marry that farm boy," she said. "I'm sorry that you never got to. For what I had to do. For all the things that I couldn't give you."

Consumed

A tear slid down Claire's cheek. "You've done more for me than anyone," Claire said. "You gave me a normal life, love, a home. You only did what you had to do to keep me safe, to keep me out of the Syndicate's grasp for as long as possible. And I may not have a farm boy, but I do have a rather intimidating elf."

Marion's eyes glistened with unshed tears. "Selene would have been proud of you," she said, "just as I am. I am sad that she is no longer with us. I wish you could have known her as I did."

"Me too." Claire's meeting with her birth mother had been all too brief.

"She was a good, gentle woman," Marion said. "She loved you as much as I."

"I saw the letters you wrote," Claire said. "I can't believe you did that."

"Well," Marion said, looking up to prevent tears from falling, "it was the least I could do."

Claire hugged Marion, burying her face in her shoulder.

Marion stroked her hair. "It's all right," she whispered. She held Claire until they were both able to hold back their tears successfully.

Claire drew back to look at Marion. "I know you don't like being holed up here, but I have to know that you'll be safe. I don't think I could bear anything happening to you."

Marion raised an eyebrow. "Isn't that *my* job? I used to be a Syndicate agent, remember? They didn't let just anyone in. I can handle myself, young lady."

Claire had no doubt that she could. But still…

"I hate just sitting here not knowing what's going on," her mother said, "while you're out there risking yourself. I don't know how I feel about your mission, but if you think it's a good idea, then I'll do what I can to help."

Claire shook her head. "I can't have you come with me," she said. "As much as I want to, I can't. I can't even know where you are. Bahkar, that madman, he can get into my mind, see where you are. I can't know."

"I see," Marion said, sighing. "What about your friend over there?"

"He's tougher than he looks." Yet, she still worried about him.

"The rumors about him are true then?" Marion asked, her interest piqued.

"Mostly," she shrugged, "but he's not as scary as he seems. Not all of the time, at least." She gave her mother a sly look. "Like someone else I know."

Marion tickled Claire on her sides where she'd always been sensitive, making her jump and yelp, giggling like a little girl. Then she drew Claire into her arms once again, holding her tight. "When will I see you again my dear, sweet, child?"

Claire hesitated. "Soon." She hoped.

"Be careful, Claire. I'll find a way to help you, somehow," she whispered.

"I just want you to be safe," she said.

"That's all I've ever wanted for you, Claire." She pulled back and looked down at Claire. "And ever will. Be careful. I know you've grown strong, but I still worry. And know that no matter what, I will always love you."

"Me, too, Mother," Claire said, hugging her once again, trying to soak in all she could in case it was the last time she ever saw her, hoping dearly that it wasn't.

14

She had never thought she would lay eyes on Stockton again. Not after what happened that night.

Claire stood at the edge of the forest to the northwest of the town, Farron next to her, the horses hidden further in the trees, and gazed out across the fields. But it wasn't the same. It would never be. It was tainted somehow. The memories were too fresh, too horrible, for her to ever feel the same about her hometown again. Flashes of that night bombarded her mind and it was exhausting trying to fight them back.

Movement stirred in the town. It buzzed with life like it had before the attack. Smoke streamed into the sky from chimneys, not horrifying piles of refuse and bodies; buildings were either repaired or in the process of being so; people strolled along the streets carefree, not running for their lives. It was surreal, to be brought back from the brink after such an ordeal. But she knew it was only because of the General and Lendon that they were able to do so, further tainting it in her eyes. It was only a small comfort if her fellow townspeople were able to pick up the pieces of their lives and somehow put them back together again. What had become of her mother's tavern? She was almost curious enough to go see, but she just couldn't bring herself to do it. Not yet.

They hadn't stayed long in the mystery town, leaving early the next morning. Very early, on her insistence, so there wouldn't be as many townspeople out to see the strange blindfolded girl. She would have loved to spend more time with her mother. There were still too many unanswered questions, stories, feelings, unshed tears. There just wasn't enough time. Her days felt numbered and she wondered how many she had left.

Dread slowly filled her as they traveled ever eastward. They'd crossed into Lendonian lands, avoiding towns and cities as much as they could. Both her and Farron were on edge, just waiting for an ambush or... something. Claire could hardly sleep at night. She felt like she was surrounded by enemies—centaurs, the General, Lord Byron, the elves, the Syndicate. There were just too many. As a result, their journey took longer than expected, having to go on roads less traveled and even foregoing roads altogether. All the nights on the hard ground and bathing in cold streams put her in a miserable state. But to risk going into town was foolish. They'd had a few close calls with some traveling guards and a small group of centaurs, but they had managed to evade them without a fight. So far.

"You sure you don't want to go?" Farron asked her again. He had been giving her pitying looks all afternoon.

"Yes," she said, giving him a tired look. "Maybe another time. Besides, it could be crawling with Lendonian guards."

He nodded, but the look in his eyes was skeptical. His gaze shifted to the forest beyond and his expression hardened.

"You sure you want to go?" she repeated his question back at him, amusement in her voice.

He sighed. "No," he said, "I'm sure that fool is in there somewhere, plotting his revenge."

Claire smiled at the possibility of seeing Aeron again. But would he feel the same? They hadn't parted on the best of terms.

"I think I would rather fight another Beast of Old," Farron said.

She could almost agree with that sentiment. Almost. "It won't be *that* bad," she said, trying to make the statement sound light.

"You're not the one they want to kill," he said, giving her a pointed look.

She swallowed. That was true. He'd betrayed his own kin, the ones that had taken him in, and the forest king himself, Ryaenon. And last she'd heard, kings didn't take kindly to traitors.

"I can go in alone," Claire said. She didn't like the prospect, but if it would keep him safe…

"No," he said, a little irritated. He turned to her and his cocky grin slid into place. "I survived your mother, how bad can they be?" He nodded his head toward the forest.

He had a point. "It'll be just as fun, I'm sure. Besides, I think Aeron may have missed you."

His grin faded. "Keep that up and you *will* be going in alone."

She chuckled as she turned to make her way to the horses. But trepidation still churned in the pit of her stomach. They were so close. They couldn't back down now.

The forest was just as creepy as she remembered it.

It was still light as they entered the Forbidden Forest, but the trees soon blocked out the sky, making it dim and foreboding. They'd circled Stockton and had entered the woods from the northern side. Not that it looked any different to Claire. When they couldn't see the outside world any longer, Farron got off his horse and Claire followed.

"We have to be prepared," he said, his posture and movements uncharacteristically rigid. "They most likely know we're here already."

Claire nodded, remaining silent, her body tense as well. It was eerily quiet. Goosebumps raised all over her body. It felt like eyes were watching them. And they probably were.

But, however dreadful she may have felt, she couldn't deny the beauty of the ancient forest, even in winter, but Claire knew better. She'd seen the dark secret held within.

"It's about time," Farron said, stopping.

Claire froze, her heart jumping. She swallowed hard and glanced out at the trees, but she couldn't see anything.

A thump sounded and it took her a moment to realize what it was. An arrow protruded from the ground inches from Farron. Farron didn't even flinch, though his shoulders tensed even more.

An elf stepped out from behind the tree several paces in front of them, a smirk on his beautiful face. He made hardly any sound as he walked toward them. His hands were empty, his weapons still undrawn. He hadn't loosed the arrow. However, he wasn't alone. Claire braved another glance, stifling a gasp as she took in the group of elves that surrounded them, all training their arrows on her and Farron.

The head elf, she assumed, spoke to Farron in their flowing language, and even though she couldn't understand it, by the tone it wasn't very friendly. Not that she expected to get a warm welcome. She just wished she knew what was being said. She supposed she was going to be in the dark for most of the visit, just like last time.

Farron replied a few words back and the other elf laughed. He had stopped a few feet away from them, his hands on his sides as he took her in. His dark hair contrasted with his pale skin, making his features seem stark and severe. His cheekbones looked lethal, but not as much as the look in his eyes.

Consumed

"I don't suppose you speak my language, do you?" Claire asked, trying to make it sound light, though she couldn't keep the slight tremble out of her voice.

The elf just raised an eyebrow at her and turned his attention back to Farron. He spoke a few words, his face a harsh scowl, then raised a hand.

Farron's shot up to the dagger hilt over his right shoulder. And then everything grew still again as if time stopped.

Claire held her breath, her pulse pounding wildly. "Fare," she muttered, "what's happening?"

But he didn't answer. His gaze rested solely on the elf in front of him.

They stared at each other for several tense moments, sizing one another up, just waiting for the other to make the first move. Claire wondered why they hadn't attacked so far. Did they know what he was able to do? Surely Aeron had told them. Perhaps they were just being cautious.

She could feel Farron's magic stir and the other elf's face twitched.

"Fare," she said carefully. "Do we have to fight?"

After a moment he lowered his hand and held it up before him in surrender. He spoke to the elf, his tone wary.

"We didn't come here to fight," Claire said and Farron relayed the words to him. "We came because we need your help."

The other elf laughed after Farron translated.

"I think it will be beneficial for you to hear us out," she said. Though standing there, surrounded by drawn arrows, the words filled her with apprehension. Was this the right thing to do? What was she going to unleash upon the world?

The elven city hadn't changed since she'd last seen it, oddly beautiful, ancient and uneven, the buildings crowding in on each other, distracting from their elegance. Curious elves lined the main avenue as they watched the captives being taken to their king. Or their dungeons. Claire could only hope for the former. They weren't allowed to talk much, so Claire hadn't been able to ask Farron what exactly was going on. The elves had taken their horses and their weapons, but she was sure Farron had a few hidden on him still.

An odd feeling came over Claire. She had made a complete circle, coming back to where her journey had started all those months ago. Everything looked the same. The never-changing city. No wonder the elves were antsy to get out of the forest. It was like they were suspended in time.

They passed the fountain Claire had admired the last time and headed right for the heavy wooden doors that led into the palace. The guards standing in front of them sprang into action and opened them, their hinges groaning. The dark-haired elf strolled through without pause, but instead of the throne room, he turned right down one of the long hallways into the depths of the building. It was just as mazelike as she recalled, twisting and turning with hardly any windows visible. The only sound came from the soft clacks of the elves' footsteps on the shiny marble flooring.

The dark-haired elf stopped suddenly in front of an unassuming door and motioned for one of his subordinates to open it. He said a few words to Farron and stood glaring at him as he entered. Claire followed, nervous about what she would find.

But to her surprise it was only a regular room—well, as regular as a richly decorated elven room could be. The door slammed behind her and she could hear the soft click of the lock.

Claire breathed a sigh of relief. So far so good.

Consumed

Farron walked to the far side of the room where an opening led out to a balcony.

"Well," she said, "that could have gone much worse." She followed Farron, slowing as she neared the balcony. It hung over the cliff with a sheer drop too far down for her comfort.

"They still want me dead," he said, turning to look at her. "Not that I can blame them."

"Is that what he said with his pretty words?"

"More or less." He shrugged. "You're the only reason I'm still alive. That and my magic."

"I was wondering why they didn't just attack," she said.

"Perhaps that fool wasn't so useless," he said, a grin sliding into place.

"See," Claire said, sidling up close to him. "I knew you liked him deep down in there." She ran a finger up his chest to rest above his heart.

He frowned.

"Do you think they'll listen?" she asked, her amusement fading.

"I hope so," he said, "Ryaenon is proud, but I think he would do anything to gain power. Besides, I sort of completed the original mission."

"If you ignore the part about rescuing the prisoner for your own reasons," she said, a grin turning the corner of her mouth.

"Well, there is that…"

"Not that I'm not grateful," she said.

He drew her close. "Are you now?" His hand brushed along the side of her neck, his thumb stroking her cheek. "I seem to recall that you weren't too thrilled that the Ice Prince had whisked you away."

"Well," she said, tracing circles over his heart, "that was before I knew that this existed."

Laughter rumbled in his chest. "I assure you, Claire, it has always been there." He bent and whispered just above her lips, "It just needed a little thawing." He kissed her then, light and sweet.

Claire slid her hands up to wrap around his neck, drawing him down closer. It was a good distraction.

The door opened with a loud bang as it hit the wall.

"So, you got the girl after all," said a familiar voice.

Claire pulled away from Farron, heat rising to her cheeks as she faced Aeron.

"I suppose my chances are pretty dismal now." He stood in the middle of the room, looking dejected in an overly dramatic way.

Farron straightened and crossed his arms, though he didn't look all that upset to see his old superior.

"Aeron," Claire said as she rushed to him.

Aeron opened his arms wide and engulfed Claire in a too-tight embrace, lifting her up and swinging her around once before planting her back on the floor. "You look as lovely as when we last parted, *mon laini*." He stepped back to take her in. Then he leaned in close and muttered, "All things considered." He nodded in Farron's direction.

Claire smiled. "I know, it still confounds me."

Aeron laughed, a rich, hearty sound. "Who knew our broody little Farron would be such a romantic?"

Farron glowered at Aeron.

"Or so deceitful," Aeron said, his mood shifting quickly, a seriousness she'd rarely seen on the elf.

Claire backed away from him, a few steps toward Farron. "Aeron..." she said, "It's not—"

He kept his gaze on Farron, his brow furrowing in anger. "The king nearly took my head for showing up back here empty handed, for letting you get away. I was kicked off the king's guard and demoted to night watch. I was spat on for losing our *Yaederri*. And now you dare show your face here?"

Farron remained quiet. The tension in the room was almost suffocating.

"I'm the reason he's here," she said, trying to keep her voice neutral.

Aeron's eyes shifted to her, the spark of anger fading a little, though not as much as she would have liked.

"What he did," she said, gesturing back at Farron, "was traitorous. And I know the reasons may not be good enough for you, or your king, but believe me when I say his intentions weren't bad. Far from it."

Aeron snorted in disagreement. "Maybe not for you," he said. His shoulders slumped, the fierce expression softening. "But what do I know about love?"

The tension left the room and Claire took a deep breath.

"I would like to think that I would do the same," Aeron said. "But I had to pay the price. I hope that it was at least worth it?" He raised a questioning eyebrow and looked between her and Farron.

Farron didn't give anything away and heat rushed to her cheeks.

Aeron laughed. "I see," he said, grinning suggestively. He leaned in close to Claire and whispered, "Is he as good a lover as he seems?"

"I-I," Claire stammered.

"Better," Farron finally chimed in, making her whole face blush.

Aeron laughed again.

"Will the king see us or not?" Farron asked, his voice cold.

"So impatient." Aeron waved a hand to dismiss the other elf. "Besides, I do not know anything more than you do. I was demoted, remember?" He gave Farron a sharp look.

Farron sighed.

"But when I heard the rumors that our *Yaederri* had returned, I had to see for myself," Aeron said.

"I'm sorry about what happened," Claire said, reaching out to touch his arm. "I didn't mean for you to get into trouble."

"You were a brash young thing," Aeron said, "Still are, I suppose, if you came back here." He glanced over her head and seemed to get a silent answer from the other elf. "And I see things with the General did not work out after all?"

Claire pulled up her sleeve to show him the damage.

Aeron's eyes widened. "He did that?"

"Himself," Claire muttered.

"And you did not kill him?" Aeron directed the question at Farron.

"Not yet," Farron said, malice dripping from his voice.

"It is unfortunate that you did not," Aeron said. "He and his little king have expanded their empire considerably. I suppose the rumors were true. We have already had to increase patrol in the forest. His men are adventuring a little too close for the king's liking."

Claire glanced back at Farron, but his expression revealed nothing.

"And Stockton?" she asked, curious if Aeron knew anything.

"They seem to be flourishing," Aeron said. "It is a shame that they are now ruled by Lendon, though. Especially after all that has happened and how it came to be." He looked at Claire, pity in the depths of his deep blue eyes. "You have not been back?"

She shook her head. "I can't. Not yet."

Aeron placed a hand on top of her head. "*Mon laini*, I wish there was a way to heal your wounds." He leaned in again, the pity replaced with a mischievous glint. "I could help ease your mind, show you what a true lover is like."

Clare brushed his hand away and sighed. He hadn't changed much.

Aeron chuckled. "Though, seeing what this can possibly do," he said, lifting up her right hand, "you frighten me a little, *mon laini*. By the way, is that other woman, the scary one, attached?" He raised an inquisitive eyebrow.

"Lianna?" How was she not surprised. "Didn't she harm you?"

A wistful look took over Aeron's face. "The only thing she harmed was my heart."

Claire rolled her eyes. "I'm afraid that you have some tough competition," she said. "You'd have to battle a king for her hand. That's if she even wanted you."

"An elf can dream," Aeron said, and he leaned in once again, lowering his voice. "In fact, I have."

Farron sighed audibly, displeased.

Aeron gave him a curious look. "She seemed to know you pretty well," he said, grinning. "Is she a past lover, perhaps?"

"That's a path best left untraveled," Claire said. It would only aggravate Farron and they didn't need that right now.

"If you say so, *mon laini*." Aeron turned his gaze back to her, studying her a little too closely. "Perhaps you can tell me, then, why you have come back instead of running off into the sunset? Have you grown tired of our little Farron so soon?"

"Not exactly," she said, unable to stop herself. "We need your help."

"I'm listening," Aeron said, his interest truly piqued.

Claire told him as much as she could about what had happened, and what they planned on doing. After she was done, it was the first time she'd ever seen him speechless—for a few moments, anyway.

"*Mon laini*," Aeron said, his voice soft, breathy, "you truly are our *Yaederri*. But I hope you know what your actions may bring."

Claire nodded. However, now was not the time to speak of traitorous thoughts and plans. She just hoped Aeron would listen to reason and agree to help them. If not, then she might yet doom the human race.

15

The elven king, Ryaenon, was as beautiful as she remembered. And as intimidating.

She knelt in the throne room before the dais where the king sat in his intricately carved wooden chair. Farron was beside her, his body as rigid as stone, avoiding the king's gaze as much as he could. Ryaenon hadn't uttered a word since they had entered the room, but his piercing gaze said everything.

Two guards flanked him, armed and armored, accompanied by the elder elf from the last time who had read from the ancient scroll. A few more elves were scattered around the room, including the dark-haired elf that had confronted them in the forest. It was dim, the only light coming from the chandeliers hanging from the ceiling and a few lanterns dotting the walls. Back when Claire had first seen it, she thought it was the grandest place she'd ever laid eyes on. Now, it seemed almost quaint.

Silence hung in the air for a while, so much so that Claire shifted slightly, uncomfortable. She could only imagine what they must be thinking, seeing her and the traitor again. And that they had come back of their own free will. She'd be baffled and suspicious, too.

Finally, the king spoke in his flowing tongue. Farron tensed next to her for a moment before rising to his feet. Claire looked up at him, questioning, but he held a hand up for her to stay. His jaw clenched, his shoulders squared, and an obstinate air surrounded him, his icy mask slipping into place. If he was nervous, it didn't show as he stared down the elven king. He hadn't lied when he'd said that Ryaenon didn't scare him. His brother was the king of an entire country. What did this one have? When Claire thought of it that way, he didn't seem so daunting. He was king of a forest. What power did he really hold? But, that could change if she were able to restore magic to the land. He wasn't so almighty now, but he soon could be.

Claire remained kneeling for the time being. They still had to be diplomatic. It was his help that they sought. That they needed. These elves held the final piece of the puzzle.

King Ryaenon rose from his throne and descended the few steps, his silk robes brushing along the polished floor. Emeralds sparkled in the low light as he walked, sewn into the deep maroon fabric in a twisting, swirling design. His dark hair hung freely down past his shoulders. He approached Farron, and he was one of the few that was able to meet the tall elf's gaze.

He spoke a few words before reaching out to touch Farron's hair hanging over his shoulder, still dyed black, but fading. A gentle movement that didn't match the malice in his voice.

Claire wished dearly for a translation. She didn't like being left in the dark.

Farron reached up and snatched the king's wrist. The guards reached for the swords at their waists and Claire tensed, her breath catching.

"Fare," she whispered.

Consumed

Time seemed to stop for several moments. Then the king laughed, a haunting sound that broke the spell. He let Farron's hair fall from his hand and Farron released him.

The whole room seemed to let out a sigh of relief.

Farron spoke, his voice sharp, his eyes glaring.

The amusement faded from Ryaenon's face. His gaze shifted over to her and Claire froze, gulping. Farron may not have been afraid of him, but Ryaenon still made her nervous.

Farron spoke and the king listened, surprisingly calm and attentive, and his eyebrow lifted as he looked Claire over.

King Ryaenon motioned for Claire to stand. She did a little too quickly. She needed to relax. She'd faced much greater foes than this. He said a few words and Farron translated.

"He wants to see it," Farron said, looking at her. "The mark."

Claire looked between him and the king and cast a quick glance around the room at the others. All eyes were on her, bringing up unpleasant memories of the last time she had been in this room. She sighed and stripped the jacket off to reveal the wild dark lines and the silver contraption. At least this time she wasn't being held by a strange, perverted elf.

Ryaenon's eyebrows rose slightly as his eyes traced down her arm. He reached out and touched her, his fingers light on her skin as they trailed along the mark, pausing before the scar. He whispered something.

Claire looked at Farron.

"He asked what happened," he said.

"How much time does he have?"

Farron muttered a translation to the king and Ryaenon's lips twitched.

Had he almost smiled? He didn't exactly strike her as the humorous type.

The king took her wrist in his hand and lifted her arm up to inspect the damage more closely. His other hand hovered over one of the silver bands as he spoke.

"Where did you find this?" Farron translated, but instead of waiting for her to answer, he did it for her.

Surprise crossed the king's face. He gave Farron a considering look and spoke again.

"He thought these were lost after the Great War," Farron said. "He finds it amusing that a human is wearing one." Farron listened as the king spoke more before continuing. "They used to put these on elven dissidents."

Claire nodded. Of course, they would be made for elves. What better punishment than to strip away their magic, make them closer to being like the humans they so despised?

"He asks why you wear it," Farron continued. Only this time, he waited for her to answer, a quiet warning in his eyes.

"So I can hide," she said. He was right. She shouldn't be telling the king about her condition. They couldn't appear weak.

Farron translated and when Ryaenon gave him a questioning look, Farron went on. Claire trusted that he wouldn't reveal too much, but she still wished she knew what he was saying.

Ryaenon's face grew serious as he muttered a few words.

Farron paused before telling Claire what he had said. "There are more." He nodded and they both looked at Claire. The king spoke again. "He thought Aeron was lying."

Aeron had met Lianna, but even he had no clue that there were even more Star Children. Claire may have been their *little hope*, but she was not their only one. And she wasn't sure if that weakened their stance or not.

Consumed

The king released her arm and stood for a moment, looking down at her before turning to Farron, his expression hardening. He spoke and the beautiful words had a sharp edge to them.

"He asks why we have come," Farron said, looking at her.

Claire nodded at him. It would be faster if he just told the king himself.

And so he did. Claire tried to look as confident as she could while she listened, but she couldn't totally hide the worry growing inside of her. She couldn't tamp down the feelings of betrayal, guilt. Was it too late to change her mind? Did she want to? She glanced around at the elves in the room once again. They're attention was focused on what Farron was saying. Not that she could blame them. Their lives were so secluded, sheltered. Just like she had been for most of her life. What Farron was saying, it was like he was opening the door to the birdcage, to their freedom.

Silence fell over the room when Farron stopped. Then all eyes were on her again.

Ryaenon's laugh pierced the air, though it wasn't exactly happy. When it died down he spoke, a grin curling the corner of his mouth, a devious spark in his dark eyes.

Farron frowned and said, "He finds it funny that even though I betrayed him, I ended up completing the mission anyway."

"Well, he may have a point," she said.

Farron, however, didn't find it as amusing. His frown only deepened.

The king spoke again, squaring his shoulders as he looked between them.

"After everything, you come to ask me for a favor?" Farron translated.

That irked Claire and she had to bite her tongue to keep from shouting. She didn't need to make an enemy of yet another king—

well, any more so. That had probably happened when she decided to steal away with the General. From the start, she had been their prisoner, and that was only after Farron had spared her life that night in the forest. It had never been her choice to go on their mission so they could use her. Their *little hope*. The ego of a king was truly astonishing.

"I believe that our offer will be beneficial to us both," Claire said, trying her best to hide the anger within. She wondered if it would have been easier to just sneak in and take the piece of tablet that they needed. But then they still needed it to be translated. Surely there were other ancient elves still alive somewhere?

The king narrowed his eyes as he listened to Farron and spoke.

"What makes you think you're in a position to bargain?" Farron translated, his body tensing. His face remained neutral, but Claire could see the gears turning in his head. He didn't like to be threatened, not even by a king. His eyes quickly darted around the room, assessing, but he made no other move.

Claire took a deep breath. They couldn't appear weak. So, being either brave or immensely foolish, she said, "What makes you believe *you* are?"

Farron looked at her for a moment, eyebrow cocked.

She nodded and he sighed before delivering her words.

The guards reached for their swords again, the dark-haired elf from the forest drawing his bow and arrow. The king just looked at them, fire in his eyes. He probably wasn't used to being challenged. Well, there was a first time for everything.

Claire's pulse sped up. It was probably foolish to threaten a room full of elves, but she was tired of feeling powerless when it was just the opposite. They needed her as much, or more, than she needed them.

Consumed

The dark-haired elf and the guards trained their focus on Farron, but he only grinned and held up his hands.

"I'm not the one you should be afraid of," Farron said.

Confusion twisted their faces momentarily before their attention turned to her. Claire tried to look as intimidating as possible, straightening her back, lifting her chin, but wasn't so sure she was succeeding. But there was a way. She held her hand out, palm up, and focused on the magic in the pendant. A blue orb formed, drawing gasps from a few elves.

"We didn't come here to fight," Claire said, Farron relaying the words, "but we will if we have to."

The king raised his eyebrows as he studied her, his face hard to read. Then he held his hand out to his guards and they eased back, the dark-haired elf following suit, though not looking happy about it.

Claire let the blue orb dissipate and relief filled her. She really didn't want things to escalate. She'd like to think that they stood a chance against the elves, but she really didn't know if they did. Not in the state they were currently in. But they didn't have to know that.

"Now," she said, "are we ready to talk?"

King Ryaenon smiled and spoke, spreading his arms out.

"Our *Yaederrí*, we would be honored to serve you," Farron said, though he couldn't replicate the darkness in the king's voice.

Claire may not have been able to understand the king's words, but she knew a snake when she saw one.

All five stone fragments sat on a table in front of her, assembled for the first time since the magic had disappeared. Claire ran her fingers lightly across them, her magic stirring inside of her, the bands growing warm. There was a sort of resonance that hadn't been there before, the power that emanated from them different, more powerful, in sync, as if they knew they were together once again. Silly, she knew, but then again, most of what had happened to her would have seemed absurd a few years ago.

After speaking to the king for what seemed like hours, and then the ancient elf, her and Farron were led through the labyrinth of the palace to a room deep underground filled with artifacts and scrolls and other treasures from the past. It was only a small sampling of the riches the elves had once had. Claire had never seen so much gold and silver and precious gems in one place. With such riches, it was a mystery why they had stayed hidden for so long. They could have bought the power that they desired. But she supposed that not even money could span the gorge of hatred they had carved between elves and humans. And she didn't think that King Ryaenon desired peace with humans so much as he desired conquering them once again.

The last stone fragment had been hidden away in an unremarkable chest deep in the vault for years, valued only by the ancient elf until Claire had shown up in the forest. The elder lit up when he discovered that Claire and Farron had the other pieces.

"You can decipher it?" Claire said, her eyes tracing the strange letters on the fragment in the warm lamplight.

Farron stood close behind her and spoke the words to the elder who was setting an armful of scrolls down on the table.

The elf nodded a little too vigorously, his dull blue eyes displaying the excitement of a child. He muttered something in his cracked voice as he leaned over the stones.

"He's a little rusty," Farron said. "It might take a little while to get the full translation."

Claire nodded. It wasn't like they had many other options.

Farron touched her shoulder. "We should get some rest," he said softly.

Consumed

She peered up at him and his eyes urged her not to argue, so she didn't. He said something to the old elf, but the elf only nodded and waved a hand absently, already lost in his studies.

Claire took Farron's hand as he led her back through the dim halls. She didn't feel entirely safe in the forest palace. They had no friends here, no allies. Not even Aeron could be fully trusted. And she wasn't sure that they wouldn't try for Farron's life. She wanted to keep him close, just in case.

"Do you trust him?" she asked when they were far enough away from the treasure room.

Farron shook his head. "But what choice do we have?" He slowed his pace a little and lowered his voice. "Our goals are the same," he said, "for now. Ryaenon is so intent on restoring elves to their former glory that he will try anything, even work with a human." He squeezed her hand. "And a traitor. As long as we are instrumental in that goal, we should be safe. We just need to be a little more, let's say, *diplomatic*, in the future." He gave her a pointed look.

"I am very diplomatic," she said, a smile tugging at her lips. "It's not my fault that kings have oversized egos."

"Surely no match for your stubbornness," he said, "but let's not threaten the king again while still under his roof. No matter how satisfying it is."

"All right," Claire said. She had gotten pleasure in seeing King Ryaenon back down from her. It made her feel truly powerful, something that she would relish. Even with her powers, there weren't many times when she really felt like that. It was exciting and invigorating, addicting. Now she knew where Lianna and Razi got their confidence from. "So," she said, changing the subject, "where did you use to stay?"

He raised an eyebrow and grinned. "I hardly doubt you want to stay the night in the guard quarters."

"Oh, I don't know," she said, "I was hoping to see if they had another, less arrogant elf I could trade you for."

He frowned. "Perhaps," he said, "but they wouldn't be as charming. You're stuck with me, Claire, whether you like it or not. But I highly suspect that you do." He leaned down close to her and jabbed a finger into her chest, his grin returning full force.

She sighed, dramatically. "Unfortunately, I do."

"Besides," he said, straightening, "I'm better looking than any of those fools."

Claire rolled her eyes as he pulled her along again, though she found it hard to argue the point, no matter how conceited it was.

❧

The room hadn't changed one bit since the last time she'd seen it. And she knew every little detail after being kept inside it for what seemed like weeks. Only this time, the doors weren't locked and there was no guard stationed right outside. They were guests, so far, and she hoped that it would stay that way.

Farron surveyed the room, slowly walking around it, inspecting everything. "It's truly awful," he said, nodding. "I can see why you would want to run away."

"Try being locked up inside with nothing to do for days on end and then see where your sanity leads you," she said, going through their packs to make sure nothing was missing.

All of their things that had been confiscated were already waiting in the room, along with food and a pitcher of wine, and a few fresh changes of clothes. She'd missed her elven made shirt and looked forward to having another; the fabric and fit were truly exceptional. And though she appreciated the treatment, she was wary of it.

Consumed

Farron opened the double doors leading out to the balcony that hung over the cliff and she turned away. She still didn't appreciate the view.

"I suppose this escape is out," he teased. He closed the doors again.

"I'm glad you are amused by my past predicament." She stuffed everything back in the packs. Nothing seemed to be missing.

"It's better than the guard quarters," he said, coming up to inspect his weapons for the third time. "But a prison is a prison."

"Besides, did you see the attendants?" she asked, remembering the stern elves that avoided her gaze at all costs.

"How could I not?" he said. "I believe I was on the receiving end of their glares on more than one occasion."

"Which I'm sure you deserved," she said, smiling.

"Well," he said, "I told you I am charming, didn't I?"

Claire laughed and appreciated the levity. And even though she wasn't too excited to see her old room again, it was pure luxury after being on the road for weeks. She couldn't wait to take a bath. Rest on an actual bed. Eat warm food served on a plate. One last indulgence before what might be the end.

16

Claire tapped on the door and waited for a response, but none came. She looked up at Farron and he shrugged.

The hall was dark and empty. They had snuck out of their room to find Aeron's quarters, which had been moved from the palace to a more modest lodging down a side alley in the cramped elven city. Following Farron through the streets lit by ghostly pale lanterns was almost surreal. The architecture must have been beautiful once, and still was in a way, before the limited space and years of additions warped the buildings into bizarre versions of themselves, twisting and looming, mismatched materials and styles. Throughout all of her travels, the few times she had actually felt foreign were in the elven forest. They were in their own separate little world.

They'd managed to avoid any guards, Farron having memorized the rounds. He'd found out Aeron's new home from one of the current guards. She just hoped that it didn't seem too suspicious that they would want to call upon their old friend. His room was on the fourth floor of a narrow building, and even though it wasn't the palace, it was well kept and nice in a simple way.

After a few more silent moments, Farron knelt and picked the lock, cracking open the door to listen before entering. Claire followed, dipping into the dark room. Farron eased the door closed with a soft click.

Moonlight shone in through a large window on the far side of the apartment, illuminating a bed and a sleeping figure in it. A table with a single chair sat to her left, a shelf with a few books and knickknacks to her right. And that was it. Guilt stirred within her. It was because she had run away that he had lost his position in the King's guard and had to move to a place like this. Though it wasn't bad, she didn't know where he had lived before. Knowing him, it would have been much more extravagant than this.

She looked at Farron and he nodded. Claire crept up to the bed, eyeing the elf in it. Was he really asleep? With the elves' hearing ability, it was hard to believe he hadn't woken up. She leaned over him. He wasn't wearing a shirt and she hoped that he wore something underneath the sheets. It wouldn't surprise her in the least if he slept in the nude.

"Aeron," she whispered. His name had barely left her lips when he reached out and pulled her down onto the bed next to him.

"Why, Miss Claire," he said, a grin in place, "I should have known you would not be able to resist." He ran a finger down her jaw to her chin.

One of Farron's blades appeared at his neck, pressing lightly on the skin.

"If you insist on joining, you are more than welcome," Aeron said, "I have always been curious what kind of lover you are."

A soft groan escaped Farron as he sheathed his dagger.

Aeron frowned. "Your loss." He looked down at Claire and the smile returned. "Or is it mine?"

It was Claire's turn to groan in exasperation. She struggled to sit up and pushed his hand away.

"As much as I would like it to be, this is not a late night tryst, is it?" Aeron sat up, the sheet pooling in his lap.

Claire's cheeks burned and she hoped the shadows hid her embarrassment. She was almost positive that he was naked under there.

Farron crossed his arms and remained standing by the side of the bed. Not that Claire could blame him.

She shook her head and his expression fell in a dramatic way.

"Well then," Aeron said, leaning back on an arm. "What brings you here in the cover of darkness? I suppose it is nothing good."

Claire exchanged a glance with Farron. He wasn't wrong.

"No," she said. "And I'm not even sure it's a good idea."

Aeron's eyebrow rose, his interest piqued. "Oh?"

"I know it's a lot to ask, but can we trust you?" she asked, her eyes pleading. They were taking a risk coming here tonight, and an even bigger one asking him to do what they proposed.

"You are asking me about trust?" He laughed. "I think you lost that when you decided to run off with that general of yours and then the Ice Prince." He looked at Farron. "And you, you," he said, anger rising in his voice, "after we took you in, you betrayed all of us. Why should I be loyal to either of you?"

"Because," Claire said, the word coming out more frustrated than she meant it to. "This is bigger than you and me and Farron."

Aeron remained quiet, waiting for her to continue.

She took a deep breath. "We need to know that we can trust you," she said. "Or we'll leave, and we can forget this whole thing."

Aeron looked her over, his eyes narrowing in deliberation. He glanced up at Farron, then let out a sigh, his shoulders dropping. "Fine," he said. "What we say here stays here."

"You have to promise me," she said, deeply serious. "Our lives depend on it."

Aeron looked up at Farron again, who nodded. "All right," he said, turning his attention back to Claire. "What is it that has you two so troubled?"

"It's about our mission," Claire said, "or more specifically what happens afterward."

"You want to restore magic to save the land," Aeron said.

"And you remember the history lesson that you taught me?" she asked.

Aeron's lips thinned into a tight line, comprehension sparking in his eyes. "Yes," he said, softly.

"You know Ryaenon's goal," Farron finally chimed in.

"I do," Aeron said. "You're asking me to betray my king…"

A silence fell over the room and Claire could see the inner battle start to wage inside of Aeron. He had been out in the world, had seen human society, and perhaps he could see the good, the potential for peace, for compromise, for alliance.

"You've seen the outside world," she said. "It's far from perfect, but it can't go back to the way it was before the Great War. You said yourself that there are others that think like you, that don't believe in the old ways."

Aeron's gaze fell to the bed in front of him, lost in thought.

Claire reached out and took his hand. "I know what I ask is hard, impossible maybe, but I believe that we can live together in peace if we work at it. It doesn't have to go back to the way it was." She placed her other hand over his, cradling it between hers. "I plan to return magic to the land regardless," she said. "If I don't then no one will stand a chance. I'm just asking you to help give humanity one."

"You are sure you can do it?" Aeron said finally. "Restore magic?"

"I hope so," Claire said. She wasn't sure if she wanted to reveal her condition to him, but a little extra sympathy couldn't hurt if it would help sway him to their side. "For my own sake, as well."

Aeron narrowed his eyes at her, his brow twisting in confusion.

Claire stripped off the jacket to reveal the wild mark, the silver chains.

Aeron's mouth fell open as he took it in. "This—" He reached out to touch her shoulder, but stopped, his fingers hovering over her skin as if he were scared to. "It grew."

She nodded. "And it won't stop," she said. "I can only slow it down for so long before it takes over me completely."

"Is that what this is really for?" He touched a metal band.

"It has more than one purpose," she said. "I wasn't lying when I said I was hiding. The other Star Children, they can sense me. This keeps them from doing so."

"I see," Aeron said. "How much time do you have?"

Claire shrugged. "I don't know exactly."

"You said General Bren did this?" Aeron asked.

Claire nodded and turned her arm to expose the mark more clearly.

Aeron's eyes followed as his finger traced the down the scar. He turned to Farron. "And he still lives?"

"For now," Farron muttered, his jaw tensing.

A snort of laughter escaped from Aeron's lips. "Surprising," he said, "since you have wanted to kill him from the beginning. Or was that only after Sanre?"

Claire tried to think. What had happened in Sanre? Heat rose to her cheeks again. The kiss. She looked at Farron and his eyes met hers before shifting away. Leave it to Aeron to make things awkward.

"Will restoring the magic stop that?" Aeron nodded to the mark.

"I hope so," Claire said. "I don't know for sure. No one does. But it's our only hope."

Aeron's hand fell limp in his lap. "As far as King Ryaenon's plans, I agree," he said. "There *are* those among us that do not want another war, more fighting. They just want to be free. Most were mad after I returned without you. They do not call you *Yaederrí* because they think that you can help them conquer humans again. They do because you gave them hope that they could leave the forest, return to the world one day, see what I have seen, live a life of their own choosing."

"You told them of your adventures?" she asked, but of course he had.

He nodded. "I told them that it was not as we had thought. We are not hated and feared as we had once been. With time, that wound could heal if we showed humans that we are not the same as our forefathers. Some even wanted to journey out on their own before the king stopped them."

"What did he do?" she asked.

"Locked them in the dungeons for a while. Made them compliant again." He gave Claire a meek smile. "There was more than one reason why the king chose to demote me. He could not outright imprison me without it looking suspicious, but he has been trying to undermine me and my tales from the outside world as much as possible. There was already a growing divide and my return only widened it."

"It seems to me that *you* are now their *Yaederrí*," Claire said.

Aeron considered that for a moment, a smile tugging at his lips. "I suppose I am."

"So, what do you think?" she asked. "Will you help?"

"I will do what I can," he said. "I do not want a return to the past either. And if our little Farron has taught me anything, it's that there are things more important than blind loyalty." He touched her chin.

Claire took his hand in hers again and kissed it. "You don't know how much this has put my mind at ease," she said. "Fare may call you foolish, but I think if anyone could rally the elves, it's you."

"Why, Miss Claire, you are already in my bed, there is no need to charm me even more."

"Thank you, Aeron," she said, trying her best to ignore his comment.

"Everything is about to change," he said. "Let us just hope that it is for the better. For all of our sakes."

She did hope for that, but nothing was ever that simple.

It took two days for the old elf to translate the stone fragments. Not that Claire was complaining too much, as it was a welcome respite from their journey, and she savored the warm baths and soft bed as much as possible.

They were back in the dimly lit vault under the palace, only this time they had been joined by the king and a few other elves that she hadn't seen before. Ryaenon was dressed simply in plain red robes, his hair loosely braided and hanging over his shoulder. It was probably the most casual she would ever see the elven king.

The ancient elf spoke and ran shaky hands over the stone fragments. They all had gathered around the table, a mess of scrolls and books and a few curious looking tools, and listened with rapt attention. Claire grew anxious with anticipation, having to wait just that much longer for the translation. What did it say? All of that time and effort, and what if it wasn't worth it? What if, in the end, it couldn't be done? She knew she was letting her fears get the better of her, but she had every right to be nervous with her luck.

"He says," Farron muttered. His hair was back to its striking platinum blonde after he'd washed the remaining dark dye out in the bath the night before. And just as she was getting used to it… "They are instructions, but they aren't exactly clear to him. He was hoping that we might know more." He looked down at her, his arms crossed in front of him. He'd gotten a fresh set of clothes, but they were just as somber as the last ones, black pants, black top. She supposed she was just going to have to live with it.

"What does it say?" she asked, nodding at the stones.

"'Only when the stars come together again will there be light in the darkness,'" he said, running a finger over the words like the old elf had just moments before. "'When there is peace or no hope left, with their essence, say these words and return the world to its true state: Stars of the night, shine your light on the world once more. Return life to the land and its children. With these keys, I release you.'"

Claire took a deep breath and released it through her teeth, making a soft hissing sound. For some reason, she'd expected more, something more mystical.

"Essence…" she whispered. "Maybe it means blood? Mine activated the map, remember?"

Farron nodded.

The rest of the elves just looked at them, the king with an annoyed look on his face. Well, now he knew how it felt.

"Maybe we really were just keys all along," she said. "That could explain why there is still magic in certain places. Maybe it's able to break through somehow, like the barrier is weaker. Perhaps it's just using me to get back to the world…" Her eyes glazed over as she spiraled down into her thoughts. It all sounded so ridiculous, but deep down she knew it was true. The magic inside of her was like a living thing, a wildcat in a cage pacing, waiting to be released. When Claire came back to the present, Farron was already translating to the other elves.

The old elf, Sabin, she finally learned his name, nodded, excitement making his eyes shine. He shouted something and turned to rummage through the pile of papers.

"Of course," Farron relayed, though his delivery was a little lacking.

When Sabin turned back, he brandished an old-looking copper dagger. He reached for Claire, but Farron's hand shot out to grab his wrist, stopping him. The other elves reached for the swords on their hips, but Sabin stopped them with a wave of his free hand. He gave Farron a meek smile and muttered something.

"He wants to test something," Farron said.

Claire nodded and Farron released the old elf's hand. She would have thought he was overreacting, but she remembered the last time she'd been here all too well. At least this time she had an idea of what he wanted to do. She held out her left hand to the elf and he took it gently, turning it palm up. With the dagger, he sliced a small cut on her thumb, and squeezed it so enough blood welled up before pressing it down onto the stone. He slid her thumb across all of the pieces then released her. Claire shook her hand, then sucked on her thumb, not caring if she looked ridiculous. It stung more than she had thought it would.

The fragment absorbed her blood and a moment later the carved letters started to glow, a soft white light. Claire's magic stirred within her, feeling the familiar pull. Then the pieces started to vibrate, softly at first, increasing until the table itself shook. The stone slowly melded together, like liquid sand, becoming one. And then it stilled once more. The room remained quiet for far too long afterward. What had once been five pieces were now one, with no sign of scars or seams. Sabin muttered something.

"Amazing," Farron said, and he matched the tone this time. He seemed as awed as the rest of them.

King Ryaenon settled his gaze on her, the corner of his mouth upturned. There were gears turning in his head and she wasn't sure they were exactly good. Claire looked down at the stone, trying not to squirm or look guilty, hoping that Aeron would be able to stop the elven king.

Sabin started to say something but stopped mid-word, perking up. All the other elves followed suit, even Farron, tilting their heads slightly to listen to something.

"What—?" she asked, but a distant horn cut her off, another blowing nearer, followed by yet another before silence fell once more. She scanned their faces, but they revealed nothing, so she turned to Farron.

"Invaders," he said.

Her pulse picked up instantly. Was it Bahkar? Had he found her? Perhaps the tablet's magic had led him here. She wondered briefly if they had blown their horns when she had entered the forest. It seemed strange to her that they would think of her as a threat. Claire the Invader. It had a nice ring to it...

The door to the vault slammed open and an armored guard marched in, the dark-haired elf from the other day—Rhian, she'd learned—close behind. He bowed quickly to the king and said a few words before gracing Claire with his stern glare.

"There's an army at the edge of the forest," Farron said, close behind her.

Well, that she hadn't expected. An army? Who would—? But, at this point, who wouldn't? She was way too young to have so many enemies.

Consumed

"Human, centaur, or elven?" she asked, trying to make it sound light.

Farron translated and the king rose an eyebrow.

"What can I say?" Claire shrugged. "I'm in rather high demand."

King Ryaenon gave his orders to Rhian and the elf stormed from the room, taking the guard with him. The king muttered to the elves at his side and they nodded. Then he turned his attention to her and especially Farron. They had a tense conversation that Claire didn't dare interrupt. She would probably only make it worse. They both fell quiet and stared at each other for a moment before the king turned to leave, taking the rest of the elves with him.

When they were alone, Claire turned to Farron. His worried expression didn't set her at ease.

"They ask for you," he said.

"Of course," she said, sighing. Who wasn't these days? "Do they know who it is?"

He shook his head. "Not yet," he said, "but they're human. I can take a guess, though."

She nodded, her stomach turning. "How do you think he found us?"

"If he was smart, he would have had spies spread throughout his empire, and even beyond. As careful as we tried to be, it's possible we weren't able to avoid them all." His voice grew soft at the end and she could tell that he blamed himself.

She reached out to touch his arm. "If it wasn't him, it would've been someone else. We have way too many enemies to go unnoticed forever."

He looked into her eyes then, a fire igniting in the icy blue depths. "This ends here," he said, his voice as sharp as his blades. "That man, his life is mine."

Casey Odell

Claire swallowed hard. It always chilled her when the *Sin de Reine* surfaced. The General may have found her, but he would soon regret it.

17

Less than an hour later, Claire and Farron crossed over the bridge and into the forest, surrounded by a squadron of highly trained elves. And yet even they were not enough to quell the storm growing inside of her. Hatred swirled with apprehension. She never wanted to face him again. What would she do now that she had to? She already knew what Farron wanted to do. Would she just let him take another life? Go down that dark path he'd been avoiding for so long?

She was so lost in thought that she missed what Farron said to her.

"What?" she asked, blinking.

It was still light out, but it was hard to tell time under the thick forest canopy.

"I said don't take your chains off, no matter what." His voice was low, serious. "We don't need any more unwanted company."

She nodded, looking him over. He'd gotten a few pieces of the shiny metal armor the other elves wore, his forearms and chest glinting as he moved. It was strange seeing him in it, though she didn't exactly hate it.

He grinned, glancing sideways at her as he adjusted an arm piece. "I hear you like knights in shining armor."

Despite everything, she was still able to blush.

"It rather suits me," he said, his face lighting up.

"No armor in the world is enough to contain your ego," she said.

He laughed and a few elves looked their way.

"Fare," she said, drawing nearer. It was her turn to grow serious. "Don't let your anger get the best of you. I can't afford to have anything happen to you."

He frowned. "I could say the same thing to you."

"I hate him even more than you do." She took his hand and squeezed it. "Don't do something you might regret."

"I have killed many men in my past," he said. "But none have ever brought me as much pleasure at even the thought of ending his life. No, I will not regret killing him. I dare say I would even rest easier at night, knowing there was one less person after you, and that his presence was snuffed out from this world."

"And if his death causes a war?"

"Then let it," he said, his voice cold.

"And you commented on my diplomacy," she said. "Let me at least talk to him." She didn't like the thought, but she wanted to avoid bloodshed if she could. Even if it meant facing one of her biggest nightmares. How was *that* for diplomacy?

He was quiet for a few moments, then he said, "Fine." Though he wasn't happy about it. Far from it. "But if he does anything," he said, pulling her to a stop. His intense gaze bore into her. "*Anything*, then diplomacy is over."

"All right," she said, her voice wavering slightly. Why was she so hesitant about killing him? Even though she hated him, the thought of more death made her uncomfortable. She was still too soft. Was always going to be too soft. She used to think that the mark was wasted on her, but after seeing what Rialla had done, why she had done it, it made a little more sense that it had found her. What better way to hide something than in a person who would be too scared to use it? Only, her theory crumbled when she thought of the other Star Children, who were anything but afraid.

He kissed her on the forehead, his lips lingering. "He's already done too much damage, Claire. Don't let him do any more."

"I won't," she said, hoping she would be right.

Someone up ahead cleared their throat. The group of elves had stopped and were staring at them, none-too-happy about their pause. Claire fought not to roll her eyes. It was her fault, after all, that trouble was at their doorstep. She settled for a sigh and continued on through the trees, her anxiety growing more and more until it threatened to suffocate her. Farron kept his hold on her hand and it was as if it were the only thing that still tethered her in the world, giving her much needed strength. He was her rock and would be until the very end, and she was grateful for every moment.

Light shone up ahead and her pulse picked up even more, her head light. She had to hold it together. She couldn't let that man know how much he still affected her. What could he do to her now? With her powers? If he even got past Farron and the rest of the elves. He was nothing. So why did it feel like she was about to face another Beast of Old?

Claire narrowed her eyes as she stepped out from the line of trees into the field, temporarily blinded by the sun. She heard the horses snorting and stamping their feet impatiently as she waited for her vision to clear. But when it did, she didn't like what she saw one bit.

A long line of armed men stood before her, a large group in the middle mounted on metal-adorned steeds. Front and center was the General, scourge of her nightmares, looking as luminous and beautiful as ever. And she hated him even more for it.

Bren nudged his horse forward and the beast took a few steps before the squad of elves drew their weapons in a frighteningly efficient flurry. About half a dozen arrows were trained on the General. He pulled the horse to a stop and grinned. As usual, his long brown hair was pulled back in a low, loose ponytail and hung over his right shoulder. His armor was scant and lighter than his men's, but much more ornate, showing his status more than it offered protection, copper with golden accents. Red clothes underneath made him stand out even more.

"Miss Claire," he said, bowing atop the horse. "It has been too long."

"I'd say it hasn't been long enough," she replied, letting her anger show, probably more than she'd intended.

Bren chuckled. "Oh, how I've missed your spirit."

"I haven't missed you at all," she said. A cold sweat had broken out over her skin. She needed to calm down, not let him get the best of her. "What do you want?" There, straight to the point. Diplomacy wasn't dead, yet, but she could already feel it circling the drain.

"I thought we could talk," he said, his face still pleasant.

Her palms itched to slap him. Her reaction to him had changed so drastically from when she'd first met him. "About what?" she said. "I don't think there is much to say anymore."

He shifted in his saddle, his smile faltering a bit. "I've heard about your recent exploits," he said. "I am rather impressed—not that I wasn't before." He flashed her a smile that would have once melted her into a puddle but now filled her with raging fire. "My lord, King Philip, grows increasingly curious about you and would like to extend an offer of alliance."

Claire couldn't stop the laughter from bubbling up and escaping. "An alliance with you?" She rolled up the sleeve covering her right wrist and held her arm up. "I think you ruined any chance of that when you gave me this."

His lips pressed into a thin line. "An action that I deeply regret," he said, his voice morose.

It was hard to tell if it was genuine or not, but she preferred to err on the side of caution and assume anything he said had some falsehood to it.

His eyes lingered on her arm, curiosity in their depths. Claire covered the mark and scar again. Would he feel true remorse if he found out that what he had done was destroying her? She doubted his feelings were anything more than a way to manipulate her. She was only a tool, would only ever be one to him and his little King Philip.

"I do not want to fight," Bren said. "I only want to talk. Perhaps we can put our past aside long enough to do that?"

His patronizing tone almost set her off, made her want to give the order for the elves to fire. Only the image of him as a pin cushion in her head calmed her enough to repress the desire. Lendon's deal with Derenan was too costly to risk it. Her desire for revenge wasn't worth the thousands of lives they could save.

"Fine," she said through gritted teeth. "Let's talk."

Bren bowed on the horse again. "Very good, Miss Claire." He glanced at her companions, arching his eyebrow as he looked over Farron. "Perhaps we could take this somewhere more private?"

Claire crossed her arms. She *really* didn't want to do that. "Forgive me, but I am a little hesitant to be alone with you after what you did."

"She isn't going anywhere without me," Farron said, his voice a barely contained growl.

"Ever the faithful knight," Bren said, his smile returning. He'd always known how to rile Farron up, even before he'd betrayed Claire. "I see now you are trying to actually look the part. Good for you."

Farron went for his dagger hilt over his right shoulder. Claire had to grab his arm to stop him.

Bren chuckled and turned his horse halfway, looking down at her. "I have taken the liberty of restoring your mother's tavern," he said. "Come with your guards, if you so desire." He kicked his horse and the line of men parted to let him through, then followed after him.

Claire stood in the field, watching them head toward Stockton. Her mother's tavern still stood. She didn't know what to make of that, especially if he had had a hand in restoring it. She wished now that it had burned down that fateful night. To face him in her old home, her safe haven filled with so many good memories, it felt tainted now. Had he gone through her things? Been in her old room? She felt violated all over again.

"Are you sure you want to do this?" Farron asked, wrenching her from her thoughts.

She nodded, even though she really didn't want to. "We need to settle this," she said. "If we run now, there's no telling what he would do."

"All right," he said, then turned to the others, giving them orders in their flowing language.

The elves nodded, although none seem thrilled to be taking orders from Farron. With that, they set out across the field to her old home. She'd hoped for a happy homecoming, not one so full of dread.

It felt surreal to step foot in Stockton after so long. The sense of familiarity had been replaced by a strange uneasiness. What had

Consumed

been burnt and damaged was rebuilt, changed, some buildings even better than they were before. Life had returned, the plaza cleared of the bodies, but even now she couldn't stop the memory of their faces from flashing before her eyes. Visions of that night danced dangerously close to the forefront of her mind. It was as if she were walking in a haze, halfway between the past and the present. She hardly noticed the stares, the slack jaws and pointed fingers, the hushed whispers as a group of beings thought long gone strolled through the middle of the town in broad daylight. They were going to find out sooner or later anyway.

Claire tried to avoid looking at anyone in particular. She didn't know if she could stand the pity. She recognized a few faces but didn't stop. What would she say to them? What could she?

The route to the Blazing Stallion was so ingrained into her that her feet took her there seemingly of their own will. Her breath hitched when she laid eyes on it once again. It was as if that night had never happened. The building had been restored with such detail, it was a little unnerving.

"Check it," Farron said, making a circular motion in the air with his hand.

The elves dispersed, diving into the alleys surrounding the tavern, leaving her and Farron alone on the street. Two armed guards emerged from the building then, holding the door open.

Claire took a breath and looked at Farron. "Ready?"

"Are you?"

"No," she said, stepping forward. This was all too much. Rebuilding the tavern, inviting her back here. What game was he playing?

The guards eyed Farron as he neared, but didn't make any movements. Just like the outside, the interior of the tavern had been restored. Claire paused in the doorway to take it all in. It gave her the creeps. In the center of the room, the General sat at a small wooden table a little too casually, a welcoming smile on his face. Two more guards stood a few paces behind him, staring forward with blank eyes. Farron stepped around her and approached the table. A few candles illuminated the uneven surface. A crystal decanter of wine and glasses sat to the side.

In one swift move, Farron reached up and drew one of his daggers and stabbed it into the wood. The guards barely had time to react. The General didn't move an inch, though his smile widened. He held a hand up to stay the guards.

"You always were hot-headed, weren't you?" Bren said, rising to his feet. "Please," he motioned to the chairs across from him, "have a seat. I only wish to talk."

It took everything she had to walk closer to that man. Her skin crawled more with each step she took. She almost would have preferred to face another Beast of Old than to sit across from him. Farron left the dagger buried in the wood and crossed his arms. Claire took a seat, not trusting her knees to support her.

"We're here," she squeezed out of her tight throat. "Now talk."

Bren chuckled and sat down, crossing his legs and leaning back, looking too comfortable. "You have grown even bolder since we last met," Bren said, his eyes gleaming with amusement.

"And you more insufferable," she retorted.

His smile faded and he sighed. "I hope that one day you will be able to forgive me, Claire. I only did what I thought was necessary. I had feared that you were working with the elves." He looked Farron up and down. "Though, your presence in the forest again does raise the same concern. What has brought you back? I would have thought that you were quite happy to live in a palace. Wasn't that your dream once?"

"It was," she said. "Once. However, things change." She gave him a pointed look. "As for my business here, it is none of your concern."

"Oh, but it is." He raised an eyebrow. "Unless you haven't heard, Lendon now controls the surrounding land, and anything that could harm the realm is, of course, my concern. Am I to believe that those elves have hidden away for years for their love of humans? That they finally ventured out when they got their first whiff of real power? After seeing what you can do, and learning about their history, no, I do not think their intentions are in our best interest. So, I will ask again, what brings you back here?"

The air hung heavy with silence. If she told him her true mission, that she was working with the elves, the very thing that he accused her of, then he wouldn't just let her go free and clear with a friendly pat on the back.

"I thought that you wanted to escape?" he asked. "Isn't that why you ran away with me in the first place? To escape from their clutches? So, why is it that you willingly went back?" He looked at Farron. "And it's even more curious that you would bring her back here. The bastard son of a king. Who would have thought? You finally managed to win her over and you didn't ride off into the sunset. Curious indeed."

Farron glared down at the General. If looks could kill...

"What can I say?" Claire said. "I was feeling nostalgic." She motioned around with her hand. "Speaking of which, why go through all the trouble to restore my mother's tavern?"

"Think of it as a gift," Bren said, turning his gaze back to her. He leaned forward and poured a glass of wine. He offered it to her, but when she declined he shrugged and leaned back in his chair again, taking a sip. "An apology. Though, I know it will take much more than that for you to forgive what I have done."

"How kind of you," she said, making the words as bland as possible.

"Did you ever find her?" Bren asked. "That mother of yours?"

Claire considered the question for a moment. There was more than mere curiosity behind his words. She had to be careful she didn't reveal too much. "I did."

"Good," Bren said, taking another sip, but it didn't hide the flash of disappointment. He had thought to use her mother against her once, would still if he could. He started to motion to the room around them. "Perhaps, she would appreciate—"

"No," Claire said, cutting him off. "You will never get your hands on her. Ever."

"I didn't mean—"

"Yes, you did." Claire sat up straight in the chair. "Your kindness always has a motive behind it, a reason. All of this," she swung her arms out, "isn't because you feel bad. It's some sort of sick, twisted mind game, or bribe, maybe both. I don't know. I'd sooner burn it to the ground than have it in your hands."

"Fair enough," Bren said, setting the glass down on the table.

"As far as answers, I don't owe you anything. Your king was never my king. I have no allegiance to Lendon, now or in the past, nor will I in the future," she said.

"I see," Bren said quietly. "That's rather unfortunate."

"How so?" she asked.

"I had hoped that we could convince you to fight for our side, to not betray your own kind. I fear my suspicions about you have been true all along." He turned the glass with his fingers. "That you went back into the forest means that you have fallen under their influence. I know not what you have planned, but it isn't in our best interest, is it, Claire?"

Consumed

Goosebumps rose across her skin. This wasn't going well. She supposed diplomacy wasn't her strong suit, after all.

"Careful," Farron said, a warning flashing across his face.

Bren looked up at the tall elf, unflinching. "I still don't know where you fit into all of this. The brother of a king, assassin, with no loyalty to anyone."

"He's loyal to me," Claire said.

"Ah, of course." Bren smirked. "You were able to let him into your heart after learning of his... past?"

"*He* never harmed me." She'd grown tired of his prodding.

"A woman's heart is a fickle thing," Bren said.

"As capricious as a man's temper," she shot back.

He stared at her, unblinking, and she managed to return the favor.

"I will extend the offer one last time," Bren said, an edge to his voice. "Accept King Philip's offer of alliance or become an enemy of the realm."

Claire scoffed. "An enemy, for what?"

"Treason against humankind," Bren said matter-of-factly.

"And then what?" she asked, becoming incredulous, or stupid. "You'll carve up my other arm? Feed me to another Beast of Old? You've seen what I can do. What makes you think you are a threat to me?"

"If I wasn't, then you wouldn't have come to talk." Bren clasped his hands together. "If you are so powerful, then you would have just gone." His eyes fell to her neck where the edges of the mark peeked above the collar of her jacket. "I have my own spies in Derenan. The rumors about you are true, no?"

Claire swallowed. So, he knew after all. "All thanks to you."

A grin tugged at his lips. "Believe me, it was never my intention, Claire. Despite everything, despite what you may think, I happen to be rather fond of you."

She laughed. "You only ever liked what I could do for you."

Bren shrugged. "Believe what you want. But regardless of my feelings for you, I cannot just let you betray us all. What is it, may I ask, that they have offered you? It can't be gold. No, you could have had that back in Derenan, could still have it in Lendon. Power? That was never your desire. Not truly. And since he doesn't have any loyalty except to you," he nodded at Farron, "then he wouldn't sway you into working with them. It definitely isn't your love for that fool we once traveled with. So, what is it?"

Claire shrugged. "Perhaps I just appreciated their hospitality, and wanted to thank them for saving me in my hour of need."

"I don't believe you."

"That's your problem then." Yes, diplomacy. She doubted the truth would matter. Even if it was to benefit the whole world, he would still see her as a traitor for working with the elves, for restoring them to power. She was having a hard time trying to convince *herself* that she wasn't. The truth didn't matter anymore as far as he was concerned. She was already a traitor in his eyes and nothing she said would change that.

Bren sighed. "I cannot change your mind?"

Claire shook her head.

"Then, on behalf of King Philip of Lendon, I, General Brennus Erolle, declare you an enemy of the realm." He stood from his chair and the guards stepped forward.

Farron went for his dagger, pulling it from the wood.

"You don't want to do this," Claire said, trying to salvage the situation, but she knew the effort was in vain.

"No, I don't," Bren said, "but I fear I have no other choice." He nodded over his shoulder to the guards and they advanced forward, the one on the right whistling.

The guards that had been outside slipped inside, closing the door behind them. Commotion sounded suddenly from the street, metal clanging, the thunk of arrows finding their targets, men shouting. Farron became a blur of motion, lunging for the guards behind him. Claire drew her dagger and held it in front of her. She had agreed not to take the bands off, so her magic was limited. The General had an idea of her fighting skills, which still weren't the greatest, not against men who had had years of training.

"Take her," he commanded the guards, looking wholly unthreatened by her. He kept glancing at Farron. Magic or no, he was a danger and Bren knew it.

The two guards came around the table. She tried to make a magic orb, but she couldn't. She searched frantically inside of herself for the threads of her magic. Nothing.

"Fare!" she shouted, backing away from the men.

"You didn't think that I was foolish enough to come unprepared, did you?" Bren said, a smile on his face. He spread his hands wide. "I made a few improvements."

Claire glanced around. She didn't see anything out of place. But he had done something. She'd been so distracted by her other feelings, she hadn't noticed how her magic had been suppressed even further upon entering the tavern. The back door that led to the kitchen burst open and men dressed all in black poured in.

Claire froze. No, it couldn't be. The Ophiuchus Syndicate. They wouldn't form an alliance with Lendon, would they? But she knew well enough what desperation could lead people to do. She had hoped she'd seen the last of them. She must have really made them mad for them to resort to working with the General and King Philip.

Men kept streaming in and soon she and Farron were outnumbered. The guards were nearly on her. She slashed out with her blade and they stopped, drawing their swords. Claire shrunk back. Swordplay had never been her strength.

The men in black surrounded Farron, a few leaping into the fray. "You can't subdue our magic forever," Claire shouted at Bren.

"I don't need to." He came around the table toward her.

Her pulse picked up. Memories of that day raced through her mind. All of this was becoming too familiar. The men made another move for her, but she slashed at them, keeping them barely at bay.

Bren made a clicking sound with his tongue. "Now, boys, she's hardly a threat." He brushed past the guards, his eyes full of dark hunger.

The look frightened her. Her hand shook. What did he want with her? "Don't you touch me!"

Bren's pace didn't slow. "Why, Miss Claire, I seem to remember you wanting me to do just that." He smiled down at her.

Claire stabbed out at him, but he dodged, laughing. She slashed again, then again, becoming too frantic. She couldn't let him have her. Not again. Anything but that.

Bren's hand shot out and grabbed her wrist. His fingers squeezed hard until she cried out, and he twisted her arm up and back until she dropped her blade. The two guards came to either side of her, taking hold of her other arm and shoulders.

Bren pulled her closer, his eyes narrowed. "You will never be able to best me, Claire."

Claire made a move to spit at him, but his other hand shot out and grasped her jaw, yanking her chin up. She nearly bit her tongue off.

"Let's not be disrespectful," he said. He handed off her wrist to a guard, then glanced over his shoulder at the scuffle between

Farron and the others. "He really is quite talented. I wonder how long he will be able to last?" He turned back to her, an eyebrow raised.

Claire jerked her chin from his grip. "Long enough to kill you."

Bren chuckled. "I look forward to the challenge then." He touched the pendant hanging from her neck, lifting it up to inspect it closer. "How troublesome." He tugged the chain hard. It snapped and he pocketed the necklace. "Come," he said, turning and motioning for the guards to follow.

The men dragged her toward the kitchen. She kicked out with her feet, tried to drag them on the floor, but it was no use. The tall guards merely lifted her up higher.

"Fare!" she shouted.

Farron called after her but was soon quieted by another round of fighting. She was on her own for the moment.

They carried her through the door and into the kitchen—only it was much different than she remembered. In fact, it wasn't a kitchen at all, just a plain room with no windows and a narrow door that led to the back alley. The stairs had been blocked off with several boards. It had all been a façade. The guards slammed the thick door to the tavern closed and slid a heavy bar across it, plunging the room into darkness.

A moment later a flame sparked to life, illuminating Bren's face, the hollows of his cheeks cast in deep shadow, making him seem gaunt. He lit a lantern and crossed the room to light another. The guards slammed her down into a chair. The only other furniture was a table against the wall with a multitude of instruments spread out atop it. She took several deep breaths to try and calm herself, but they weren't successful. What did he plan to do?

Bren went to the table. "I didn't want to have to do this again," he said, running his finger over the tools. "Here, now, so rushed. But I'm afraid I have no choice."

"You do have a choice," she said, her voice shakier than she liked.

"No," he said. "I don't. The Syndicate only agreed to help if I turned you over unharmed." He looked at her. "They came to me, you know, after you and your friend devastated their ranks. You took almost everything they had." He grinned. "I'm more impressed than anything, really. That kind of power." He picked up a long, thin metal piece with a wooden handle and a pointy end.

She eyed it, her skin breaking out in sweat as he came for her.

"I saw with my own eyes what you did in Teren, the corpses. You single-handedly annihilated the main centaur force, our empire builders. A shame, really. Thanks to them, Lendon has grown to almost four times its previous size. But I'm not mad. Not truly, just disappointed." He stepped closer, the dark hunger in his eyes again. "But with you… there's no limit to what we could achieve. Pledge your loyalty to Lendon, to King Philip, to *me*, and your little elven lover will live and your flesh will stay whole."

"Never," she snarled, squirming in the chair. The guards had shifted their hold on her. One knelt and held her ankles, the other stood behind her with her wrists in his grip.

Bren ran the point of the metal tool across her cheek and down to her neck, and with it lifted the collar of her jacket away to reveal the edge of the mark.

"You are in no position to refuse, and yet you do." His eyes lingered on her throat. "Together we could rule the world."

"I have no desire to do so. It sounds rather exhausting."

He snorted a laugh. "Such power is wasted on you."

"No," she said. "I thought that once before I learned the truth. It was hidden in us to keep it away from people like you."

"Was it now?" Bren lowered the tool. "That hasn't stopped that council of old men in Derenan, has it? They have found a way to use you, and the others like you. I will do the same." He gripped her chin again and wrenched her face up to meet his. "I told you before, I will not stop until I make you mine."

"Then you will have to kill me." She met his eyes with a fire of her own. She didn't like the thought, but it was better than the alternative. "Oh, but you have already seen to that."

He released her. "It's true, then? The mark, it consumes you?" He tucked the tool into his belt and grasped the lapels of her jacket. With the same urgency of a lover, he pulled her jacket down to reveal the mark and the damage that he had wreaked. "My, my…" he muttered, reaching out to touch her shoulder.

Claire jerked back as much as she could. She wanted him to touch her as much as she wanted to pluck out her own eye. But she could only move so far back. The guards tightened their hold on her. Bren slid his finger over the dark lines, his touch leaving a trail of fire in its wake. She squirmed.

"All of this because of me," he whispered in awe.

"You understand now why I can't accept your offer," she said, her voice sweet poison.

"And these?" He toyed with a dangling silver chain.

"Why don't you take them off and see?" Another prospect she didn't like, but it would get her and Farron out of a jam—and possibly into another. But perhaps they could slip away in the chaos.

But Bren didn't take the bait. "The Syndicate informed me of this." He dropped the chain. "Ingenious little contraption." He fished the chain and key out from around her neck and lifted it over her head. "Curious, why you still wear it after you escaped their capture?"

"I like the way it looks." She shrugged her shoulders.

"Or it could have something to do with this." He lifted her right arm.

Well, he wasn't wrong. "You've always been a shrewd one."

He yanked her arm up and leaned in close, his eyes searing. "Leave us," he said.

"But, sir…" the guard at her feet said.

"You heard me," Bren growled. "Leave!"

The guards hesitated before scurrying out the door to the alley.

The room was silent except for her heavy breathing.

"Claire," Bren muttered, running his fingers down her jaw to her chin. His other hand gripped her wrist harder, pulling it up further. She leaned back in the chair to try and get away from him, but his hand shot out and gripped her neck and began to squeeze. She clawed at his arm but his hold on her didn't relent. His eyes became wild, the hunger back, like a hunter about to devour its prey.

A sound escaped her throat, a sort of stifled scream.

"Relent to me, Claire!" Bren breathed, his face inches from hers. "You were once almost mine." He pushed her back in the chair until it tipped back, its front legs leaving the floor.

Claire struggled to breathe.

"Say it," Bren growled. "Say you will be mine!"

She kicked out with her legs, thrashing until they connected with something, anything. He grunted when her foot struck near his groin, his grip faltering just enough for her to squirm away. The chair tipped and she fell to the floor. Air ripped down her throat, her shoulders heaving as she coughed. Bren lunged at her. Claire crawled away toward the door. She didn't even know which one, just a door, any way to get out and escape from him. He was going mad, his lust for power blinding him.

His hand slammed down on her ankle, halting her in her tracks. She clawed at the floor as he dragged her back toward him.

"No!" she screamed hoarsely, her terror causing tears to well and spill down her cheeks. "Let me go! Please!"

Consumed

"Claire!" Farron's muffled shout came from the other side of the door, followed by a pounding. But the thick wood barely budged.

"Farron!" she shouted as the General's hands found their way to her waist.

He turned her over and straddled her legs, trapping them under his weight. Claire writhed, scratching at his hands, his arms, his face, anything within range. She opened a bloody gash across his cheek. He smiled. It only seemed to drive him more. He leaned over her, capturing her wrists in his grip. She couldn't stop the sobbing.

"Stop this," she pleaded, "Please."

"Relent," he said, "Say you will be mine."

"Claire!" Farron shouted again, the door shaking as he rammed it.

"Never," she whispered.

Bren transferred her wrists to one hand and took the sharp tool from his belt. He ran the tip across her skin, up to her neck where the mark's tendrils curled.

"No," she begged. "Please, don't…"

"If you won't be mine, then no one should have you." He pressed the tip into her skin. Claire tried to twist away, but he only pressed harder. "Not the elves, not those old men, not your lover…"

The door shook again and again, the pounding relentless.

A disturbance sounded from out in the alley, the sound of fighting. It wouldn't be long before she was found, she hoped. But would it be too late?

"Stop this!" she shouted at him. "You will never have me."

"No," he said, his voice emotionless. "And no one else will either."

He pressed the tip into her skin, piercing the surface.

Claire yelled, writhing. How was this happening again?

Bren drug the sharp tip down her neck to her shoulder, slicing through the mark.

"You made me do this," Bren growled. "If you would only yield."

A scream ripped up her throat. Her body bucked underneath him, twisting and turning as the sharp metal carved a crooked line down over her shoulder. Claire paused to gather her strength, and with one big burst of energy, she turned her body to one side, breaking his grip on her momentarily. But it was enough. His rage had made him careless. She ripped one of her hands from his grip and clawed at his face. She caught his left eye and he reared.

"You bitch!" he shouted.

She struggled out from under him and started to pull herself away. But only a moment later he was almost on her again. Claire kicked at him. It didn't slow him down. He was relentless. And that's when she remembered, she wasn't entirely defenseless. She drew her right leg up to her chest and fished the slim blade from her boot. She held it up just as he lunged at her again and the blade slid into his stomach.

Bren froze and looked down at the growing red stain on his shirt, darker than the surrounding crimson cloth. Claire was motionless as well. The room fell into silence. The pounding on the door paused. The world seemed to slow to a crawl around her. Blood dripped down the blade to her hand. She gasped and released the dagger.

Bren smiled, a pained look on his face. "He taught you more than I thought."

Claire scurried away from him, her back pressing up against the wall. The sobs came freely, her whole body trembling violently, her breath raspy. Her shoulder stung, her blood soaking her shirt. Her throat already felt bruised.

Bren collapsed to his hands and knees, his own breathing becoming laborious. He chuckled slightly before falling onto his side.

Claire just stared at him for several moments. Was he dead? Had she just…?

The pounding and rattling of the door brought her back to the present.

It took all of her strength to stand again and push aside the bar blocking the door.

Farron stilled when he took her in, his eyes widening. "Claire," he said as she stepped out from the back room into the tavern.

Bodies littered the floor and she didn't know if they were dead or just unconscious, or if she cared. She was lost in another daze. Shock. Something she was all too familiar with. Nothing seemed to be real at the moment.

Farron ran his hands over her, inspecting, when she didn't answer him. He stopped at her shoulder, a sound deep in his throat escaping. "What did he do," he whispered. He disappeared for several moments.

Claire just stood in the middle of her mother's old tavern, where she had once experienced such happy memories, now filled with misery and death. It would never be the same again.

"Claire," Farron said, coming around her. "Are you all right?" He bent to examine the red spot on her stomach where the General's blood had dripped.

"It's not mine," she uttered. "Not there."

"We need to leave," he said, his voice remarkably calm. "Can you do that?"

She nodded. Anything to get far, far away from here. And hopefully never return.

Farron took her hand and led her to the door. Claire tripped over a body, but his grip steadied her. There was going to be no end to her nightmares.

Chaos filled the street. Elves fought humans. Townspeople fled. That night replayed in her mind, flashing before her eyes as Farron pulled her along, dodging and slipping through the crowds just like her mother had. She didn't know where he led her and didn't care. Anywhere was better than here.

Farron knelt in front of her. He wiped her hands on a cloth, staining it crimson. She sat on a rock in the dim shade of the forest canopy. The elven forest. It was far too quiet and eerie to be anything else. Her body shook, her extremities were numb, her mind still in a haze.

"You're fine," Farron whispered, "You're all right."

"Fare," she said, tears streaming down her cheeks. She didn't know what she wanted to say, but just uttering his name seemed to give her strength. He was her rock, her steadying force, the bright light in the darkness.

"You're all right, Claire." He brushed her hair from her face.

Her skin was cold and clammy with sweat. She was sure she looked completely terrible. "Are you?" she asked, her voice weak.

He nodded. Aside from a few bumps and scrapes, he looked fine. "I've fought a legendary Beast of Old, a horde of centaurs, and faced your angry mother," he said, a grim expression on his face. "And none of those have scared me as much as hearing your screams on the other side of that door."

Claire looked down at her hands. The blood was gone, but they were still tinted red. "I killed him," she said.

"If you hadn't, I would have." He took her hands in his, smothering them with his warmth.

Consumed

"So much for diplomacy." She tried to smile, but a sob escaped her mouth instead. This was surely going to strain relations with Lendon. Without their help, the lives of too many were now at risk. It was all in her hands now. Her blood-stained hands.

"It doesn't matter now," Farron said. "It's done."

He rose to inspect the wound on her shoulder. Claire winced, sucking in air through her teeth when he pulled the cloth of her shirt away. He muttered a few elven curses under his breath.

"Is it as bad as it feels?" she asked.

He hesitated longer than she was comfortable with. "The wound itself isn't too bad. It will leave a scar, though."

Great, just what she needed. "It seems I'm acquiring quite the collection. It'll soon rival yours."

"I hear they add character." He leaned down and kissed the top of her head. "As far as the mark… How does it feel, your magic? Is there anything different?"

He dug in his pocket and took out her pendant. He fiddled with the chain before slipping it around her neck, along with the silver key. A weight seemed to lift off of her when he did. She closed her eyes and took a long shaking breath. She felt calmer already.

"It's hard to tell at the moment," she said. "I'm still too shaken up. But I'm sure it's not good." She looked up at him. "I'm sorry, Fare. I never should have dragged you down there, never should have insisted that I try to talk to him." She looked down at her feet. "What did I expect to happen? That he would listen to reason?"

He knelt in front of her again. "If one good thing came out of it, it's that we don't have to worry about him anymore. If it starts a war, we can worry about it after we restore magic. *They* can deal with it." He nodded toward the elven city deep in the forest. He stood and took her hands in his to pull her up. "Come," he said. "We need to get you cleaned up and mended before this gets any worse." He motioned to her shoulder, worry clear on his face.

Claire nodded and let him lead her back to the elven city. In the end, she'd only managed to make things worse. Bren was dead. By her hands. She wanted to feel relieved. It was one less madman after her. But all she felt inside was numb.

Numb was better than the alternative. Her soul had never felt heavier. She'd killed before, but that was under the control of her magic. But Bren, that had been all her.

Claire stood out on a wide balcony, the same one where she'd encountered Farron and had pleaded with him to let her go, swaddled in a robe that was half a foot too long. Cool air nipped at her still damp skin. The bath had warmed her, returned the feeling to her body, soothed the aches and pains. She no longer trembled. The shock had worn down to a barely perceptible presence, regret and guilt taking its place.

The sky had grown dark and ghostly lanterns along the rails and walls came to life. The palace had been abuzz since their return. War with the humans was on the horizon. Their peaceful solitude had been broken. They had no choice but to prepare for the inevitable. Another weight to add to her shoulders. If it hadn't been for her, they could have kept hidden from the world just a little bit longer.

"There you are," Farron said from behind her.

She glanced over her shoulder at him. He'd cleaned himself up and wore a crisp white shirt instead of his usual, darker attire. After their return they'd been separated, Claire rushed to the healers, Farron to report to the king.

"I looked in the baths and you weren't there," he said, leaning in close. "A shame." He kissed her lightly. "How do you feel?"

"Better," she said. "Not good, but better."

He drew her into his arms and hugged her tight. She buried her face in his chest. His warmth was more comforting than any bath.

"It'll get better," he said, stroking her hair. "Day by day, it will."

Claire slipped her arms around his waist. "Thank you, for everything. I couldn't do this without you."

"Hmm," he hummed, resting his chin on the top of her head. "I assure you it's for purely selfish reasons."

She gave his side a pinch and he laughed. He pulled back enough to look down at her and cupped her cheek with his hand.

"Selfish reasons," he muttered and bent to kiss her again, pressing his lips against hers more urgently. The kiss deepened, becoming more and more passionate until they were both out of breath. "Don't scare me like that again."

"I'll try not to."

"You keep saying that," he said, straightening.

"What can I say?" She shrugged. "I live a dangerous life."

A smile tugged at his lips and he sighed. He pushed the neck of her robe down from her shoulder, revealing the bandage the elves had wrapped around her after her bath.

"Does it hurt?" he asked, his smile turning into a frown.

"A little." She tried to move her right arm but stopped when a sharp pain shot through her shoulder. She winced and let her arm fall to her side. "They put some sort of salve on it that seemed to dull most of the pain. Then they stitched it closed with silk. I dare say my shoulder is worth more now than my entire wardrobe growing up."

"And your magic?" He seemed hesitant to ask her about it.

And she was just as reluctant to answer. "Well," she said, "it's not better than before. And I can only assume that it will speed up the mark's progress."

Farron pulled her robe back into place, spending a little too long adjusting it. When that was done, he quietly drew her back into his embrace. He didn't need to say anything. They were both thinking the same grim thoughts. Her days had already been numbered, but now they were even more so.

18

"Do you trust them?" Claire asked, wincing as she pulled her shirt on.

The numbing effect of the salve had worn off overnight and the wound throbbed, sending a particularly sharp pain through her whole body whenever she moved just so. She would have to visit the healers again before they set out to get some more of it.

Farron shrugged as he donned his dark attire once again. "I don't think that it matters much," he said. "Ryaenon insists on sending his elves. I say let him. Our goal is the same anyway. The less trouble we have to deal with, the better. We don't have the luxury of any more setbacks." He gave her a look, the same look he'd given her all night, his eyes lingering on her shoulder. He was eager to take the bandage off and reveal the damage done, to see if the mark had grown even wilder. "Besides, it wouldn't hurt to have a few more allies on our side."

She couldn't argue that point. They may have had one less enemy, but there were still plenty more in line. And what better defense than a squad of highly trained elves? She just hoped that they didn't suffer the same fate as the last group tasked with accompanying her.

Claire sat to pull on her boots, freshly cleaned and mended. It was unfortunate that they had to leave the luxury of the elven city behind, but her time was running out and they couldn't waste any more dawdling, no matter how much she wanted to. So, her and Farron had agreed to leave as soon as they could. On possibly her last journey. She paused for a moment, letting that thought sink in.

"Claire?" Faron asked, bringing her back to the present.

She shook the thought from her head, glad for the interruption. That was a dark road that she didn't like to go down. But she found herself doing so more and more lately.

"Well," she said, standing. "Let's get this over with."

They were to meet the king in the throne room for a final send-off, and hopefully wouldn't be subjected to public spectacle like the last time. She glanced out the window to the plaza below and noticed no crowd, much to her relief.

After gathering their things, she took one last look at the room, already missing the plush bed. Farron led the way through the maze of halls to the throne room. Aeron stood just outside, a sad smile on his face.

"You leave so soon," he said.

"You sure you can't come with?" Claire asked, hoping. He would make the journey a little more bearable.

He frowned. "With how the last mission turned out, I am lucky his majesty did not take my head." He held his arms out wide and engulfed Claire in a too tight hug. "Besides," he muttered, "I think it best if I stay here."

Claire hugged him back, then withdrew, nodding. She understood what he meant. If he were to succeed at all with what she had asked of him, he couldn't come with her, no matter how much she wanted him to.

"A shame, really," Aeron said, grinning. "I know how much our little Farron wanted me to come along. I know how fond he is of me."

"I'm devastated," Farron said, his voice monotone.

Aeron laughed and stuck out his hand. Farron took it and they shook. "Safe travels, old friend."

"Don't do anything too foolish," Farron said, a smile breaking through. Despite what he said, Claire had a feeling that he liked Aeron more than he let on.

"I make no promises." Aeron gave her a sly look and then it melted into a more somber one. "I really hope to see you again, Claire."

"Me too," she said, her eyes stinging.

Aeron ruffled her hair and let his hand fall back to his side. "Well," he said, gathering himself up. "You should not keep his majesty waiting."

Claire shrugged. "I quite like making kings wait."

Aeron laughed. "You have gotten braver, Miss Claire. Do not let anyone tell you otherwise."

She smiled. "Take care, Aeron."

He bowed and Farron pushed open the heavy doors to the throne room. With a final wave to her elven friend, she turned and entered the crowded room. Too many eyes watched as she entered. So much for a quiet exit.

The doors clunked closed behind her. She approached the king on his throne and knelt, Farron doing the same. To either side stood a group of well-armed elves. Her new travel companions? She didn't recognize any of them. Did Farron? Not that it mattered too much, she supposed.

The king said a few words, the crowd silent, listening in earnest. Sabin, the ancient elf, stood behind and to the left of the king. His eyes met hers momentarily before shifting away once again to stare blankly ahead. She wondered if he looked forward to the return of magic. Had he been alive when it disappeared? She'd never had a chance to ask him.

Farron responded to the king and stood. She followed, resigned to being lost and not understanding. If it was important, she hoped Farron would tell her.

The king stood and spoke again. He motioned to the armored elves with a regal sweep of his hands.

A loud boom sounded outside from what seemed like the plaza and the floor trembled beneath them. Startled gasps broke out among the crowd of elves. Claire looked at Farron, but he just shook his head, a concerned look on his face.

Another loud crash sounded out in the hall followed by yelling that was cut short a moment later. All attention now focused on the entrance to the throne room. The crowd closest to the doors shrank back. Half of the armed elves surrounded the king, while the others took up positions near the entrance and drew their weapons.

Farron moved in front of Claire, his hand on the dagger over his right shoulder. Claire's pulse jumped up to her throat. What now? Was Lendon attacking? Retaliating for the death of their general? If it was them, how had they managed to get through all of the elven guards to the city without causing any alarm? No, if that were the case, they would have heard about it. Judging by everyone's reactions, this was a surprise. And there weren't too many people that could do that.

"Fare," she whispered, her dread growing. Her stomach sank down to her knees.

Consumed

A shout sounded right outside the doors and that too was cut short, only this time she could hear a sickening gurgling sound. The armed elves braced for action. Farron grew tense, his grip tightening on the hilt of his dagger. The doors slowly pushed open, the hinges groaning, and an unnerving laughter filled the room.

"No," Claire whispered. She knew that laugh. It had haunted her dreams for months. Still gave her chills. How had he found her?

Bahkar stood in the doorway, a deranged smile in place. "My flower," he said, his voice disturbingly unsteady. "Why have you hid from me for so long?"

Her body already trembled, her fear paralyzing. How? The question repeated in her mind over and over again. She frantically replayed the events of the past few days in her head to find her mistake. When had she slipped up? The silver contraption hadn't left her arm at all. *Then how?*

The elves closest to him pointed their swords and arrows at him. Bahkar blinked and looked at the elves, his gaze sweeping over them. Then he grinned.

"Look out!" Claire shouted at the elves. She had already grabbed Farron and was pulling him back.

Bahkar raised his arms and sharp spikes shot up from the floor. Three of the elves were impaled, and the others barely managed to get away in time. A barrage of arrows rained down on Bahkar. A thin marble shield stopped them and they clattered harmlessly on the floor. His laughter filled the room.

"New friends, I see," Bahkar said, hiding behind his defense. "I would spare their lives, but I do not think that they will just let you go."

Claire whirled around, looking for another way out. They couldn't stay here. The throne room was too closed in for battle. And if she lured him away then maybe it would be possible to lessen the destruction, the lives taken.

A few steps back and she spotted a door behind the great wooden throne. A small one not meant to be seen by visitors. She nudged Farron.

"Where does that go?" she asked, nodding to the door.

"The king's private chambers," he said. He drew his dagger, his eyes locked on the invader. "But there's a way out on the other side."

Claire pulled him by the arm toward their exit. She felt bad leaving the elves to fend for themselves, but the longer she stayed, the more damage done. They were halfway up the dais when the king shot them a look. His words were sharp and he pointed an elegant finger toward Bahkar.

Farron exchanged a few tense words with him, the look on the king's face growing angrier by the second. His guards all drew their weapons at the same time, their uniformity a little unnerving. Claire turned to look at Bahkar. He'd stepped out from behind his shield, his eyes wide and wild.

"Is that any way to treat a guest?" he said, deep and angry.

The crowd had retreated to the edges of the room, pushing their backs against the walls, some even cowering with their arms covering their heads. The elves that were attacking him moved to the center of the room and stood at the ready. It probably wasn't every day that they encountered a foe they couldn't easily best in combat.

Claire pulled on Farron's arm, but he resisted. "Fare," she whispered.

"He thinks he can reason with that madman," he said, his words hushed.

"Tell him he can't, no one can."

"I did. There's no reasoning with him either."

"Well, if he wants to try, let him." The ego of kings truly astounded her. Did he really think he could use Bahkar as well?

The king raised his hands in a signal for his guards to lower their weapons.

A mistake in Claire's book.

He spoke briefly, a smile spreading on his face.

Farron sighed and translated. "We do not wish to fight," he said, the anger in his voice contradicting his words.

Bahkar tilted his head to the side. "You don't?" He held a hand out to Claire. "Then you'll hand her over freely?"

King Ryaenon's pleasant façade faltered slightly. He muttered to Farron.

Farron tried to argue with the king but was stopped with a silencing hand. "We cannot do that, but—"

Bahkar's laugh cut him off. "Another king thinks he can use me?" he said, more to himself. His laughter stopped and his face grew serious. He fixed his wild eyes on the king. "You have no power over me."

Farron took a step back, then another, easing away slowly so he didn't draw attention to himself. Claire dug the silver key out from her shirt. She didn't want to, but she may have no other choice. King Ryaenon frowned and flicked a finger at his guards. They raised their weapons.

The king spoke, his voice authoritative, but Farron didn't translate. He moved back toward Claire.

"Save your words," Bahkar said. "I can't understand you anyway." Fire from the candles and lanterns started to drift to his hand. "I did not come here to negotiate with anyone. I came to get my flower. You are but insects to be crushed."

Farron ran his hand down the back of his dagger and sparks engulfed the blade. A few elves glanced his way. Claire saw a few elves sneak out of the throne room through the broken door behind Bahkar, the rest too scared to move. She grasped Farron's wrist. They needed to leave. If Ryaenon wanted to be foolish then let him.

"I will not let you use me or her," Bahkar muttered, holding up the flame in front of his face, his eyes mesmerized by the warm light. "She belongs to me."

He threw the flame at the king, but a guard dashed in front of him and it engulfed him instead. King Ryaenon barely flinched. The elven guard writhed on the floor, grunting and groaning until the fire was extinguished. He lay still on the floor, his breaths heavy and shaking. No one made a move to help him.

The king gestured again and another volley of arrows rained down on Bahkar. He raised another marble shield to block them. The guards in the center of the room rushed him. More stone columns shot up from the floor, but they were nimble enough to avoid them. Bahkar laughed and more spikes dropped down from the ceiling, and a few from the walls, crisscrossing every which way. No one was able to dodge them this time. With sickening cries, the elves fell limp, held aloft by the spikes that impaled them. This room was a death trap.

Bahkar lowered enough spikes for him to step through. Red splatters glistened on his cheek. He ran a finger through it and looked at it. "Elves bleed red," he said. "Though, I already knew that." He grinned and looked at Farron.

The guards around the king moved slightly, drawing Bahkar's attention.

"So eager to join your friends," Bahkar said. He dropped to the floor and slammed his palms on the stone.

Farron pushed Claire to the small door. The last thing she saw before the door slammed closed behind her was the back of the wooden throne, a massive spike piercing it and dark red blood dripping off of the sharp tip.

Consumed

The rooms were a blur as Farron pulled her through them at a dizzying pace. Shock was struggling to take hold in her. The elven king was dead. More lives had been taken because of her. This needed to stop. Claire let her anger chase away the fear. The world came into focus once again, her mind clearer.

Farron stopped suddenly and she crashed into the back of him.

"Do not think I will let you escape me," Bahkar said. "Not this time."

He stood out on a wide balcony, the forest behind him. Farron lowered into a fighting stance. His dagger still sparked in his right hand. A four-poster bed stood in the middle of the room between them. The king's bedroom, she guessed by the size and ornate decoration.

Bahkar dissolved in a cloud of dark mist. Claire and Farron spun. He could attack from anywhere. With shaking hands, she unlocked the silver bangles. Her magic swelled inside of her. The rush left her breathless. Her arm tingled, the mark coming to life, the blue glow bright. Already she felt close to the edge. What the General had done, it had definitely made things worse. Her magic was like a dark storm barely contained within her.

Bahkar materialized a few feet in front of her. He closed his eyes and breathed in. "Yes," he said, his voice euphoric. "The power..." He opened his eyes and looked at her. "You bloom even more beautiful, my flower."

Farron rushed him, but Bahkar dodged. The madman's hand shot out and grabbed Farron by the throat. He lifted Farron up, his hand squeezing. Farron stabbed at him, but Bahkar caught his wrist.

Claire's magic rose sharply inside of her. "Don't!"

Bahkar looked at her and smiled. "Do not worry," he said, turning his attention back to Farron. "I will not kill you... yet. You still have a purpose."

Bahkar threw Farron. Farron crashed and slid across the floor. When he slowed he rolled into a crouch, his left hand going to his other blade. He drew it and slammed it onto the other. The sparks spread to both.

Bahkar came for her and Farron rushed at him. She dropped to the floor, but before her hands could make contact with the marble, Bahkar was on her. Dark smoke swamped over her, swirling winds obscuring her vision. His hold on her was strong as her feet left solid ground. She screamed. But it was too late. She was his now.

19

She hit the ground hard. A grunt escaped her and she rolled onto her back. She blinked a few times to clear her eyes. A gray cloud-covered sky hung low over bare trees. The air was chilled, cooler than the elven forest. She watched the puffs of her breath rise and dissipate in the air for a few moments. She needed to stay calm, or at least try to.

Heavy footsteps approached her. She rolled over and pushed up onto her hands and knees. Her body trembled already. What was he going to do with her?

"Welcome, my sweet flower," Bahkar said, leaning over her. He spread his hands out wide, a smile on his face. "To your new home."

Claire glanced around. Dreary castle ruins stood around them, ravaged by nature and time. Half of the walls were knocked down, the ceiling and upper floors missing or caved in. Vines and dirt covered nearly every surface, tree branches stuck in holes in the roof. Old furniture was piled against the walls.

"How," she said, her voice faltering, "how lovely." She tried to make it sound genuine. She couldn't afford to upset him.

"Hmph," he grunted. "It was once. It will be again." He crossed his arms and looked around him, his eyes wistful and the least insane she'd ever seen them. He looked almost normal at that moment. But it didn't last long. Anger furrowed his brows and his mouth tilted in a snarl. "Earnehard will pay for what he did."

It took a moment for Claire to realize who he was talking about. The late king of Derenan and Farron's father. "Earnehard…" she said, trying to keep her voice even. "Earnehard's dead."

Bahkar blinked and looked down at her, anger turning to confusion. "Yes," he said, "that's right…"

Claire remained crouched on the floor, her body as still as possible. She didn't want to draw his attention any more than she had to. As carefully as she could, she glanced around at the room, or what was left of it. There was hardly anything useful. Not against him, anyway. She thought about calling out to the others, Lianna and Razi, but he would feel the surge in her magic and know instantly what she was up to. But perhaps just the absence of the silver contraption would be enough to alert them.

A glint of metal caught her eye.

Bahkar held the bracelets up in his right hand. "Curious…" he said, looking them over with the awe of a child. "This is how you have hidden from me all this time."

Claire swallowed, not sure what to say.

"Why?" he asked.

"I-I…" she stuttered. Her fear was getting the best of her.

"Why?!" he shouted, looming over her.

"I didn't hide just from you," she said, her pulse pounding too hard in her chest. "I hid from the others as well."

Bahkar frowned and was silent for a moment. Then he smiled. "Running off with your little elf lover?"

"Yes." It was mostly the truth.

"But you've been busy," he said, playing with the bracelets. "Busy, busy." He turned and walked toward a stone fireplace, surprisingly intact. Ashes covered the bottom. A stack of freshly cut logs stood next to it. He bent and carefully placed some wood inside with a peculiar attention to detail, adjusting them until they were just right.

While his back was turned, she used the opportunity to really look around. A doorway to the left led deeper into the interior of the castle. The one on the right was half-collapsed and impassable. Behind her stood two thick double doors, weathered but still sturdy. Who knew where they led? Up wasn't an option unless she suddenly learned to jump really high. Flying was another, but he was much more adept than her at it. He would catch her too easily. Besides, she still had no idea where she was. She had to come up with a plan, wait for a moment, an opening. Hopefully, it would come soon.

A bright flash lit the room, followed by the crackling of the fire. Bahkar stood staring into it for several moments. Claire watched his back. Waiting. Her breath held. She didn't know what to do.

"Yes," Bahkar muttered. "He will pay."

Claire shifted back onto her knees, freeing her hands. Her dagger hung at her side still. The stiletto blade was tucked into her boot, though she was hesitant to take it out after what had happened. Even with the weapons, she felt utterly helpless against the madman. He was too powerful and unpredictable.

Bahkar spun around and fixed her with a wild stare. "You will help me."

"I—" Claire took a deep breath to help calm her nerves. "I will." Arguing with him would do no good.

Bahkar nodded, a grin pulling at the corners of his mouth. He stalked over to her and pulled her to her feet. His hands grabbed her shoulders, his fingers digging into her skin. "My flower," he said, gazing down at her. "Together we will do great things."

Claire nodded, not trusting her voice enough to speak. She clenched her teeth to keep from wincing. The cut on her neck started to sting.

"Yes," he said, releasing her.

She stumbled a little, her legs unsteady. Bahkar walked to the double doors and said over his shoulder, "Get some rest, little one. We shall act soon." When his hand was on the handle he turned back to look at her, a dark glint in his eyes. "And remember, no matter how far you run, I will always find you."

A chill raced through her body. He wasn't wrong, and that terrified her.

A short burst of laughter erupted from his lips as he opened the door and swept through it. The door slammed closed behind him, shaking the dust from the walls. He wasn't going to lock her up. He didn't need to. Somehow he was able to find her even with the silver contraption, which he now held in his possession. There was only one way to escape from him. But would she be strong enough to do it?

Claire hobbled over to the fire, her body stiff, her mind heavy. Not even the flames were enough to warm the coldness within her.

She felt his presence even in her dreams. Claire stirred awake, sore and even more stiff from the hard floor. The fire had died down to a few glowing embers. Darkness had fallen over the room, making it seem eerier than before. But what scared her the most was the warm buzz of power sitting close behind her. Too close. Her pulse increased, but she remained lying on the floor, too nervous to move. His fingers brushed a few stray hairs from her cheek. It took everything she had not to jump or cringe away.

Consumed

"Do not be afraid, my little flower," Bahkar said, his voice soft, though far from soothing.

"What—" Claire stuttered, "what do you want from me?"

"You know what I want." An edge seeped into his voice.

Claire didn't, not exactly, but she wasn't going to push it too far. She sat up and stretched, trying to make it look as relaxed as she could. She yawned and covered her mouth, but couldn't keep her hand from shaking.

"The power inside of you…" His eyes swept over her, but not in a leering way. "They will learn to fear us. To obey *us*. They will not try to control us any longer."

"Who?"

"Earnehard."

"You killed King Earnehard," she said carefully. "Don't you remember?"

His eyes narrowed as he stared into the fire. "Yes, that's right. I did. He wanted to control me. I wouldn't let him. Not after what he did to Father…"

"What did he do to your father?" Not only was Claire curious, but the longer she could keep him talking, the longer it would delay whatever plans he had for her.

"He used him," Bahkar said, his eyes glazing over as he relived the past inside his own head. "Earnehard the Great," he spat out the name. "Father was loyal. Father was wealthy. A noble knight, a lord. But that didn't matter. None of it mattered. Not to that bastard. He let father rot away up here, his body and mind decaying with the castle. After everything that he had done in the name of the king. I was too young, too strong-headed to understand. I wanted to be a knight, like Father. He tried to use me, too. But I wouldn't let him. I made sure that he couldn't use anyone ever again."

"What did you do?" she whispered, trying not to break him of his spell.

"I did what any good son would do. I did, Father. Earnehard has paid for what he did to you." He affixed her with a cognizant stare, back in the present. "Only now there are others. They want to use us, what we are. We are not weapons for them to use!" He clenched his hands into fists.

Claire tensed. Well, wasn't he using *her*? But she didn't dare point that out to him. Not now.

"That son of Earnehard, he's no better," he sneered. "He has *that woman*. She has fallen under his fae spell. And then there's that Salí." He shook his head. "We will make them see. We will free them."

She gulped and nodded slightly. He wasn't wrong about Razi being used, but at least Razi was aware of it now.

"I noticed that they have others there now, at that place, that damned palace. Was that your doing?"

Claire shook her head, hoping he wouldn't see through her.

Bahkar looked at her for a moment, his eyes narrowing, but didn't say anything. "We shall free them, too."

"And how are we going to do that?"

"Together," he said, a smile twisting his lips, revealing yellowed teeth. "You and I, our powers, we will be unstoppable. We will destroy the palace, free the world of that damned fae and Council. Then we will move onto the next one. Everyone will know freedom soon. We will be their saviors."

"And then what?" she asked, carefully. "What will you do after?"

He frowned. "I will return here."

"And me?"

"You may return here as well, if you wish. My home is big enough for all of our brothers and sisters. It will be a sanctuary for our kind. A safe place where no one will bother us ever again."

Consumed

It sounded a little too much like the compounds that the Syndicate had kept the Star Children locked away in. Would he ever let her or the others leave? She had a feeling that he wouldn't. His idea of freedom was just another cage.

"I see," she said, at a loss for words again. Of course, none of this was going to happen. Not if she could help it. "Do you have a plan?"

"Of course!" he exclaimed as he hopped to his feet. He paced the room, back and forth, his hand rubbing the top of his head. "You," he said, glancing at her, "they trust you, that woman and boy. You can get inside the palace. Move freely within. I know." His voice dropped lower and his hand gripped his graying hair. "I watched you before. Sensed you. But you were always under their protection. But not anymore, no, not anymore." He said the last part more to himself.

A shiver went down her spine. Perhaps she had been safer at the palace than she'd thought.

"When you're inside, there you will kill that bastard Earnehard."

"You mean Líadan," she said, unsure if she should even bother at this point. "Earnehard is dead. You said you killed him, remember?"

He hit himself on the forehead a couple times, so hard that it surely knocked a few more things loose inside. "Yes, yes!" He stopped pacing and looked at her. "He paid for what he did."

She nodded.

"Now it is his son's turn."

Claire wondered briefly if Bahkar knew that Farron was also Earnehard's son. If he didn't, she certainly didn't want to bring it to his attention.

"You will kill that bastard fae while I distract that woman and the other ones." He started pacing again. "And when he's dead, together we will destroy the palace, bring it down level to the ground. Earnehard's legacy will be nothing but rubble when we're through."

"All right," she said. "It sounds like a good plan." It was—however, not in the way that he thought. He would essentially be delivering her back into the safety of Lianna and Razi. She just had to pretend to go along with it until then.

"You will do it, then?" He paused to look at her, his eyes studying.

She nodded. "They have tried to use me in the past, like I was just some sort of weapon. Held me prisoner against my will. I have no soft spot for them. Not anymore."

Bahkar grunted, a grin tugging at the corners of his mouth. "You lie, my flower. But that's all right. I have collateral. You will do as I ask or that little elf lover of yours will join the rest of his kin."

Claire stilled. Did that mean he knew of Farron's lineage?

He laughed, a full-throated, bellowing sound, and threw his head back. "Of course I know who he is, girl. Practically the whole realm does. Earnehard's bastard was no secret. I'm sure there are a few others running around out there as well."

So, he knew, and he was planning on using him as leverage against her. That was the reason he hadn't killed Farron back in the forest palace. Could he find him though? Of course, he didn't have to, because Farron was coming for her, no matter what. It was only a matter of time before they crossed paths again. Claire had to be extra careful. One wrong move could prove disastrous. If only Farron wasn't so stubborn and had listened when she had tried to push him away. She was too dangerous to be involved with. If she wanted to protect him, and everyone else she cared about, then she had no other choice. She had to end Bahkar once and for all.

Her hand brushed down her boot, felt the outline of the dagger it concealed. She didn't like the thought of taking another life, even if he was a murderous madman. But it was necessary. It was what she had to do to protect the ones she loved, and other innocent lives. She had to be careful about it, though, and wait for an opening. If she failed, she wouldn't be getting a second chance. That she felt sure of.

He paced again, the laughter fading. "Yes," he said, his eyes flashing with excitement. "It will finally come to pass, Father. You will get your revenge."

"When do we leave?" Claire asked. She didn't think she could last too much longer wherever they were. The fire could only keep so much of the cold at bay when the walls and ceilings weren't exactly whole. And the sooner she could be rid of him the better.

"Rest up, my little flower." Bahkar stopped and trained his gaze on her, lifting his chin, squaring his shoulders. "Earnehard's reign ends tomorrow."

It was still dark when she awoke from a fitful dream. A light sheen of sweat covered her body and a shiver soon set in. The fire had died down and she had only found a makeshift blanket among the furniture that might have once been a curtain. She laid on her side in front of the fireplace and curled up into a little ball. It was too cold to move and try to start the fire up again. And she didn't dare venture further into the old house. Who knew what she would find? Instead, she just waited, staring into the embers, for the time to come. Watched as the sky started to brighten.

It was curious, though, that no one had come to get her so far. Surely they had felt her presence again after taking off the silver contraption. Had Farron gotten in contact with Lianna? Perhaps they were trying to come up with some sort of plan. Bahkar was too powerful to face off against unprepared. The magic within her was a warm buzzing presence, a predator waiting to pounce. She'd forgotten how alive it felt. How much peace the bracelets had given her. She needed to get them back and soon. The pendant around her neck could only do so much. The added damage that the General had inflicted on her was definitely starting to take effect. The wound stung unbearably. A trip to the Haven sounded like a good idea, even if she would have to face Maria and her daughter once again.

The sun was just above the horizon when the double doors creaked open. Claire tensed under the blanket. His footsteps were heavy on the wooden floor as he approached her.

"Are you ready, my flower?" he said, his voice low, ominous.

She wasn't, but she said, "Yes." It wasn't like she had much of a choice in the matter anyway. She was his tool now.

"Good," he said, his excitement rising. "Then come, my flower. Let us go and liberate the people of Derenan."

Claire sat up and eyed his outstretched hand for a moment before taking it. As soon as they touched, the winds started whipping around them. She hoped that the only one to die that day would be him.

20

When the winds cleared, she found herself in the palace courtyard. Bahkar loomed over her, his eyes ablaze, a grin forming on his lips. Clouds covered the morning sky. A thick fog just beginning to disperse made everything more ominous. The palace was eerily quiet. Surely the others knew they were here. She scanned the area, looking for any movement.

Bahkar grabbed her wrist and yanked her close. "Remember, my flower, your purpose here." He leaned his face down to hers. "Or else."

She nodded, letting her fear show freely. She had to be careful because he truly meant what he said.

He gave a short snort of laughter and turned around to face the great doors of the palace, the frozen clock above. "That didn't take long."

Claire followed his gaze. Lianna stood, hands on hips, in her full leather armor, an annoyed look on her face. Relief filled Claire. It was good to see a friendly face. If anyone could match Bahkar in battle, it was Lianna.

"At least you have saved us the trouble of seeking you out," Lianna said. "Come, Claire." She held her hand out to Claire.

Claire hesitated, not sure what to do. Bahkar's hand tightened around her wrist. "We have come to liberate you," he said. "All of you." He glanced over his shoulder.

Claire did the same. Razi had appeared behind them, blocking the entrance to the courtyard. Unlike Lianna, he wore a simple shirt and slacks, with only his dagger at his side. A frown formed on his face. His hand went to the hilt of the dagger, but he didn't draw it, yet.

"Release her," he said, his voice rising with anger.

Bahkar laughed. "You fools," he said. "You are mere tools. But together, we could be more. We could be free."

Razi's face twitched. He was well aware of his predicament. But Claire didn't think he would help Bahkar any more than she would. She hoped…

"I am no damsel that needs saving," Lianna said. "Now, let her go and leave, or we will fight you."

"I was hoping that you could see things my way," Bahkar said. "But I look forward to a challenge." He released Claire and she took several steps back from him. His magic rose sharply within him, causing her own to stir inside her. "Have it your way then."

Lianna's mark came alive, the purple glow illuminating the ground around her. Razi's did the same. The power within the courtyard became suffocating. Claire took a few more steps back. This wasn't going to be good.

A burning sensation flared along her scar, and the fresh wound at her neck throbbed even more, her mark reacting to all the magic. She didn't want to use it, but she might not have a choice.

A fireball suddenly exploded around the madman, engulfing him in bright orange flames, shaking the ground. Claire recoiled,

Consumed

holding her arms up to shield herself from the intense heat. She glanced around. Where had that come from? Then she saw him. Atop the eastern wall, Farron stood, another arrow nocked, the tip blazing with fire, aimed and ready to release.

Although she was glad to see him, she had mixed emotions about his presence. Not only did Bahkar want him dead, but the Council did as well. Once again he was putting his life on the line to rescue her. Not that she could stop him, but she sure didn't like it.

The flames died down and the ground shook as the stone barriers Bahkar had erected slid down back into the earth. The madman laughed, unscathed.

"You've come for your flower, I see." He shot Farron with a glare and started to kneel down.

"Oh, no you don't!" Claire yelled and dropped to her knees, slamming her hands to the hard stone of the courtyard. Spikes burst up in a line toward Bahkar and he jumped back.

Razi rushed him then, Lianna disappearing into a dark cloud. Farron jumped down off of the wall, rolling as he hit the ground. He got to his feet swiftly and took aim again. He stood opposite from her, the madman between them. He loosed the flaming arrow, but Bahkar blocked it with another barrier. The madman turned just as Razi was almost on him. Razi drew his dagger, running his hand down the back of it. Sparks shot out around the blade as he swung it at Bahkar. The madman leaped back, narrowly avoiding each attack. Claire sent another volley of spikes after him to try to block his escape, but he just dispersed into a black cloud. His laughter echoed through the courtyard.

"Do not forget my words, my flower." His voice crawled along her skin. A lightning bolt struck close to Farron.

Farron jumped to the side and rolled away. Claire's heart leaped up to her throat. That was too close. She scanned the sky for any traces of the madman, but in her panic couldn't find him. Taking a deep breath, she ran for the massive wooden doors that led into the palace. Farron followed, avoiding another bolt of energy. He helped her push open the doors and then close them once they were inside. The ground shook again, the doors vibrating.

"That was close," Farron said, trying to make it sound light. He pulled her close and looked her over. "Are you all right? Did he do anything?"

"I'm fine," she said, trying to catch her breath, her pulse still hammering in her chest. "Mostly. He wants to destroy the palace and kill your brother. Well, he wants me to kill your brother. Said he would kill you if I didn't."

"I feel like everyone wants me dead these days," he said with a grin.

"You shouldn't have come back here." There was a thunderous boom outside and the ground shook.

"You know that wasn't an option," he said, his face serious. "That man, he dies here today."

Claire nodded. It wasn't often that she agreed with him about killing, but this was an exception.

"Do you have a plan?" she asked, hoping that they did.

"Sort of." He shrugged. "I only just got here. Lianna and Razi said that they felt your presence as soon as you took the bangles off. They appeared in the forest soon after that man took you. They saw what he could do. We only came back here to regroup before going after you. But then he saved us the trouble. So, not really according to plan. We are improvising now."

"Where are the other Star Children? He may go after them next."

"Hidden in the bowels of the palace. They should be safe down there for the time being."

"And your brother?"

Consumed

He shrugged again. "Lounging in a bath, for all I know."

It wouldn't surprise her in the least if the king actually was in a warm bath at the moment. But it did worry her that he wasn't accounted for and hidden away somewhere safe. He was the king, after all, and his life was currently in danger.

"In any case, it might not be the best idea for you to know his whereabouts," Farron said. "If that is Bahkar's goal."

Claire nodded, feeling stupid for forgetting how Bahkar could dive into her memories. When he finds out that she wouldn't kill the king, he was surely going to go after him himself. And Farron. They needed to end things quickly.

"What now?" She looked up at Farron.

"I guess we see how tough he really is."

"I can't ask you to hide by any chance?"

He lifted an eyebrow.

That's what she'd thought.

Farron's head jerked to the side, his eyes flashing before he suddenly pushed her to the side, out of the way as rubble came crashing through the doors. He jumped in the opposite direction at the last moment. Dust filled the air. Claire rolled over on the floor.

"Fare?" she called out, not seeing him.

"I'm fine," he said. He came around the wreckage and pulled her to her feet. "That was close." He took her hand and started to lead her down the hall. "Come."

They raced through the maze of halls until they burst out into Lianna's garden, brown and dull from the winter cold. Farron scanned the sky while she closed her eyes to try and pinpoint the others. She felt the tug of magic just around the side of the palace and it was moving, fast.

"There," she whispered. "They're coming this way." She turned to Farron. "We'll need to work together to bring him down. Be careful."

"You, too." He leaned down to kiss her on the forehead.

"If you can, try to stay out of his sight. He won't hesitate to kill you."

He nodded before slinking off. If anyone could hide from Bahkar, it was the King's Shadow.

Claire jogged to the center of an open area and cast out a small amount of magic, hoping to draw Bahkar to her. A moment later, his magic collided with her, the sheer power of it knocking the breath out of her. He materialized before her, the wind stirring the bushes and sending her hair flying about her head.

"My flower," he said, frowning. Blood dripped down the side of his face. "Why aren't you off killing that bastard fae?"

She gulped. The wind died down and the silence was unnerving.

"Because I'm not going to," she said, her throat too tight.

A gust of wind brushed her back. "He is tougher than he looks," Razi said.

Claire glanced at him to make sure he was all right. He looked a little winded, sweaty, a few cuts and bumps, but nothing too serious.

"But not invincible," Lianna said, stepping out of the dark whirlwind to Claire's other side.

"You are all fools!" Bahkar shouted, his face contorted into a snarl. "Together we could end all of them! Earnehard has to pay!"

Lianna cocked her head, a confused look crossing her face. "King Earnehard? He has been dead for years."

"He's mad," Claire said, keeping her voice low. "He keeps confusing them."

"I see," Lianna said and shrugged. "No matter. His plan ends here."

"Do you have something in mind?" Claire asked, hopeful.

"Yes," Razi replied instead. He exchanged a glance with Lianna.

Lianna sighed. "Yes, yes," she said in a dismissive manner before charging at Bahkar.

The two vanished in a cloud of dark haze, lightning flashing, the deafening crack echoing off the palace walls.

Razi rushed over to Claire. "We will wear him down, you draw him in. He underestimates you, it seems."

Claire nodded. Farron's lessons were coming in handy. She just had to come up with a plan. Before she could ask Razi, he had disappeared. She took a deep breath as she watched the battle. An opening… How was she supposed to know if she could hardly keep up with them?

"Any ideas?" She glanced over at Farron as he stepped out of the shadows.

A light sprinkle of rain began to fall, sending shivers through her body.

"Close combat is dangerous," he said. His eyes narrowed as he watched the sky. "He's too fast for ranged attacks." He looked over at her. "When he had you, did he lower his guard at all?"

She nodded. "I *should* have ended it then. I just couldn't…"

Farron took her hand in his and squeezed it. "Lucky for us, I think he underestimates us both. That will be his last mistake."

The palace shook as they raced down the halls once more. How much damage were they doing? By the day's end, there might be a pile of rubble in its place, whether they won or lost.

Farron and Claire split up, each going their separate ways, a plan in place. It was risky. She just hoped that it worked, for all their sakes.

She had had Farron tell her the location of the king and had given him a look, hoping he would get her plan without her having to say so. She wasn't sure how much Bahkar could see in her memories, but she was hoping that in a moment of haste, he wouldn't get her thoughts with everything else. Thankfully, Farron only took a few moments to get what she was implying. His hesitance would only help.

The map chamber underneath the palace—that was a convincing place as any for a king to seek out safety during an attack. She had asked Farron to find the king to protect him for her memory, had tried to make her voice as frantic as possible. Bahkar had to be persuaded for this to work. She let the sequence play over and over again in her mind to keep it fresh. It would be close quarters, but she was hoping the surprise would catch him off guard enough for him to hesitate long enough for an attack.

She didn't like the fact that Farron was bait, putting his life right in the line of danger, but it was all they had at the moment.

Claire rounded the corner and slammed into a solid, heavily armored man, so big that the hallway felt cramped. She stumbled back a few steps. And then her heart dropped. In the middle of a regiment of guards stood the king, an exasperated look on his beautiful face.

"Oh, no," she whispered. She looked away quickly, but it was too late. The memory was already imprinted into her mind. "What are you doing here?" She didn't mean to sound so impudent, but her plan was now ruined. What now?

The king arched an eyebrow. "And where is it I should be?" He waved a hand and the guards in front of him moved to the side as he stepped forward toward Claire. "My home is currently under attack. Should I be cowering in the cellars?"

"Yes!" she shouted before thinking. "That man, he wants you dead. He killed your father and he won't rest until he does the same to you."

"What did you say?" His eyes narrowed and focused on her. "That man, *he* killed my father? How do you know this?"

"He told me. Said that King Earnehard had known about his powers and had tried to use him. So, he killed him. He's mad. His mark, it has corrupted his mind."

The palace rumbled around them, the floors shaking. The king didn't flinch. Perhaps he was made out of stronger stuff than she'd thought.

"I see," he said, his eyes trailing down her arm.

Claire shifted uncomfortably. He thought the same would happen to her. Not that she could blame him. It was something she feared as well.

"I will not hide," he said, the authority in his voice not belying any fear. "This is my home. Let him come for me."

"But you're—"

"I will be in my quarters," he said as he glanced back at the guards.

With a nod from the king, they fell into formation again and led him down the halls.

Claire just stood there and watched as he turned the corner. What should she do now? Her plan had fallen apart. There was no time to search for the map room deep in the bowels of the palace. It would collapse on top of them by the time she could get there.

A loud crash brought her back to the present, the rumbling more violent than before.

The safest thing would be to stay away. She was a liability. But she couldn't let Lianna and Razi risk themselves when she could do something, *anything*. She ran toward the commotion. If anything, she could at least provide a distraction.

Claire turned another corner and skidded to a stop. Light poured in through a gaping hole in the outer wall of the palace. She inched near it, the view making her head spin. The ground fell away, dropping sharply down a cliff side of jagged rocks, the town too far down below for her comfort. Claire pressed her back up against the opposite wall. Debris and dust dulled the shiny marble floor. Bricks of the wall still crumbled away, falling down, down, down…

She took a deep breath. There was no time to panic. There were more important matters at hand. She closed her eyes and focused her magic, reaching out, searching. They weren't far. All three were like burning torches in her mind. A slight relief touched her. At least there were still three.

Claire had barely had time to move when she felt his presence. Her eyes snapped open, a gasp escaping her.

"This has gone on for too long," Bahkar snarled. His shoulders heaved. A gash crossed his left eye, blood streaming down his cheek. "Where is Earnehard?"

"He's dead," Claire said. She reached out with her mind for the others, her magic spiking, the sting along her scar intensifying.

Bahkar surged forward and slammed a hand on the wall behind her. The walls shook and stone shot up and down, closing the hole, cutting off Lianna and Razi's approach. It wouldn't hold for long, but it was precious moments wasted.

Claire turned in an effort to run. She couldn't let him into her mind. Bahkar smashed his fist into the wall, cracking the marble, trapping her in place. She reached within for the strings of her magic and conjured up a blue orb. She shoved it into his chest. He barely flinched, the only sign of pain his clenched teeth.

Consumed

Bahkar grasped her neck and slammed her against the wall. Her head hit the stone hard, stars dancing along the edges of her vision. Then his other hand was on her forehead, followed by the sharp pain as he dived into her memories. A scream ripped up her throat. Her feet kicked helplessly as he lifted her up off the floor. She struggled to breathe, her hands clawing at his arms in vain.

Memories flashed in her mind, too quick to distinguish one from the other clearly.

"You thought you could trick me?" Bahkar muttered. He leaned his face close to her ear. "You disappoint me, my flower. Together we could have built a whole new world, free of tyrants, free of those that wish to use us. It could have been ours."

His hand squeezed harder around her throat, cutting off her screams.

"There," he whispered as the memory of the king from moments before replayed. "That fool. So much like Earnehard. Today will be his last."

He released her suddenly and Claire slid to the floor, coughing. When she looked up, Bahkar was already gone.

"No," she whispered. She got to her feet and ran, hoping she was going in the right direction. It could already be too late.

21

The sound of shattering glass echoed down the hall as Claire ran. She slowed as she approached the throne room and eased up to the entrance. The massive wooden doors were mere splinters. Bahkar stood in the middle of the cavernous room, glass falling like twinkling snow around him. His laugh filled the air.

"Come out, come out, Earnehard," he said in a sing-song voice.

Silence followed.

"Don't be a coward like your father," Bahkar shouted, anger replacing the joy. "Your reign ends here."

More silence.

Where were the others?

The room grew still, and the falling glass froze, hovering in the air. Bahkar turned slowly, his eyes scanning. He paused when he spotted her, but made no other move. She was inconsequential to him, a non-threat, especially compared to the others. What could she do to him?

Claire remained in the doorway and opened herself up to the others, Lianna and Razi, but she couldn't sense them. Their spark of magic was gone, like it had disappeared from existence. Fear stabbed through her. Did that mean…? No, they couldn't be dead. She had just sensed them minutes ago. There was no way Bahkar could have killed them in such a short time.

But there was another possibility. Her silver contraption dangled from Bahkar's belt, but that didn't mean that it was the only one in existence. Had they found more? She knew Lin had worn one when he was in the Syndicate's grasp, and there was a great chance that the others Lianna and Marion had liberated had worn the contraptions as well. A faint glimmer of hope rose inside of her. Even though she didn't know their strategy, the bracelets could tip the scales in their favor.

The sound of a door slamming echoed through the throne room.

"Earnehard's reign ended long ago," came a familiar voice.

Claire's stomach sank as Farron stepped out from behind the throne. What was going on? He was supposed to be in the map room. Or had this been a part of their plan all along?

"Thanks to you," Farron said. His hand was outstretched, his fingers splayed. Was he controlling the glass? He stopped at the top of the dais. His eyes met hers for a brief moment, but they revealed nothing. One of his daggers was grasped in his other hand.

Not knowing what else to do, Claire crouched in the doorway, readying for whatever came next.

"I have no fond memories of my father," Farron said, his voice turning ice cold. "But you have threatened everything that I care about." He started to slowly descend the stairs to the dais, not taking his eyes off of the madman. "Kidnapped the woman I love, invaded her mind, used her as a tool for your own gains, almost taking her life." He reached the bottom of the stairs but didn't stop. The glass shards shifted in the air and began to swirl above Bahkar.

The madman started to crouch, but a stone spike shot up inches from him, another rising behind him, halting him momentarily.

Consumed

Farron stalked toward him, his eyes revealing only a hint of anger, but it was enough to send a shiver down Claire's spine.

"And for that your life is mine." Farron's hand closed into a fist and the glass shards descended on Bahkar, thousands of twinkling razor-sharp pieces, slashing, piercing flesh, tearing at cloth.

Bahkar screamed as red started to stream down his skin, soaking into his clothes. Farron drew his other dagger and launched at the madman, but as he sliced at him, Bahkar vanished in a cloud of black fog. The glass shards fell lifeless to the floor, the sound almost deafening.

Claire slammed her hands to the floor and erected a barrier behind her to block his escape. Stone began to cover the destroyed windows and the light in the room dimmed until it was pitch black. Claire could feel Razi's presence suddenly below in the bowels of the palace. Was he doing that? They must have had a plan in place. Lianna was still missing from her senses, but she probably wasn't far.

The throne room grew quiet again, the only sound her own breathing and heartbeat in her ears. Claire remained crouched, trying not to make a sound. She couldn't see a thing. Could Bahkar? If he couldn't, Farron had the advantage. She hoped.

Bahkar's laughter filled the air, slithering along her skin. "You think the shadows can protect you?"

The floor shook and a deep rumbling surrounded her, followed by a whoosh of air. Claire gasped, the spikes missing her by mere inches. She reached out and felt the stone columns all around her. They probably covered the entire room. She wanted desperately to call out to Farron, to see if he was all right but knew even if he was, he wouldn't risk exposing himself. He was smart enough to have prepared for this. He knew what that madman was capable of.

There was a reason that Bahkar had spared her in the attack. He wasn't done with her yet. Despite the fact that she had defied his orders, he still had plans for her. As long as there were people out there that she cared about, he could exploit her for his own gain. Claire reached out, searching. He circled the room, like a cat in a cage, around and around, burning furious and bright. He attacked a covered window, but as soon as a ray of light penetrated the darkness, stone would replace the damage, plunging the room into shadow once more. The spikes slowly lowered until the floor was smooth. Bahkar let out an exasperated growl.

Claire felt his presence back in the center of the room. A bright white orb formed in his hand, illuminating his bloody figure. His whole body heaved from breathlessness and anger. He slowly circled and launched the orb, then formed another, throwing it into the air, then another, repeating the process in order to find the elusive elf. He let out another growl when his search came up empty.

"Are you a coward like your father?" Bahkar yelled into the darkness. "These tricks, are you afraid to face me without them?"

There was no answer.

Silence hung heavy in the air.

Claire held her breath. What could she do to help? Her magic was dangerously close to the edge already. Too much more and she would lose control and very likely bring down the palace herself. But perhaps there was another way, something she could do.

"They are no different than your own dirty tricks," she said, breaking the silence, her voice quivering slightly. She stood up, her hands feeling out around her for any surprises.

Bahkar snorted in laughter.

"All the killing, the manipulating, trying to use me, my powers, and all for what? Some personal vendetta against a dead king?" She took a few steps in his direction. "There's a reason I have remained hidden all this time."

"I told you," Bahkar said. "I do this for all of us, for our freedom!"

"No," Claire snapped, using her anger to fuel her confidence. "You do this for your own gain. You desire power like the very kings you wish to kill, like the one that you have killed. You are no different from any of them."

Bahkar let out an enraged shout. "Do not test me, girl!"

"You claim you want freedom for all of us, but you do not hesitate to use me as your weapon. How am I to believe that will change if you reach your goal?"

"Shut up!" he shouted, his voice becoming more maddened.

"You have used me for your own desires. You are just like them."

"No!" The air vibrated with his shout.

Claire froze, not sure if she should continue.

But she didn't have to. Lianna's presence burst into her mind, bright as the burning sun. The floor shuddered and a blinding flash of lightning lit up the center of the room. Claire ducked instinctively, blocking the flash with her arms over her head. Stone walls had shot up around Bahkar, trapping him as the lightning struck. A moment later a flaming explosion engulfed the trap, the intense heat radiating along Claire's body. Bahkar screamed and all of the flames and lightning dissipated, plunging the room into darkness once again. And then it was a confusion of different lights, flames here, lightning there, orbs thrown. Energy crackled along Farron's daggers as he attacked in a flurry of dizzying strikes. Lianna attacked from the opposite direction, shifting in and out of the smoke from one place to another so quickly that if it wasn't for Claire's ability to track her by her magic, she wouldn't have been able to at all. Spikes shot up from the floor every now and then to throw Bahkar off balance.

The fight was intense and way too out of her league for her to jump in. She would just make things worse.

The battle went back and forth across the room for several tense moments and then Bahkar let out a deafening howl. Claire barely had time to move when she felt his presence close behind her. His arms wrapped around her, lifting her off the ground. A hand gripped her throat, his mark glowing bright, his palm growing warm. The rock covering the windows lowered letting in a dim light, but even that was a shock to the senses after so much darkness. She narrowed her eyes at the sudden brightness.

Farron skidded to a stop several feet in front of them, out of breath, blood dripping from a gash on his left arm. His daggers still sparked with lightning. Lianna appeared out of a dark fog to their right, looking winded as well. Bahkar's body trembled against Claire's. He had been pushed to his limit. He was only taking her hostage as a last resort.

"Let her go," Farron breathed.

Razi appeared to their right, dagger in hand, ready to pounce.

"Give it up," Lianna said. "You cannot win against all of us."

Bahkar snorted, his grip tightening on Claire.

Claire kicked violently, using it as a chance to dig the stiletto blade from her boot before he stilled her with a shock of energy. A warning. He was desperate enough to hurt her. The others kept their gazes firmly on the madman, not betraying her move. She held the blade close to her body. She only had one chance to get this right. She looked at Farron and his eyes shifted to hers momentarily; a slight twitch of his eyebrow all the signal she needed.

Claire twisted in Bahkar's grip and drove the blade up into his chest toward his heart, putting as much of her strength behind it as she could. Bahkar released her, letting out a sharp gasp. Farron rushed forward, Lianna dissipating, Razi dropping to the floor. All at once, a spike shot up from the floor, impaling the madman in the stomach, a shock of lightning struck him from above, and Farron's blades sliced into his sides up to the hilts, between his ribs, lightning crackling.

She remained pressed between the madman and Farron, her hand still on the handle of the blade. Warm blood dripped down onto her fingers. She released it and Farron pulled her back into his embrace, away from Bahkar.

A sad laugh bubbled up from the madman's lips, followed by convulsive coughing. Blood began to stream from his mouth.

"You are all fools," Bahkar rasped as he slumped forward.

The marble spike slid back into the floor and Bahkar sprawled lifelessly across it, blood pooling around him. They all stood around him, watching in tense silence, waiting to see if he moved again. When he didn't, Farron turned her around to look her over.

"Are you all right?" he asked.

Claire nodded. "I should be asking all of you that." She turned to look at the others.

Razi stood, flexing his hands and shrugged. "Nothing I could not handle."

Lianna put a hand on her hip. "Good riddance." She took a deep breath and released it. A sheen of sweat covered her skin, dust sticking to it in a layer. A few light cuts here and there were the only damage Claire could see.

The same could be said for Razi. Farron by far looked the worse for wear. Sweaty, bloodied, and worn out, his shoulders slumped. It looked like he'd been through an entire war. He stepped around Claire to retrieve his daggers from Bahkar's lifeless form. Claire had to turn away.

"I am now," Farron said.

A slow clapping sounded from the far side of the throne room. Claire looked up at the dais as the king stepped out into the light.

"An impressive display," he said in his silky voice.

He glanced around the room, his mouth twitching into a frown before his eyes came to rest on them, the expression within them hard to decipher, though Claire saw a hint of hunger, a flash of desire. If there was one thing a king wanted more than land or gold, it was power. The flash of emotion was small and lasted but a moment, but it was enough to sow the seeds of doubt in Claire. Were his intentions as noble as he said they were? He was an elf, and he would gain an immense amount of power if she restored magic back to the land. All elves would.

She glanced back at Farron. He glared at his brother, daggers in hand as blood dripped from them onto the shiny marble floor. Would he be enough to keep the king in check? Would he want to? Her mind was too tired at the moment to try and puzzle it all out. She had to hope there was good in the elves, that they had changed in the century since the Great War. The only alternative was the genocide of the elven race, and that didn't sit well with her at all. There was already way too much blood on her hands.

In any case, she could at least sleep a little easier at night, knowing that Bahkar wasn't going to hunt for her anymore. One less worry. One less nightmare.

22

Sleep didn't come easier.

Claire tossed and turned in her old palace bed, the room untouched from the earlier battle. Bahkar's haunting laugh echoed through her mind. Visions of his lifeless bloody form on the cold floor filled her thoughts every time she closed her eyes. She sat up and Farron stirred next to her. It wasn't the first time she had killed, and she didn't even really regret it, so why was she having such a strong reaction?

Bahkar's body had been taken out of the throne room by a group of guards. Where they had taken him, she had no clue. A red stain remained on the white marble, but it was far from the only damage. She didn't want to know how much it was going to take to repair it all. But it wasn't for her to worry about. She was just relieved that no one else had been killed, or even majorly hurt.

Lianna had joined her for a bath later on that night—awkward for Claire, but Lianna seemed way too comfortable with the situation to cause a fuss over it. There, Claire was able to see the many bruises and bumps forming on her too-perfect body.

"Thank you," she had said to the other woman.

Lianna waved a dismissive hand in the air. "It is what we do," Lianna had said as they soaked in the warm lavender water. "We look after one another. We are all in this together. Even Razi has come around. He did not like that our little Claire was taken by that man."

A flush had spread through her body, the steam making it harder to breathe. Lianna had laughed. She still enjoyed torturing Claire when the opportunity arose.

"Do you trust him?" she had asked Lianna. "The king, I mean." She had once asked her before if the king's intentions were as good as he portrayed, but after today, she needed the reassurance. Whether or not Lianna told the truth was questionable. Her loyalty was to him as long as it served her goals.

"My answer has not changed since the last time you asked me this," Lianna had said, studying Claire's face. "But I do see where your concern comes from. He is a king, an elven one, ruling over a kingdom of humans. If you manage to restore magic, would he be like his ancestors before him? I do not know. I hope as much as you do that he is not. His intentions are good, but that kind of power… I know what it can do to someone. As do you." She had given Claire a pointed look.

Claire had nodded.

"But, just because the power is there does not mean he will be corrupted. You know that, as well."

Claire had watched as the water swirled with her hand movements. Lianna was right. Just because the temptation was there didn't mean that he would abuse it. She had trusted Aeron to do the right thing in the forest. He stood to gain as much as the king if magic returned. Even Razi, who was as power hungry as they came, had changed his views for the better.

"Will you still be here?" Claire had asked Lianna.

Consumed

"I hope so, unless he tires of me." A sadness had crept into her voice, one that Claire had never heard from Lianna before. Despite what it may have seemed, she cared deeply for the king, and Claire believed that he returned those feelings.

"Well," Claire had said, trying to make the situation lighter, "I'm counting on you to keep him in line."

Lianna had smiled. "I think I can manage that."

A guard had been posted outside of her room when she had returned from her bath. Farron was already waiting for her inside. The guard wasn't for her; it was for him. His brother was taking the threat against his life seriously. Though Farron felt a little insulted. The infamous *Sin de Reine* didn't need a guard. Claire could only laugh. She was surprised that the palace was big enough to hold his pride inside.

"How do you feel?" he'd asked her, concern apparent on his face. He had inspected the mark and scars to see if they had spread, grown even wilder.

But she had a feeling he'd asked about more than her physical wellbeing. "I don't know," she'd said. She felt more numb than anything. She'd felt guilty after the General's death, but Bahkar, it was mostly relief. But that only created more conflict inside her head. She felt guilty for being relieved instead of ashamed that she'd taken another life. Farron had been right when he said that it wouldn't ever be easy—only easier.

She'd asked him as well if he trusted his brother with his potential power. His answer had been much more hesitant than Lianna's. In the end, he was uncertain, which hadn't helped to ease her fears.

"Was all of that part of your plan?" she'd asked him.

He had grinned. "Sort of. We couldn't tell you for obvious reasons."

"But what if he dived into Lianna's or Razi's minds?"

Farron had looked at her and he didn't need to say a word for her to understand.

Razi and Lianna were too skilled and powerful for them to let Bahkar into their minds. There was a reason that madman had come for her. She was the weak link in all of this. Farron had taken her hand in his and squeezed it tight before bringing it up to his lips.

"I didn't expect you to do that in the throne room, however," he'd said, "distracting him the way you did. That was brave of you."

"I suppose," she'd replied, feeling deflated. "By the way, how did you avoid all of those spikes?"

"The new council dog isn't as useless as he seems. He was able to fend off enough of them for me to avoid the worst of it."

Claire had let out a long breath. "That scared me." She had grasped his hand in hers. "I didn't know if you were alive or dead at that point."

"I'm not that easy to kill, Claire." He'd grinned and she'd nudged him with her fist.

Claire shivered. The heavy drapes covering the balcony didn't completely keep out the cold. Farron rolled over and looked up at her.

"Can't sleep?" he asked, drowsy.

She shook her head. How was he able to?

He rubbed a hand up and down her arm. "You only did what you had to," he said. He drew her down into his tight embrace. "If you didn't do it, I would have. Or Lianna. Even Razi. He wasn't going to leave this palace alive."

Claire hugged him back, reveling in his warmth. His words helped a little.

"Now all we have left to do is to restore magic to the land," she said, pulling back enough to look at him.

"Is that all?" He raised his eyebrows.

She smiled slightly. "After everything we've been through, it couldn't be too hard, right?"

"Like learning to swim."

She nudged him again. "That was a little terrifying."

He brushed a hair from her face, his expression growing serious. "Are you ready for what's ahead?"

"I don't know if I have much of a choice." In the bath, she'd noticed that the mark had spread even more. She'd donned the silver bracelets once again and Lianna had recharged the pendant with more magic. It held the mark at bay for now, but who knew how long it would last?

Farron was quiet for a few moments.

"What do you think will happen after?" she asked.

"I suppose I'll be even more dangerous than I am now." He grinned, a brief flash before it faded. "But so will the others. I hope that we have all learned from the past and will be able to live in peace with each other, or else the cycle will continue. It's been so long since magic ran through the land, it will be new for everyone. Different. If it wasn't for this…" He traced a finger down her arm, following the dark wild lines of the mark. "I would have just run off into the sunset with you a long time ago, and never looked back."

"I suppose we still could, after."

"Where to?"

Claire considered the question. She really didn't know. "Why not everywhere? I've always wanted adventure."

"You've had quite the adventure so far."

"I think I'd like to have one where I'm not a prisoner or being hunted relentlessly."

Farron chuckled softly. "Everywhere it is, then."

She snuggled close to him again, feeling a little more at ease. The future, adventure, a land renewed—it was all nice to think about, but she didn't want to get her hopes up too high. There was still a chance that she wouldn't see the new world she would help to create.

"How does it work?" Lianna asked, leaning over the table to look over the stone tablet.

"I'm not entirely sure," Claire said. "The old elf, Sabin, he was only able to translate it. The elder elf at Uru Baya was killed before he could tell us much more."

They had gathered in the study, Claire, Farron, Lianna, Razi, and the king, to look over the artifact and plan their next move. King Líadan had gathered all of the scrolls he'd collected over the years that even hinted at Star Children and what had happened at the end of the Great War for any clues. The grand desk was buried underneath it all.

"How strange," Lianna said, running her hands over the letters. "I have seen this strange rock in here countless times, felt the draw, but never would have guessed its significance. Perhaps it was your fate all along to do this." She glanced at Claire.

Claire took a deep breath. She didn't know if she liked the pressure that implied.

"I too have felt it, but I ignored it. I did not think it would be possible to restore magic again." Razi crossed his arms.

"How did you get it to fuse with the other stones?" the king asked.

Claire exchanged a look with Farron. "My blood." She'd told them all about Uru Baya and the map room, how she'd drank the water and the vision she saw. "Our blood just might be the key to all of this. *We* might be keys." She looked between Razi and Lianna.

Consumed

Without hesitation, Razi drew his dagger and slit his palm. Blood welled up quickly, then he held his hand over the tablet and let it drip onto the surface. The stone absorbed the red droplets and moments later a few random letters started to glow. Everyone leaned in closer.

Lianna held her hand out to Farron and he produced a dagger from somewhere. She pricked her thumb and squeezed, letting the blood gather before rubbing it across the tablet. The same thing happened—the stone soaked it up, and a few more letters illuminated.

"Keys..." the king muttered, staring at the tablet, the glow reflecting in his eyes.

"Blood," Farron said. "Is this why you have been gathering the Star Children?" He turned to his half-brother.

The king shook his head slightly, coming back to the present. "There were hints that I needed to bring them all together." He waved a hand over the scrolls. "But never anything concrete about why. Now we know why the Syndicate was so adamant about keeping you separate, and so secret." He looked at Claire.

Claire nodded. How much did the Syndicate know about restoring magic? About what had happened? She doubted if they knew that they would be much help anyway.

"The cave that you saw," Lianna said. "Do you know where it is?"

"No," Claire said, shaking her head. "In the vision, I was already inside of it."

"Perhaps," Razi began, hesitance lacing his voice. He glanced around at everyone, pausing when he looked at Farron. "If we were to see it ourselves, we may be able to help."

That was the reason why he was reluctant. He wanted to dive into her mind again. A prospect she wasn't thrilled about, but if it would help with their mission, it was worth a try. Farron crossed his arms but remained silent.

"I suppose we could try," Claire said.

"Do you feel any pull?" Farron asked. "Like you did with the stone fragments?"

Claire frowned. "No," she said. "But I've been rather preoccupied lately."

"Perhaps if we all tried together," Lianna said. "If the spell requires all of us, it may take all of us to find the place as well."

"I guess it couldn't hurt," Claire said. "And if we do find it, what then?" She looked at the king.

King Líadan straightened. He'd posted a guard outside the door. He didn't trust the Council any more than they trusted him. If they got wind of what they planned, it could cause trouble, perhaps even lead to war. They all had to be careful who knew of their plans. The Council would be all too happy to oust the king for good. "Then we do whatever it takes to get you to that cave. We cannot risk failure. If we lose any one of you, then we would have to start the hunt all over again. And that is a delay that we cannot afford. Too many are already suffering." He ran his fingers across a map in front of him. "It won't be much longer until there will be nothing but suffering, and then not even that."

Everyone fell silent.

Razi nodded. "I have seen the damage wrought, by the beasts, the dying land. I was too caught up in the Council's ambitions to truly understand what was happening. Whole villages, towns, falling into ruin. Brown lands that were once green and full of life."

"Do not fear, *Mien Anaire*," Lianna said, leaning over the table toward Claire. "We will get you to that cave."

Claire nodded, the fierceness in Lianna's voice inspiring hope within her.

"We need Bahkar's blood," Farron said, drawing their attention. "I hope you didn't completely dispose of his body."

Consumed

The king shook his head. "I will have some men show you where he was taken."

Claire shuddered. She hoped that she didn't have to go along on that little mission. The very prospect roiled her stomach. She never wanted to see that man again, alive or dead.

"I hope his blood still works," she said.

"I suppose there is only one way to find out," Lianna said.

Claire looked down at the tablet, the glowing letters started to fade. If it didn't work, she was doomed. They all would be.

23

Under the cover of night, Lianna had gathered all of the Star Children deep underground in the map room. Candles illuminated the space, casting dancing, somewhat eerie shadows across the ragged, rocky ceiling. A few more towns had been crossed out along the western coast since Claire had last laid eyes on the carved map. Multiple guards stood at attention along the corridors leading to the room and right outside of it, but not so many as to draw unnecessary attention. Hopefully.

Farron had left the palace earlier in the night to seek out Bahkar's body. A mission he'd insisted on doing himself to make sure that they got what they needed. They couldn't afford any mistakes.

All of them sat in a circle around the map, the two children, Lin and Leah—looking much better than the last time Claire had seen them—and the dark-skinned woman, Maya, her clothing just as bright and colorful as ever. Razi sat to Claire's left, Lianna to her right. The only one missing was the madman.

"Do you think this will work without…?" Claire muttered to Lianna.

Lianna shrugged her shoulders in the elegant way she did. Concern shone in the children's eyes. Claire hated having to involve them. They shouldn't have to worry about such things at their age. But it couldn't be helped. Maya watched with curious, cautious eyes. She'd expressed interest in restoring magic after Claire and Lianna told the others of their plan. According to her, all she'd ever wanted was to be rid of the mark and lead a normal life.

"We can only try," Lianna said as she held her hands out to her sides for Claire and Leah to take them.

Claire took her hand and then Razi's. The circle was completed, all of the remaining Star Children connected for the first time since the magic had disappeared. A rush of power surged through her and she could hear the others gasp. They felt it, too. She'd taken off the silver bracelets before their little experiment so there wouldn't be any added hindrances, but now she wasn't sure it had been a good idea. Her magic swirled to life inside of her, rearing its wild head, reacting to the others' magic. Her mark started to glow and she took a deep breath to try and calm down. The others' marks started to illuminate as well, soft at first, then growing in intensity. A rainbow of colors chased away the darkness, overpowering the candles and torches. The king, the only other presence in the room, stepped closer to the circle, his eyebrow arching inquisitively.

"Open yourself up," Lianna said softly. "Think of that cave, the start of it all. Let your magic guide you."

Claire closed her eyes and thought of that fateful night so many moons ago. The visions flashed through her mind. The sharp pain of the others entering her consciousness stabbed through her head.

"I see," Lianna whispered when the memory faded. "Show us the way…"

Claire let her guard down almost completely. Her power surged within, the others' mingling and brushing against it. She concentrated on the cave, opening herself up to the world around her, searching for the telltale pull of magic. With the combined power of the other

Consumed

Star Children, her senses were heightened, the world transforming around her. She could hear the slightest sound, sense the littlest movements, feel the life flowing through the earth itself. It was overwhelming.

"Where…" Claire whispered. She gasped as her magic surged, almost taking over, like a swelling wave. Then it subsided, and in its wake she felt it. It was faint, but it was enough. "There!" she shouted. "To the north, do you feel it?"

"Yes," Lianna said, "barely, but I do."

"Toward Isailo," Razi said.

A short burst of laughter sounded from the king. Claire peeked at him, her concentration faltering. What was funny about that?

The pull grew stronger. Claire tried her best to memorize the feeling for the future. Sweat started to drip down her skin. The effort to maintain the connection was far more difficult than she'd thought it would be. Lin broke the connection as he leaned back on his hands, breathing heavily. Leah and Maya fared better, but both looked more tired than before. Only Razi and Lianna didn't seem to be affected, perhaps because they used their powers more.

"Isailo," King Líadan said as he stepped into the circle, looking down at the map. He stood over a mountainous region in the north of Derenan. He turned to Claire, a fierce look on his face. "How soon can you leave?"

"I can leave tonight if you wish." The sting started along her scar and new wound. Her mark was growing.

The king smiled, a slight tug at the corner of his lips. "Good. Li, Razi, be prepared. Things are about to get quite interesting."

Claire swallowed hard, her stomach falling to the floor. Quite interesting indeed.

It only took a couple of hours for her to get ready. As ready as she'd ever be on a mission to change the world and restore magic to the land. With Marla and Lianna's help, she'd packed as lightly as she could while they waited for Farron to return. Lianna charged the pendant with some of her magic and helped Claire don the silver chains once again, calming the mark down. But exhaustion already weighed heavy on her body, like a wet blanket.

"Is that it?" Claire asked when he'd entered her room and produced a small glass vial filled with dark red liquid. A shiver went through her. She really didn't want to hear any details of his mission.

Lianna and Razi had gathered the rest of the Star Children's blood in similar containers. It was impractical to bring all of them along, especially the children, without raising suspicion. As per Farron's suggestion, it would be best to travel light. Claire and him had done so successfully for the past few months without much trouble. The king had insisted on assigning them some men, ignoring their protests. It was too important a mission to risk it, the king had said.

When all was ready, Razi, Lianna, and the king met Claire and Farron in her room for their goodbyes.

"Be careful, my dear little Claire," Lianna said, tears gathering in her eyes. "Do not hesitate to call upon me if you need it."

"And me," Razi chimed in. "If *anything* goes wrong, send for us." He looked between her and Farron.

"Will you be all right?" Lianna touched Claire's arm.

Claire nodded. Anxiety churned her stomach, making her nauseated. "I don't think I have much of a choice either way."

Lianna squeezed her arm and gave her a hug. "I hope to see you again shortly, m*ien anaire*."

"Thank you, Lianna, for everything." Claire didn't know where she would be without Lianna's help.

Consumed

Lianna tightened her arms around Claire for several moments before reluctantly letting go. "Safe travels, Claire."

When Lianna released her it was Razi's turn to pull her into a too-tight embrace.

"*Me chaqana*," Razi whispered. "Thank you for showing me the way." He stepped back and touched her chin, tilting her head up to look at him. "Without you, I would still be in the dark."

"Thank you for everything," Claire said, her eyes feeling wet. "If you can, get your family as far away from here as you can."

Razi nodded, though he probably didn't need to be told that. "May your mission be successful." He bowed and touched the back of her hand to his forehead. When he released her, he actually shook Farron's hand, something she thought she would never see. "I wish you well."

"Show those Council bastards you are a force to be reckoned with, magic or not." Farron squeezed Razi's hand tight before letting go.

Both Razi and Lianna stepped aside for the king. "Brother," he said, opening his arms wide.

Farron glared at him but accepted the hug.

"I know our time together has not always been… *agreeable*." King Líadan pulled back to look at his brother. "But I would not be where I am without you. And for that, I will always be thankful, though I may not always show it. You have strengthened my tenuous rule in ways you will probably never know. Council or not, you will always have a home here and throughout Derenan." He released Farron and looked at Claire. "The same for you, my child. What you are doing for the land—for everyone—successful or not, we will never be able to repay you. When we meet again, the world will never be the same, for better or worse. I wish you both success on your mission. All of us are counting on you."

Well, no pressure there. Claire took a deep breath and released it, not knowing how to respond to that.

"Just try to keep the Council off our trail as long as you can," Farron said. "They will do whatever it takes to stop us."

The king nodded solemnly, then grinned. "You're not the only son of Earnehard they need to fear."

Farron matched his brother's grin, silent words passing between them.

After their goodbyes, Farron led her through a labyrinth of halls under the palace, going deep under the earth. The passages were crudely carved, damp and musty. They finally emerged through a door into an empty alleyway somewhere in the city below. A group of men atop horses awaited them, dark cloaks hiding their armor and weapons. Farron's horse and Azra stood to the side, already saddled and ready for their late night ride.

"Ready?" Farron asked her as he closed the small wooden door behind him.

"Not at all," she said as she walked to her horse. "Let's go."

24

Claire was afraid to get to know the guards after what had happened with Hamza and his men. Not that she had the time to interact with them much anyway. They rode the entirety of the first night and slept only a few hours before they were on the road once again. Breaks were few and far between and exhaustion hung over the party like a dark cloud. More than a few times Claire found herself sleeping atop a horse, either hers or Farron's, as they made their way north to Isailo.

She had thought that the name sounded vaguely familiar and had wondered why the king had found it so amusing when he'd heard it. Farron had a similar reaction, though there was a touch of sadness in his expression. Isailo was where he'd grown up, spent his formative years honing his skills, learning to fight, to kill, so he could become a tool for kings. Claire didn't know much about that part of his life; he still was hesitant to talk about it and she didn't want to push until he was ready, if he ever really would be.

The party stuck to backroads, occasionally avoiding roads altogether, bypassing towns and villages, to avoid raising any suspicion. The Council had eyes everywhere, according to Farron and the men. Everyone wore dark cloaks pulled down low over their faces, a foreboding and intimidating sight, scaring the few farmers they happened to come across.

Five days passed before they ran into trouble.

A day's ride outside of the last town, in the middle of the forest, plumes of smoke rose up into the sky, too many to be ordinary travelers.

"An army," Farron whispered, after he and a few men returned from scouting.

The party had stopped in a clearing far from any roads, out of sight.

"Whose?" Claire asked.

Farron glanced around at the gathered men and then his gaze rested on her. "I don't know."

Claire's stomach sunk a little. If Farron didn't know, then it couldn't be good.

"There's no standard to identify them or who they serve. Based on their armor and state of their weapons, they look to be made up of mercenaries," said a gruff, middle-aged man with dark blonde hair, Isak, who was the leader of the group of men as far as Claire could tell.

"Is there a way to find out?" Claire asked.

"Does it matter?" chimed in a dark-haired man—Timor, if she remembered correctly. "We should just move on, avoid them."

Claire didn't exactly hate the idea. Their time was limited and they couldn't use the delay. But still, it was a little concerning to come across an army of mercenaries in the middle of nowhere.

"It's up to you, Claire," Farron said, and everyone's attention settled on her.

She shifted uncomfortably. Why did she have to make the decision? "Although I am curious, we can't risk getting caught." A few of the men nodded silently. "But," she said, almost regretting the word as it left her mouth, "this army… it could mean trouble. If we could find out who they are working for and what their purpose is, we could warn the king. If you don't know who they are, then they aren't his, and if they aren't his, then that could be a problem."

Claire didn't know why she cared so much. Kings, councils, politics, the struggle for power, it was too much for her to keep up with. If they wanted to fight, then let them. Only, innocent people were the ones that always suffered the most.

"It's decided then," Farron said, looking at the men, his expression hard. "Nightfall isn't too far off. We will wait until then and do some reconnaissance. In the meantime, rest up, but stay alert. They could have scouts."

The men nodded, some mumbling, as they shuffled off to their horses. Farron remained behind.

Claire took a deep breath. "Do you think this is a good idea?"

Farron shrugged. "I don't like stopping for so long when there are more important matters at hand." His eyes wandered down to her neck where the mark grew ever wilder. "However, a mysterious army is not a good sign. If I were to go by my instincts, I would say that the Council is up to something."

"You don't think…?"

Farron nodded. "Who else has the gold and the motivation? Líadan has been suspicious about them for quite some time now. Perhaps they are finally acting." He was silent for a moment. "But then again, it could just be a territory dispute between some northern lords. We can't know for sure until we find out more." He touched her chin and tilted it up. "Get some rest, Claire. There's still a long road ahead."

Long indeed. But the closer she got to the cave, the more she could feel its pull. It was calling to her. A siren luring a ship to crash among the rocks. Deep down inside, she didn't mind the delay, maybe even wanted it. The old elf's warning played constantly in her head. The shadow of impending death grew larger with each passing day. But still, she marched on, because she had little other choice. A slight chance was better than none at all.

The sun was just setting when Farron suddenly perked up.

"What is it?" Claire asked. She and a few of the men had gathered close to play a card game to pass the time while the others patrolled the woods. Farron had stood watch over their small clearing like a silent sentinel for the past several hours.

Farron didn't answer. Instead, he tilted his head up to search the skies.

Claire's pulse quickened. What was it now? She didn't like when he remained quiet like that.

Without a word, Farron raced to a tree and began to climb it, the men staring after him in confusion. Farron ascended swiftly, only stopping when he nearly reached the top. The trunk swayed slightly under his weight. He knelt on the branch and steadied his balance before quickly drawing his bow and arrow. He aimed at an unseen target, tracking it through the sky. Then Claire heard it, the distant cawing of a bird. A moment later Farron loosed his arrow. The bird cried out, followed by silence. Farron descended the tree at a dizzying pace.

"With me," he said as he strode past the men, not stopping before disappearing into the woods.

The two men across from Claire jumped up to follow after the elf. Their fear of him was evident in the quickness of their pace. No one dared to anger the infamous *Sin de Reine*.

Consumed

About twenty minutes later they emerged from the trees once again. Farron held a large black bird in his grip, an arrow still protruding from its lifeless form. A small leather pouch was tied to the bird's leg.

Everyone gathered around as Farron laid the bird down and removed the pouch. From it, he took out a rolled parchment with a wax seal. Farron drew a blade and carefully slipped it under the seal to break it and unroll the paper. His eyes quickly scanned the contents.

"What does it say?" Claire asked.

"It's coded," he said, handing the paper to the man next to him. "But the seal looks vaguely familiar, I just can't place it…"

"I believe it may be the symbol of the Pylen mercenary group," one of the men said. "I worked with them a few years ago before entering the palace guard."

"Can you make sense of the code?" Farron asked him.

The dark blond man shrugged. "I can try, but I was never high enough rank to be privy to the secrets of the group."

"I can help, perhaps," chimed in a dark haired man. "I always was good with riddles."

Farron sighed and nodded as the men shuffled off with the paper.

"That was very impressive," Isak said. He looked Farron up and down. "That bird was quite far off. My men are right to be cautious of you."

A slight grin tilted Farron's mouth. "I've faced mightier foes than a bird."

Isak laughed. "Well, perhaps you could teach these fools how to aim." He nodded toward his men.

Farron looked over his shoulder at them and turned back to Isak. "I think I could teach them a lot more than that."

Isak grunted a laugh. "I may just take you up on that offer one of these days. Though, I have to admit you're not as terrifying as the stories make you out to be."

"I must be slipping then," Farron said, a frown replacing the grin.

Isak laughed again and walked over to join his men that were trying to break the coded message.

"You certainly are slipping," Claire said, sidling up close to him. "But, I don't mind."

"Yes, but I don't want *them* to know that." He tilted his head toward the men. "A little bit of fear is good sometimes."

Claire fought not to roll her eyes, but he might have had a point. A little bit of intimidation was a good motivator.

"Do you think they can figure it out?" she asked him, lowering her voice.

He shrugged. "I wouldn't count on it, but who knows?" He lowered his voice even further. "After dark I can sneak in, do a little snooping on my own."

"Do you think it's worth it?"

"Maybe," he said. "I guess we'll find out."

The night was too cold to not build a fire. Claire huddled around it under her cloak, the warmth outweighing the risk. The men took turns patrolling and standing guard. Farron had left about an hour earlier, when full darkness had settled in, with Isak and the dark haired man to scope out the mercenary camp. Claire's only company since then were two sleeping men she didn't want to disturb. She wished she could get some herself but her worry kept her weary eyes open.

Consumed

Claire sighed and reached for the small scroll of paper the bird had carried. The men hadn't been able to figure it out. The mystery made her even more curious. She unrolled the stiff, yellowed parchment and angled it so she could see in the flickering flames. Dark ink formed foreign letters in a rushed, scribbled manner. Claire furrowed her brows. What could it say? She had never been good at figuring out puzzles or riddles.

She leaned back and drew her knees up, her mind returning to Farron and the men. She didn't like just waiting around. Her hands played idly with the paper, the fire illuminating it from behind. And that's when she saw it. It took her mind a few moments to comprehend what she was seeing. It was faint, but it was there. The letters were now complete, and best of all, understandable. Claire perked up, her pulse racing as her eyes gobbled up the message.

Most of it might as well have been gibberish, talking about troop movements and mentioning names she'd never heard of. It was only the last few sentences that made her breath leave her.

"They plan to overthrow the king…" she whispered.

Goosebumps spread over her skin. The king had been right to be suspicious of the Council. Their thirst for power was too great to ignore. Was that the reason the king was so eager to restore magic to the land? Sure, he had other motives, to save his people and the land, but he also stood to gain an immense amount of power, and just like the forest king, King Líadan wouldn't hesitate to use it to help secure his rule. But to overthrow the sitting king…

Movement caught the corner of her eye. Claire glanced up and froze. Across the fire from her, the blond-haired man that had been sleeping now stared at her. They locked eyes for several moments. The look in his gaze not entirely friendly. She didn't know what to do. She slowly lowered the paper and set it aside. The man watched her every move like a hawk.

Definitely not a good sign. Claire swallowed hard, wishing Farron was there. If they had a traitor in their group, then the Council knew of their little mission. Was this all some sort of trap? The army camped so conveniently on the way to their destination?

The man sat up and stretched. "You were the last person I expected to figure it out. The elf maybe, but not you."

Claire's hand went to the dagger hilt at her side. "What was the cost of your loyalty?"

The man shrugged. "More gold than the king was willing to pay. The promise of a better world not ruled by those fae bastards," he sneered. He slowly got to his feet. "What you want to do is a betrayal of every human that had to die for our freedom."

Claire's stomach twisted. How much did he know?

"We can't regress to those times again." His voice grew more fiery.

"If we don't restore magic, then no one will have a chance. The land is dying."

"That's what they want you to think," he said. "But have you seen it with your own eyes? Or just took their word for it?"

"I—" Claire thought for a moment. Had she? Besides the refugees in the city, she hadn't seen much. There was the mountain town, but that could have been abandoned for different reasons. Razi had the motivation to back up the king's claims now that he was no longer a friend of the Council. Had she been played this entire time? She had been so caught up in her own reasons for restoring magic and doing the right thing, she hadn't stopped to think about the possibility that she was being used to further the ambitions of a different king. Lianna trusted him, but was that enough? She had her own aspirations for power.

Her mind swam with all of the possibilities. She didn't know who or what to trust. There was one thing that she knew at the moment. The man standing in front of her meant her harm. She glanced down at the other sleeping man, who hadn't stirred. Would he help her? Or was he another traitor?

The dark blond man scoffed. "He won't be joining us anytime soon."

Claire's body went cold. "What did you do?"

"I just slipped him something to help take the long dark sleep." He shrugged, his nonchalance sending chills down Claire's spine.

Claire stood and drew her dagger. She didn't want to have to use her small supply of magic on him, but if it couldn't be helped…

The man clicked his tongue. "Let's not make this more difficult than it has to be." He started toward her. "I know all about your fighting prowess… or lack thereof."

"Stay back!" she shouted, holding the blade up in front of her.

The man grinned, his pace unfaltering. Claire's pulse jumped. He thought she was helpless. A mistake. Farron's lessons were becoming more and more invaluable.

The man lunged at her and Claire jumped back just out of reach. She slashed at him, but he ducked under her attack. He came for her again and Claire was just able to dodge him. He was quick. She wouldn't be able to avoid him forever. If she wanted to end this fast, she needed to use magic. She reached within herself, searching for the threads of her power. The pendant around her neck grew warm, but the power faded and eluded her grasp.

"What's wrong?" the man sneered.

Claire searched inside again for her power, for the magic residing in the pendant. But the same thing happened. The flame snuffed out before it could catch.

"You won't be doing any of that," he said, and drew the short sword at his waist. Symbols etched into the blade pulsed with a dull indigo glow. "There was a reason Illanor was able to succeed when so many others had failed." He admired the blade in his hands. It looked old, nicked and worn along the edges, but still sharp enough to do harm. The intricate symbols clashed with the simple, utilitarian design of the hilt and pommel. "A gift from human sympathizers. It absorbs any nearby magic. King Líadan isn't the only one with an eye for relics of the past."

Well, that wasn't good. Claire's panic rose sharply. It was only her and her dagger. Without her powers, she felt too defenseless, weak. Something she hadn't missed one bit.

The man approached her again, his pace slow and deliberate, the blade hanging in his right hand by his side. "By order of the Council," he said, "you, Claire Tanith, are to be taken into custody and be judged for your attempted betrayal of all of humanity."

"And what about your treasonous lords? Are they to face judgment, too?"

The man laughed. "We are only taking what is rightfully ours, what was rightfully won all those years ago in the Great War. We have already paid the price, in blood and flesh, for the right to rule ourselves."

Though he had a point, Claire couldn't just let him take her. She would rot in the prisons under the palace for the rest of her life if the Council had any say. Unless she agreed to become their new pet. They were too conniving to not try and use her magical gifts for their own gain. Not that she would live long enough to see that come to pass.

"You don't want to do this," Claire pleaded, taking another few steps back. "The Council, they're using you. They won't be any better than the current king. Besides, you don't want the wrath of the *Sin de Reine* upon you. If you take me now, he will never stop hunting you."

Consumed

His expression faltered, his eyes flashing with fear. "I believe the others are taking care of him as we speak."

"What do you mean?"

"Their little reconnaissance mission is nothing but a trap. Isak has probably alerted the men already. A squadron will circle this camp soon enough. There will be no escape for you this time."

So, Isak was a traitor as well. King Líadan really needed to assess the loyalty of his soldiers. How deep did the Council's talons penetrate?

Claire glanced around at the woods, the dark shadows dancing in the firelight. How true were his words? Were they surrounded? Was Farron all right? In any case, if she were to stand any chance, she had to get away from the magic sealing sword. Running into the dark woods, though not ideal, was her best bet. She'd done it before. Successfully avoided a centaur. What were a few human mercenaries?

After a few more steps backward, Claire turned and sprinted into the woods as fast as her feet could carry her. The light from the fire faded too quickly and she had trouble dodging the dark forms of the trees, her hands hitting and scraping along the rough bark of their trunks. She stumbled a few times over roots and rocks and uneven ground, but she rebounded quickly, her life and freedom depending on her escape. Total darkness soon surrounded her. The moon was only a sliver in the star-filled sky. With her hands splayed out around her, Claire felt for the nearest tree and ducked behind it, kneeling on the ground. Her ragged breathing was the only sound in her ears besides the rapid beating of her heart. She closed her eyes to focus her hearing, trying to even out her breaths. A slight rustling sounded several paces away, coming in her general direction. Another rustle made her freeze, only this one came from the opposite direction. She held her breath, her body protesting, and heard yet more footsteps.

The man hadn't lied. She was surrounded.

Her hands starting to shake, she slowly turned in place, trying to count how many she heard, wishing she had Farron's exceptional hearing. She guessed about twelve men, though she couldn't be sure. Should she remain still? Her clumsy footsteps would only give her away. They were just as blind out here as she was. But she could evade them for a little bit if she went up.

Claire spun toward the tree and stood. Her hands felt around the trunk, but she couldn't find any good branches. She let out an exasperated breath and scurried to the next dark blob she hoped was a tree. After four frustrating tries, Claire finally found a tree that she could climb. The sounds of the mercenaries had come closer, urging her up the tree faster.

The man with the sword called out in the distance, though he was still too close for comfort. "You can't hide forever!" Then, in a lower voice, "Spread out and find her."

Claire climbed higher, trying her best not to make too much noise, glad that she couldn't see the ground beneath her in the darkness. She only stopped when she could feel the sway of the tree in the breeze and see the stars above her. If this had worked for a herd of centaurs, then it could work for a few men, right? Although the centaurs hadn't been hunting for her at the time.

The footsteps came closer and closer, the crunching of dead leaves under boots. Claire held her breath and became motionless as one passed directly beneath her. When he didn't pause, she let out a quiet sigh of relief as he faded away back into the forest. Their haste made them sloppy. Claire used her moment of reprieve to search inside for her magic once more. And again it was snuffed out. The sword was still too close.

She had to come up with a plan. Night wouldn't last forever and with winter, the tree's foliage was too scant to provide enough cover in the light. They would discover her for sure. That is, if the cold didn't kill her first. Her panic had masked the plummeting temperature. Her body shivered, but she wasn't sure if it was from her nerves or the cold.

Waiting for her body to recover a bit from the climb, Claire looked up at the sky. Dark gray columns of smoke obscured the stars not too far off. Was that the mercenary camp?

She climbed up further to get a better look, but the forest blocked any good view of the camp. There was only the faint glow of several fires and their smoke plumes rising up into the night sky, deceptively peaceful.

Bright orange caught the peripheral of her vision. Claire carefully turned on the thin branch she perched on. Through the trees she saw the fire, catching the dead brush and leaves, spreading fast. Shouts from men all around her were followed by more fires being set. They were trying to lure her out. She either faced them or risked being burned up in a tree. Neither option seemed all too thrilling.

It only took a few minutes for the first drifts of smoke to reach her nose, the air already warming. The fire had formed a perimeter around her and was closing in fast. There was only one gap in the burning wall of flames, a trap for her with the men surely awaiting her on the other side. Not wanting to be a roasted piece of meat, Claire began her descent. Even if they captured her, at least she would live to see another day. Another day was another chance to escape.

She dropped down to the ground with a heavy grunt, her bones and muscles aching already. There was no escaping the light of the fire now, its heat. The men had surely spotted her. She covered her nose and mouth with her hand to guard against the smoke and began to walk. She wasn't in that much of a hurry to get captured.

"There you are," said the man with the enchanted sword, the traitor. "I told you there was no escape. Now, come with us like a good girl before we have to burn down the entire forest."

Armed mercenaries surrounded her, the fire casting harsh shadows across their faces, making them seem more intimidating than they probably were. Claire remained silent as they disarmed her, even taking the stiletto blade from her boot. She was too outnumbered to do anything now. She had to plan, wait for an opening. Something she wasn't very fond of.

The man with the sword approached her and touched the pendant around her neck.

"What should I call you, traitor?" she asked him.

The man grunted a laugh and cut the chain of the pendant with the sword and held it up to the flames to admire it. "Does it matter?"

"I would like to know who to get revenge against in the future."

The man laughed and pocketed the pendant. "You may call me traitor all you want, but I think history will remember me a little differently." He turned and motioned to his men.

A few came forward to grab ahold of her. Again, she didn't struggle. She needed to preserve what little energy she had.

The coldness seeped back into her bones as they drew further from the flames and into the dark shadows of the night. She tried not to think about her future, trapped in the dank dungeons at the mercy of the Council. It was still too early to resign herself to that fate. She would find a way out of this. She had to.

The men formed a column in front of and behind her as they trekked through the forest toward their camp. Darkness had almost completely surrounded them, the distant fires like mere candlelight. Claire opened her senses, her hearing, though she would never hear *him* coming. If he would…

No, she couldn't think like that. She had to believe Farron was out there. Even without magic, he was the most formidable warrior she'd ever met. There was a reason tales were told of him. He was the king's shadow. He'd faced a Beast of Old, an army of centaurs,

Consumed

and a whole fortress of the Syndicate's men. A mere mercenary army was nothing. She hoped. These men had tricks up their sleeves she had never expected. The Council was a resourceful bunch, it seemed.

When she came back to the present, she didn't immediately notice that the footsteps of the mercenaries seemed fewer. She held her breath for a moment. A few seconds later a muffled grunt sounded from the back of the line. The mercenaries came to an abrupt halt and drew their weapons. Claire could barely make out their shadows in the dim light. The group of men surrounded her, the two holding her tightened their grips, their fingers bruising.

"What is it?" whispered one of the men.

Claire smiled in the darkness. This was his domain now.

One by one, grunts and shouts sounded from the men around her as they fell. The mercenaries closed in around her, their fear emanating off of them.

"It's not too late to run," she said. "Am I really worth dying over?"

One man took her advice and laid down his weapon before sprinting off into the trees.

"Tray, you coward!" a man shouted out. "You better ru—"

Tray's muffled scream in the distance shut the other man up.

"I know you're out there, Shadow," the traitor shouted. "Impressive that you were able to escape a whole army of mercenaries. Without magic."

Farron's deep laughter echoed through the forest. "I don't need magic to kill such dismal warriors."

Claire's body and mind eased a little just hearing his voice. He was all right. Good news for her, not so much for the men around her.

A man next to her shouted and doubled over before falling limp to the ground. The mercenaries shifted, murmuring and gasping. She could practically taste their terror.

"We need light!" the traitor shouted.

The men pulled her back toward the blazing fire. Only about half of them remained. The light might give them a chance against Farron, but only barely.

Claire savored the warmth of the roaring flames as they drew near. The mercenaries stopped in the harsh light, the shadows seemed even darker than before, forming a foreboding ring around them. Especially knowing what they contained.

Their backs to the fire, the mercenaries held their weapons up at the ready toward the darkness as if facing the night itself. Claire took the opportunity to writhe carefully out of the men's grips. They were so focused on the line of trees that they paid her no attention anymore. They were prey being hunted, the rabbit caught in the wolf's sight. Their minds were too frantic to think clearly. Not that she could blame them. She'd been in their shoes more than she'd liked in the past.

"Come face us in the light," the traitor said.

A moment of silence fell over the area, the cracking of the fire the only sound.

"If that's what you wish," Farron said, emerging from the darkness. The shadows seemed to cling to him. He had his bow in his hand, a grin on his lips. Smears of blood stained his clothes and pale skin. Claire didn't want to know if it was his, or not...

The mercenaries dropped into fighting stances. Claire backed away toward the fire. Without weapons or magic, she would just get in the way, or worse, serve as leverage for a desperate man. Six men remained, hardly a challenge for the elf.

Farron stopped a few paces away. Tension hung heavy in the small clearing, each waiting for the other to make the first move.

With a shout, the man to her left lunged at Farron, his sword in hand, ready to strike. Farron dropped his bow and drew both of

Consumed

his daggers. He dodged the man's attack and stabbed him, felling him in mere moments. Farron stepped over the limp man toward the others. They backed away from him.

"Stand your ground!" the traitor shouted.

"We don't get paid enough for this!" the man in front of Claire said, before running off into the trees.

A moment later, another man quietly joined him.

Farron advanced on the remaining three who bravely—or foolishly—stood their ground.

The traitor made a motion with his hand and the other two circled around Farron. Farron stopped, his daggers hanging limply at his sides, his eyes focused solely on the treacherous man before him. With the same terrifying display of skill she'd seen before, Farron dispatched the two mercenaries as they advanced on him simultaneously. Their dying groans were sure to haunt her dreams. But even after all that, the traitor still held his ground, magic sword at the ready. Unless it had other hidden abilities, it would do nothing to protect him.

"What you're doing, your mission, it's wrong," the man said.

Farron shrugged. "She's the only thing I care about," he said. "The world can burn, for all I care."

"It will do just that if you return magic to the land."

"Then so be it," Farron said, lunging at the man.

The man barely managed to avoid the attack, but Farron was too quick for him to keep up. Farron's dagger drove into his chest, hilt deep, and the man sunk to his knees.

Farron kept his grip on his blade and bent over the dying man, his face an emotionless mask, the Ice Prince returned. "As long as she's in it, I don't care what happens."

Claire swallowed hard as the man fell to the ground, lifeless. Farron stood over his body, his daggers dripping blood, the fire casting a sinister dancing light upon him—the *Sin de Reine* in all his terrifying glory.

Her breath hitched for a moment. No wonder tales were told of him, and men quaked in their boots, lords slept with one eye open. The elf standing before her was like a force of nature, full of deadly skill. Claire was just glad he was on her side.

When he looked at her, the icy façade melted away, replaced with the Fare she knew.

"Are you all right?" he asked, his voice hesitant. He still worried, even now, about scaring her away.

She nodded, though she'd be lying if she said he didn't intimidate her even more now. She knew of his skills but was always left in awe when face to face with them.

Farron knelt and took the sword from the traitor's hands. He held it up to examine it. "Illanor's blade," he said. "I thought it was just a myth. But I guess even myths have basis in truth." He looked at her.

"What a troublesome thing," Claire said, reluctantly approaching—not because of him, but the dead still unsettled her. She knelt next to Farron to search for her necklace, finding it in the man's breast pocket. She had to tie the chain together where it was cut, and slipped it back over her head. It would have to do for now. She quickly stood again, not wanting to be so close to death more than necessary. "What of the others?"

"They've been dealt with," he said, standing, the finality of his voice halting her questions.

Claire only nodded. She didn't need to know the details. "Should we warn the others? The Council, they plan to overthrow your brother. I doubt that this was their only move."

Farron was quiet for a moment. "As much as I don't like to involve myself in courtly schemes, I hate the Council more. They will destroy the kingdom, magic or no, if they get total power." He stabbed the sword into the dirt by the man's head. The symbols were dormant, as lifeless as the traitor. "But first, let's leave this place."

Claire couldn't agree more. She wanted nothing more at the moment than to leave this nightmare behind.

25

They rode until dawn touched the eastern sky. Their horses were still near their camp, thankfully, when they'd returned to it after the fight. Farron had found her weapons on one of the men in the dark woods, along with some other supplies they'd need for the journey ahead.

And then they rode, nonstop, their bodies and minds weary and aching. They needed rest but didn't dare stop until they were far enough away from the camp. Farron hadn't dealt with all of the men in the mercenary army. That would have taken too long, according to him. Claire noted that his ego wouldn't allow him to say that it would have been an impossible task altogether. It was only a matter of time before the mercenaries regrouped and sent word to the Council of their failure, and of Claire's and Farron's escape.

The urgency of their mission had only grown more dire.

The terrain had grown hillier and rockier the further north they journeyed. And it was only going to get worse. A dense, towering mountain range took up the entire northern horizon, an intimidating visage.

The pull of magic had grown stronger the closer they drew to the cave. It was as if someone had tied a string to her mind and was tugging on it. It invaded her dreams, the visions of that night—the humans and the elves, Rialla and her haunting message.

"We need to keep moving," Farron said when Claire protested waking after only a few hours' sleep. "They aren't far behind."

He didn't need to clarify who. She already knew. But what else was new? She'd had someone after her ever since the centaurs had burned her town down. Whether or not restoring magic took her life, she looked forward to some peace and quiet after so long on the run.

"Should we tell the others?" she asked. "Lianna and Razi. Your brother should know what the Council plans."

Farron considered her words for a moment. "He already knows. He's suspected for years that they would try and do something like this."

"Only now they finally are. Summon Lianna or Razi, or both. They could help with the army, keep them distracted long enough for our escape."

"We can summon them," he said, "but they will be as effective as you or I against them. They have a way to block our magic, remember? Why do you think I wasn't able to take care of the camp? With magic, I could have ended it that night."

"So, the sword wasn't the only trick they had up their sleeve…"

Farron shook his head. "It seems our friends on the Council have been busy."

"So, our only option now is to run," Claire said, sighing. "Hope to get there before they do."

"Just like old times," he said with a grin.

"Did I ever tell you how dull my life was before all of this?" she said. "Dull, but quiet. Peaceful. I never thought I would actually miss it."

"You said you've always dreamt of adventure."

"This wasn't exactly what I had in mind."

Consumed

He laughed, but it was a little strained. His body was tense as he started to gather up their belongings and ready the horses. Not that she could blame him. Her own body was riddled with anxiety and it was all she could do just to function. A peaceful, dull life… Oh, how she missed it.

"Tell me about your time here," she asked him as they climbed into their saddles. She needed something to help keep her eyes open, her mind distracted, and learning more about his mysterious past would surely keep her attention.

Farron shrugged as he eased his horse onwards.

Or perhaps not.

"There's really not much to tell." He clicked his tongue and spurred his horse into a trot.

Claire followed close behind. "You weave such fantastic tales," she teased. "Please, tell me more."

He looked back at her, an eyebrow raised, unamused.

"Please, go on…" Claire yawned, her eyelids heavy.

"My childhood wasn't like yours," he said, slowing his horse a little for her to catch up. "I didn't have a loving mother, adopted or otherwise. I grew up in a cold place. Trained every day. Master Lorian was the closest thing I had to a father. And if you think *I* am an Ice Prince, he was the king."

"Was it far from here?" she asked. "That… place?"

He looked at her, the corner of his mouth ticking up into a sly grin. "We were taught from a young age that if we ever revealed the location of the fort, we would be hunted down in the night."

Claire gulped. She wouldn't want someone like Farron after her. "So, there were others?"

Farron nodded. "A few. I was the youngest by far."

"Where are they now?"

Farron shrugged. "I don't know. And I think they would rather keep it that way."

Claire nodded, not knowing what to say to that. "What about your master—Lorian, was it?"

"He passed years ago."

"I'm sorry."

Farron shrugged again, but his face hardened, his mask slipping into place. "We won't be crossing paths with that place on our journey, I assure you. I don't even know if it still exists, honestly."

Claire watched him, his eyes lost in the past. It was probably as much as she was going to get out of him on the subject for now.

He shook his head, coming back to the present, and said, "We still have a lot of ground to cover." And he spurred his horse into a gallop.

Claire did the same, her apprehension growing by the second. But at least the fear kept the exhaustion at bay. For now.

"That should throw them off our scent for a little bit," Farron said as he watched the horses trot off into the trees.

Claire watched her breath rise in puffs of white in front of her. She didn't like the idea of trekking through the cold forest on foot, especially after three days of being relentlessly chased with little rest, but if there was no other way… Her body was almost to the breaking point, her limbs like lead, her mind a dark cloud, her magic prowling in the background waiting to pounce—waiting for her to drop her guard, to become too weak to resist. What little sleep she did get was riddled with nightmares.

Consumed

He hiked the large pack onto his shoulder more securely and turned to her. "It's not much further. Even I can feel it now..." He glanced behind her and took a deep breath.

Claire closed her eyes for a moment. The draw was strong. She could get there blindfolded if she had to. She opened her eyes and looked at him. "Yes."

He took her hand and gave it a squeeze before pulling her along up the mountain pass.

The sun was just dipping below the western horizon, the mountains having plunged them in shadow for the past hour or so. The temperature was dropping fast. Claire pulled her cloak tighter around her. They couldn't risk a fire tonight. If they even stopped. With the enemy so close, they might not even be able to chance sleeping.

The climb was difficult on her sore and tired body, her feet merely shuffling along. Farron's hold on her hand was the only thing keeping her upright. Her mind receded into itself, falling into a trance, and the hike quickly became a blur.

It must have been hours later when she came back to the present. Farron had stopped and squeezed her hand tight, shaking it a little to get her attention.

"Claire," he whispered, so quiet she nearly missed it.

She followed his gaze. They stood on a slight outcropping, the sky dark but alit with millions of stars and half a moon. It was hard to make out, but the contrast was clear enough. Below, the trees were lush and full of leaves, unlike the surrounding bare branches. It was like a pocket of spring in the middle of winter.

Claire's breath hitched. This was the place. The magic hum throughout her body told her so.

"Do you feel that?" she asked.

"Yes."

They stood for a few moments looking down at the area. Trees obscured any cave, but it had to be there. Farron tugged her to the side as he searched for a way down. Claire followed reluctantly, her nerves starting to make her knees weak, her hands shaking.

The climb down wasn't as bad as she thought it would be, but not entirely safe, her feet slipping on loose rocks. The ground leveled out just before the line of green. There was an abrupt cutoff between the different areas, the dead giving way to life. They paused before it.

"Do you think it's safe?" she asked. There could be traps like there had been with the stone fragments.

"I suppose there's only one way to find out." He looked down at her.

Claire reached out with a hand and took a step toward the verdant forest. Nothing happened, but she did feel...warmth.

Slowly, Claire entered the area. Grass and wildflowers grew abundantly, and the air was sweet and warm. Within a few steps, she'd entered a different realm. She took a deep breath and slowly released it, her body defrosting, feeling somewhat revived. She glanced back at Farron. He hesitated at the threshold.

"Here goes..." he said, and took one long stride into the area. He paused again and looked around.

They both held their breath, waiting for something, anything to happen. When nothing did, they both sighed, their shoulders going slack.

"Don't let your guard down," Farron said as he stepped past her.

Claire nodded and followed after him. The night grew darker underneath the green canopy. Claire relied on Farron's exceptional senses to guide them through the forest. They both remained quiet on their trek, the tension never completely leaving them. There had to be some sort of test or trap. It couldn't be this easy. But the forest around them remained silent, the only sound the whispering breeze through the leaves.

After what seemed like an hour of walking, tiny pinpricks of light caught her eye in the distance.

"Are those...?" she asked, pointing.

"*Fijärilin*," Farron whispered. "The magic is strong here, indeed."

A few minutes later they emerged into a clearing. The tiny blue *Fijärilin* filled the area, hundreds of them, flitting about like butterflies. Claire reached her hand out and they swirled around her.

"I think they like me," she said. A few landed on her skin and a shock shot through her body, her scar stinging slightly.

When Farron didn't answer her, she looked up and followed his gaze. Looming before them was a steep cliff. A cave cut a dark gash into the rocky face. The blood drained from Claire's face and she gulped hard. She'd never been here before, but she knew this place, had seen it in the vision Rialla had shown her. This was it. There was no turning back now. Her stomach sunk and twisted itself into knots.

❀

Farron turned to her, worry in his eyes. "The end of the road," he said. "We should rest a little while we can. Who knows what awaits us inside."

Claire would have loved to do nothing more than to curl up under her cloak and sleep, to delay the inevitable, but could they risk it? "We're so close," she said. "The others, they can't be far behind. What if they discover us?"

"The horses should buy us some time," he said, lowering his pack to the ground. He looked almost as tired as she felt. "Neither of us can fight in our condition. We're too exhausted."

"Do you really think there's something inside there?" She eyed the cave. Memories of the blood-red eyes of the roain came flooding back, of the giant bird-like beast guarding a piece of the stone fragment. Nothing good came of caves, in her experience. Perhaps he was right.

"It would be better to be prepared," he said, stripping off his cloak. "Just for a few hours. I'll hear if anything approaches."

Although Claire was apprehensive about stopping, she was more nervous about going into that gaping darkness. In the end, her exhaustion won. She wasn't going to argue with the elf. Not when she was this tired. Besides, it might be nice to spend what was possibly her last night with him in such a beautiful, peaceful place under the stars.

Claire set her own pack down, her shoulders sore and stiff from hauling it for so long. She took off her cloak and spread it across the grass. Farron did the same beside her. She would have loved to bask in the moment, to enjoy his presence one last time, but her eyes closed as soon as her head hit the ground, and sleep pulled her into its depths.

26

It felt like her eyes had just closed when Farron nudged her awake again.

Claire yawned and stretched, only slightly refreshed. But 'slightly' was better than 'not at all.'

"Is it time?" she asked, her voice still laced with sleep.

Her body went cold, stiffening when she saw the expression he wore, the folded parchment in his hand. She hadn't wanted him to discover that, not until after…

"What is this?" he asked, his voice cold, emotionless. He held the paper up between them.

Her mouth became dry, her words escaping her. She knew exactly what it was. But how would she explain it to him? She hadn't wanted to in the first place; that's why she'd written it down in a letter. Her cowardice wouldn't let her face him with the truth.

"Fare, I—"

"Is it true?" The first hint of anger seeped into his voice, his eyes flashing in the dim moonlight.

"You read it then." She'd written the letter back at the palace, had hidden it deep in her pack for him to find long after she was gone. *If* she died. If not, then she would have destroyed it. But now the secret was out. It was a goodbye letter, there was no mistaking it. And in it, she had told of what may happen to her, that she was sorry that she had kept it from him.

"Is it true?" he repeated.

Her throat became tight. How could she have been so careless? "Yes," she managed to say, her voice barely a whisper.

He was quiet for a long moment, his icy mask slipping into place. He stood and crumpled the letter up. "How long have you known this? Kept this from me?"

"I-I—" she stammered

"How long?" he snapped.

She stood, taking a deep breath to help calm her nerves. "Since Uru Baya," she said, finding her voice again. She had to face the consequences whether she liked it or not.

Farron made an exasperated sound and turned away from her. He ran his hands over his face. "You kept it from me all this time? What might happen to you?" He turned to her again, his mask gone, a mixture of anger and despair on his face. "Why didn't you tell me, Claire?"

"I was afraid you would try to stop me," she said. "That you wouldn't help me. I know it was selfish of me—"

Farron cursed in that beautiful elvin language, but it couldn't hide his rage.

"If you knew, you would have tried to find another way," she said, pleading for him to understand.

"How do you know there isn't?" He started to pace in front of her.

"There isn't."

"We could have looked." He spun back toward her. "We could have at least tried."

Consumed

"No," she said, her voice surprisingly calm. "There was never enough time. You know that. The mark covers almost half my body. I can feel the madness on the edges of my mind, my magic, waiting to consume me. At least," she paused, "at least this way something good could come from all this."

Farron scoffed, a scowl on his face.

"We've come too far to stop now." She took a step toward him, an imploring look on her face. She had to make him understand.

"You've made sure of that, didn't you?" he said. "Does she know, your mother? Or is there another letter in there for her?"

"No," Claire said, wincing at his question. She felt awful for keeping this from him, and from Marion.

Farron began to pace again in the clearing.

"There's no guarantee that it will happen," she said, trying to reassure him, and herself. "What the elder said. It's just a possibility."

"I don't like it, Claire."

"You think I do?"

He stopped to look at her, his angry expression falling.

"I'm scared out of my mind to go in there." She pointed to the darkness of the cave. "That these could be my last moments, the last time to see the stars, the moon, to taste the sweetness of spring. That I may never see my mother again or give her a proper goodbye. That I never got to do half of the things I wanted to do, or see the places I wanted to see. That my last words with you were a fight."

Farron came to her and framed her face in his hands. He bent and brushed his lips lightly against hers, the kiss quickly deepening, their anger and frustration giving way to desperation, sorrow, a need to devour, experience and memorize one another before it was all gone forever.

"This won't be the end," he said, drawing back. "It can't be."

Claire wanted more than anything to believe him, but her fear was like a whirling storm inside of her, blocking all the light, dimming her hopes and dreams.

"It won't be," he repeated, as if he were trying to reassure himself, too. "Are you sure you want to do this? There could be another way?"

"I don't have much of a choice, Fare."

"There could be..." A touch of desperation sounded in his voice.

"Fare," she whispered, not knowing what else to say. She ran her hands up and down his arms. "Will you try to stop me?" She had to know. If he did try, then it was all over. Though she'd be lying if she didn't admit that, deep down inside, a tiny part of her wished that he would. She had never been very brave.

Farron was quiet for a few moments. He pulled back to look at her, his expression hard to read. His fingers played along her jaw. "A world without you in it," he murmured, "is not one I wish to live in. But if there's a chance, even a small one, that you can be saved, then I will do whatever it takes." His fingers slid down to her chin and he looked her in the eyes. "I do not like that you hid this from me. I do not like that, after everything, this may not work. I don't like any of this."

Claire nodded ever-so-slightly. "I'm sorry, Fare, I should have..."

"Yes." He dropped his hands down to her shoulders. "You should have." He sighed. "I understand why you did it. I don't like it, but I understand. If I would have known," he said, his voice becoming softer, "I would have tried searching for another way. Would have gone to the ends of the world to do so."

"I know."

Consumed

"And your magic would have consumed you while I did it." He slid a finger over the mark on her neck, tracing the dark lines, the fresh scar. "I just want a little more time, Claire."

"So do I." Tears welled up in her eyes again, stinging.

He pulled her into his embrace, his arms encircling her tightly. She slid hers around his waist. Her tears escaped and soaked into his shirt. So many thoughts ran through her mind, she didn't know where to begin. In the end, she supposed, all everyone wanted was more time. More time for love, for life, for adventure. Just more.

When it seemed her tears had run dry, Claire reluctantly pulled back, still sniffling. She knew she looked miserable, not heroic like a woman who was about to save the realm.

"Make sure the tales don't include how I look right now," she said, a smile cracking through the sadness. She wiped her face with the edge of her cloak.

Farron frowned. "Don't talk like that. You'll be around to spread the tales yourself."

"But if I'm not…"

He let out a sigh. "Then I'll make sure you're fierce and mighty. And tall."

"I'd like that."

"Do you have any words for your mother? In case…"

She thought for a moment. She'd wanted to write her mother a letter as well, almost had, but what could she say? Only true death would let Claire escape her mother's wrath from keeping such a thing from her. "Tell her that I love her. And thank her for everything that she did for me. Nothing else I could say would be enough."

Farron nodded, a solemn look on his face.

Claire took a deep, shaky breath. "Well," she said, "I suppose there's no point in delaying any longer."

"Are you sure?" Farron gripped her shoulders hard.

"No, but we've come this far. And besides, if I wait any longer, I might lose my nerve. Then what sort of hero would I be?"

Farron drew her close and kissed her, long and deep, his hands burying in her hair, brushing along her cheeks, her neck, her waist, memorizing her. Claire did the same, hoping that this wouldn't be the last time she'd be able to do so.

They were both breathless by the time they pulled away from each other. Without a word, Farron gathered up the packs and took her hand. Then, he faced the dark, looming cave. Claire squeezed his hand, holding on like it was the last real thing in the world—her anchor, her strength. She tried not to feel anything as he began leading her toward that darkness, but her fear started to bubble up to the surface from deep inside. Her skin grew cold, sweat beading, making her shiver.

This was it. She wasn't ready.

Unlike the cave in Uru Baya, this one seemed wholly natural. The floor was rough, rocky, no stairs hewn into the stone. Rialla hadn't built this. No, it was as old as magic itself, carved by nature a millennia ago. How or why they had chosen this place to perform the ceremony, Claire would probably never know. That was a secret that would forever be lost to time.

Goosebumps sprouted up across her body as they crossed the threshold into the cave, her magic awakening inside of her despite the amulet and bracelets. The magic coming from the cave was so strong it was almost suffocating.

"Do you feel that?" she asked, gasping.

"Yes," he said, squeezing her hand. "Are you all right?"

"As much as I can be, I suppose."

Farron led the way into the darkness, his steps slow and steady, his head tilting every now and then to listen. They were only a few

Consumed

yards into the cave when Farron stopped and turned back toward the entrance.

He cursed under his breath.

"What?" she asked, her heart rate hitching even higher. Had they triggered a trap? Was it another Beast of Old awakening to protect its lair?

"It looks like our little diversion didn't last as long as I thought it would."

Claire stilled, listening. She didn't hear anything, but she didn't doubt the elf one bit.

Farron looked down at her, his brow gathering with worry. "They found us, this place."

Of course, none of this could be easy. Why would it be?

"Can you hold them off?" she asked, though she really didn't want to part with him yet—or not at all.

"I could, but—"

Claire pulled him down and smothered his mouth with hers. "Be careful, Fare." She pried the packs from his grip and hoisted them onto her shoulders. Her body cried out, exhausted. She looked up at Farron and her heart broke. She'd never seen him so sorrowful. She could have sworn she saw tears in his eyes, but it was too dark to tell. "I love you."

"We will meet again, Claire. I will make sure of it." His hand went to the hilt over his right shoulder. In a flash, he drew the dagger and slipped out of the cave and into the night.

She didn't have much time. Though she trusted in the elf's abilities, there were too many of them. He wouldn't be able to hold them off forever, not without his magic.

With a deep breath, Claire continued deeper into the cavern. Without Farron's eyes, she didn't know where to go, she was practically blind. If only she'd thought to bring a torch. But she did have something better. She searched inside for threads of her magic, surprised to find she could. Either Illanor's blade was far enough away, or the cave kept its sealing powers at bay. The pendant around her neck grew warm as a blue orb formed in her palm. It pulsed, growing dimmer and brighter, as if it were fighting against the oppressive darkness. It wasn't much, but it would have to do. The weight of the packs and her exhaustion made the trek more of an ordeal than it should have been. Her feet shuffled across the uneven rock, stumbling and tripping every now and then, her palms becoming scratched and bloody, her knees bruised.

She followed the curve of the cave as it descended into the earth. Her breath filled her ears, her footsteps echoing. Silence from the forest outside did nothing to ease her urgency. Seconds seemed to stretch into minutes, minutes into hours. Just when she thought that the darkness would go on forever, faint light caught her eye at the end of the tunnel, silvery and dim. Moonlight. Just like that night in her vision. Chills wracked her. The end of the line…

Claire paused at the end of the tunnel, the magic orb finally sputtering out, losing its fight to the surrounding magic. The cave opened up into a massive chamber. The ceiling was open to reveal the night sky. The tiny blue dots of *Fijärilin* flitted in the dark air. Like the forest outside, there was green everywhere, only the plants seemed overgrown, unrestrained. Vines covered rocks and climbed up the walls. The ruins she'd seen in the vision had all but disappeared underneath it all.

Claire stepped into the cavern, her boots sinking into the plush moss. The *Fijärilin* swarmed around her as she walked to the center toward the ruins. What they had been used for, she didn't know. They'd looked old already in the vision Rialla had shown her. When she reached the ruins, she stopped and lowered the packs to the ground.

Consumed

"Well…" she said to the empty air, though it didn't *feel* empty exactly. Magic prickled along her skin. "I hope this works."

Claire dug the small silver key from her shirt. She didn't know if she had to undo the bracelets, but it wouldn't hurt. Her hand hovered above the first lock, hesitating. Her magic was going to react, she knew—it was inevitable. She just wasn't sure if she would have the strength to keep it at bay for long. After thinking it over for a moment, she let the key fall back around her neck. She should figure out what needed to be done, first.

She turned to survey the area, her eyes struggling in the dim light. If only Farron were here…

In the vision, Rialla hadn't used the ruins, but that didn't mean Claire wouldn't need to. Why couldn't she have left more clues behind? With a sigh, Claire knelt and took out the vials and the stone tablet, setting them on the soft moss. She had all of the parts, but what should she do with them?

A scream out in the forest made her jump. Farron's handiwork, no doubt. She didn't have time to dawdle; she had to figure out what to do, and fast. She rose again and made her way to the center of the ruins. The ground was hard and flat beneath the plants and moss. Pillars stood around her in a circle, most of them only half standing. There had to be something here, or else why would Rialla do the ceremony here in the first place? Why would the tablet point her here?

In order to figure anything out, she needed to be able to see. She didn't have Farron's eyesight, no matter how much she wished it in the moment. Her hand grasped the key once again, taking a deep breath. She needed her magic or the orb wouldn't last long enough. One last time…

With shaking hands, she undid the silver bracelets holding her magic at bay. When the contraption fell to the ground, her mark stirred to life, the indigo glow flaring at the edges. A rush went through her body, her magic rearing its head. She closed her eyes and waited for the initial wave to recede a bit so she could push it back down again.

Another shout outside the cave jerked her back to the present. That one had been closer.

Quickly, she searched for a small thread of power and formed an orb in her hand, bigger than the last one, more powerful. An eerie blue light filled the chamber. The *Fijärilin* drew nearer, circling around the orb like moths to a flame. A few landed on her arm along the glowing mark, tickling her skin. Her mind struggled to keep her magic from taking over, holding the dam in place, but already the cracks were showing, leaks springing.

She slowly turned to look over the ruins, her foot sweeping over the ground, tapping and feeling for anything unusual. Not that *any* of this was usual...

And then she saw it. In the back of the circular area, what she had thought was a pillar was something else, square instead of round like the others, buried under thick layers of vines and lichen. Claire approached it carefully, her magic illuminating it, and began to tear the vegetation away. Underneath lay a peculiar altar of sorts—or at least that's what she guessed it would be in a place like this. Like the fountain in the cave in Uru Baya, the top was hollow, shaped like a bowl, but unlike the other one, this one's surface was jagged and rough, as if something was missing...

Claire whirled. Just like the back of the stone tablet. She rushed back to where the artifact and the vials lay on the ground. She launched the blue orb up into the air where it hovered high above her. A grunt escaped her as she lifted the tablet. It was heavier than it looked. There was a reason it had been in Farron's pack. She lugged it over to the altar, more shouts from out in the forest spurring her on, her fear pushed to the background to focus on the task at hand.

Consumed

She hefted the slab up and leaned it on the edge of the altar, taking a deep breath.

"Now or never…" she whispered.

With some maneuvering, she fit the tablet back into its rightful place. For a moment, nothing happened. Claire's stomach twisted, wondering if it was all for naught. But then there was a soft grinding noise and the ground shifted slightly beneath her.

"I suppose it's too late to turn back now," she said as she fought to steady her feet. She rushed back to grab the vials. She tried not to think too hard about their contents. It still made her a little nauseous. When she returned to the altar, the letters were already starting to glow, faint and white. Her mind frantically tried to recall how to pronounce the ancient words.

She undid the cork from one of the vials. Whose was this? She had refused to label them. It would have been too morbid for her tastes. She poured the blood onto the stone. Like before, it soaked it up and a few letters began to shine brighter, almost blindingly so. Her hands trembling, she unstopped the next container and even more characters illuminated. When she was on the fifth bottle, shouts sounded again, but they were closer, echoing.

They had reached the cave. Her time was running out. She slammed the last vial onto the tablet, the glass shattering, slicing her fingers and palm. She pressed her hand down harder on the stone, hoping her blood would be enough.

The shouts grew nearer—they were at least halfway down the passageway now. Claire could see the flickering glow of their torches.

The last of the letters came alive then, their brilliance illuminating almost the entire cave. Claire shielded her eyes with her free hand. The ground shook again. The *Fijärilin* circled wildly. The shining script pulsed, waiting. She took a deep breath.

This was it. What she'd fought so hard for all these months. Her last chance. Her last moments. This would be the end, whether she lived or not.

The words were stilted as they came out of her mouth, her lips and tongue unfamiliar with the foreign language. She'd practiced them before, a few times. But that was before, just practice. Her nerves made her stumble, repeat, forget.

The men were almost to the end of the passage. One screamed out in pain. Farron's work, she guessed. But it all faded into the background. Her magic thrashed inside of her, wanting to be free. It took all she had to contain it long enough to say the incantation.

When the last word left her lips, the world around her dimmed. Everything suddenly sounded miles away, muffled and garbled. Her mark came to life, the vines crawling across her skin, the blue radiance battling the light from the tablet. The *Fijärilin* descended on her, swarming her body. Her skin stung where they landed, a thousand tiny pinpricks.

"Let magic flow freely across the land once again," she said as she fell to her knees. "Bring life and hope to all."

The tremors spread throughout the cave, growing more violent. The tablet let out a bright light, like a star that had fallen to earth.

And then it just blinked out, an invisible force sweeping past her and beyond. The trembling stopped and the world grew quiet. Numbness crept into her hands and began to spread up her arms.

Claire held her hand out in front of her. Slowly, the glow of her mark started to fade, and the lines grew still once more. The magic inside of her calmed and for the first time in months, she felt at ease. She closed her eyes and reveled in the feeling. Her body and mind were so tired. Now she could finally rest. No more nightmares waking her up in a cold sweat, no more magic pressing up against her mind like a dam ready to burst, just serenity. She'd almost forgotten what it was like to feel normal. To just be… Claire.

A strange tingling started on her right hand and along her mark up her arm. She opened her eyes again. The dark line of the mark had begun to fade from her skin. Tears welled up in her eyes, and flowed down her cheeks. It had been a part of her for so long now, had caused so much trouble, but now that it was going away, she was going to miss it. The power it gave her, the strength, both of body and mind, the confidence. What would she be without it? With the mark, she was someone, powerful, able to change the world. But without? She hadn't thought too much of what came after. She'd been so afraid, so sure that there wouldn't even *be* an after. But what if there was? What if…?

She watched as, inch by inch, the dark lines of the mark receded, leaving only the scar as a reminder. But as her magic was waning, the world around her was coming to life. The vines entwined with the ruins and along the ground stirred and began to crawl, twisting and turning, growing and consuming all in their path. Claire's body grew cold, her limbs turning to lead. She couldn't have moved even if she wanted to. All she had wanted to do for so long was rest. Find peace.

A voice sounded in the distance. Something about it was familiar, but her muddled mind couldn't quite place it. The vines edged closer to her, the tendrils wrapping around her ankles first. She should have been afraid, but where they touched grew warm, easing the pain and cold emptiness in her body, like a warm summer day after a blizzard.

The shouts grew closer, more insistent. Was that Fare…? She tried to turn her head, but her neck was like stone. Her head was so heavy…

The warmth spread up her legs and to her waist. The vines began to squeeze and consume her. But still, she didn't fight it. They drew her into their peaceful embrace.

"Claire!" yelled the familiar voice.

Hands began to pull at the vines, trying to take away her safe haven.

"No," she whispered. She wanted to go. To rest. Just for a little while. It had been so long.

"Claire, talk to me!" The voice was merely a murmur in her ear.

More tugging, but it wasn't enough. The vines were too strong. Claire laid down, accepting their sanctuary.

The familiar voice grew more frantic, desperate. The hands wrenching the vines even more so.

The world grew dim, the darkness closing in on her.

"Get off me!" the voice shouted.

Other voices joined in, but they were too far away, too fuzzy to make out.

The ground rumbled, the very core of the earth trembling. Rocks began to fall around her. She couldn't hear them, but she could feel it. She was one with the rocks, the vines, the moss, nature itself. New life had been breathed into the earth, the land, like rain in a desert. Igniting hope once again. Her life for the lives of thousands. That was a fair trade. She was just a silly little barmaid, after all.

The familiar voice began to fade away. Tears fell freely down her cheeks. Would she ever hear that voice again? See his face? Feel his warmth?

The darkness was settling in around her, pulling her into its abyss. But she wasn't afraid. Not anymore.

Magic coursed through the land once more. It was up to the rest of them to make it work, to live in peace. Her job was done. Was she going to be remembered a hero or traitor? Only time would tell.

Consumed

Two faces flashed in her mind before the shadows swallowed her up. She hoped the new world was kinder to them than the old one had been. She wouldn't be seeing them again in the end. But knowing that they would have a fighting chance was enough for her. It would have to be.

The darkness pulled her down into its depths and she knew no more, except peace and quiet.

Epilogue

It had been six months since the light had gone from his life.

Farron splashed cold water on his face, like he did every morning. It was the only way for him to wake up, to feel something, even if it was just the rush of gooseflesh. He dried his face on an old cloth then tossed it aside. Six months. It felt like years. He'd only been able to tell by the scratch marks on the wall. Six months to the day since she…

He didn't allow his mind finish the thought. It would do no good. There was nothing he could do, nothing that he could have done. His guilt tried to tell him otherwise. He could have found another way. Maybe if one of the other Star Children had gone into the cave instead of her…

But she wouldn't have had it. She was too stubborn to have done it any other way. She wouldn't have asked anyone else to do something she wouldn't do herself. She used to say that she wasn't brave, wasn't strong, but she was wrong. What she had done for the realm, for humanity, for them all… Some called her a traitor, but they weren't left standing long in his presence.

What she had done was far from traitorous. Magic had returned back to the world, lifting the dark veil that had covered it for so long. It flowed through the land, giving life where it had begun to fade. He could feel it in his bones, the power, as natural as breathing. The earth's fate had been reversed. What they decided to do with it was up to them—the outside world, the humans, and the elves. They'd been saved and most of them didn't even realize it.

But what good was it all without her?

Farron sat on the edge of his cot to pull on his boots. The room was small and bare but it was all he needed. He had never thought he would find himself back here after so many years. But it was the only place he could go to escape. He hadn't lied when he'd said he didn't want to be a part of a world that she wasn't in. And so he wasn't.

The old Haven was more of a fortress than any place of healing. Cold and dreary, but it was different than when he'd been here last. The fountain in the middle of the courtyard had started to flow for the first time since the Great War had ended. The magic here was palpable. The others here felt it as well. They were confused, surprised, in awe. Like a piece of them that had been missing all their lives had finally been returned.

When he'd returned to this place, he'd wanted to hide away from the world, his past, everything. But after observing them—the students, his old masters, he knew that it was up to him to try and teach them how to use their newfound powers, and to not abuse them.

She would have thought it amusing, the scourge of Derenan, the infamous Sin de Reine now a humble teacher.

He got up and started to strap on his daggers and pull on his gloves. The early morning sun shone through the window. A commotion caught his ear. What was it now? He was usually the first to rise, to revel in the quiet before everyone else stirred.

Consumed

Farron opened his door and stepped out onto the balcony that circled the interior courtyard. The guards had opened the thick main door and were escorting a hooded figure. A group of curious students had gathered in the shadows, whispering. Farron leaned on the railing looking down at their visitor. Their clothing was rich, black velvet with gray fur trim, the hood pulled down low over their face. Over her face.

The hooded figure paused in the middle of the courtyard, ignoring the guards, her hands going up to her hood. She looked up at him and drew it back.

Farron's stomach sank. He hadn't seen Lianna in months. Why was she here now?

"She's here for me," he said, loud enough for the guards to hear.

The doors boomed closed as he made his way downstairs to greet his guest. His mind raced. What did she want? Was this a friendly visit? Had his brother sent her? Had things gotten so bad out there?

"Fare," Lianna purred, her voluptuous lips forming a grin. She reached out to him and drew him into a hug, squeezing him tight. "My little Fare." She drew back to take him in, her eyes sweeping over him. "You look… better."

He managed a meek smile. He supposed he was better than he had been the last time she had seen him.

"You cut your hair," she said, frowning.

He ran his hand over his head, self-conscious. He'd cut it all off after he'd come here. He wanted a fresh start. It was the shortest it had been nearly all his life.

When he didn't say anything, she said, "Is there a place we can talk?"

He nodded and led her to the small common room. A fire already burned in the giant hearth on the far wall. A few students that were eating got up and scurried away when they saw him approaching. Everyone gave him a wide berth. His reputation preceded him even here.

When the room was empty, he sat at a table near the fireplace. Cold usually didn't bother him, but the warmth felt nice.

"What brings you way out here?" he asked, getting to the point. "Is my brother in trouble already?"

Lianna came around the table, stripped her wool gloves off, and held her hands up to the fire. "No," she said. "Your brother is doing just fine. Though, he does miss you." She gave him a pointed look, which he ignored.

"The Council?"

Lianna shrugged in that graceful way she did. "They are of no consequence. After the attempted coup, most were ousted from their seats, with new figureheads to replace them. But they are all too frightened to make a move since the magic has returned. The king's new powers are keeping them in line."

"How are the people taking it?"

"Well enough. Not much has changed. A few protests have happened, instigated by the Council, no doubt." She frowned. "But once they saw the effect it had on the land, how it was being healed, given new life, many of them threw their support back with the king. His seat is secured for the time being."

Farron nodded. At least his brother was handling it all well. Only time would tell if he would start to abuse it. If he ever did, however—well, even kings weren't safe from the Sin de Reine. It had been her wish to keep peace in the realm. He would ensure that it happened.

"Any word from the forest?" he asked.

"Not much," she said. "After Ryaenon's death, they have been scrambling to find a new leader. Many have left, according to your friend. Aeron, is it?"

Consumed

Farron grunted. "Friend…"

"He seemed rather fond of you," she said with a smile.

"Does he know about… her?"

Lianna's smile faded and she nodded. "He sends his condolences. He has stepped up to try and lead, as she had asked, but it is hard. Their way of thinking, it is difficult. Fights have broken out. Many want to retake the human world, others want peace. It will be a long road, but I believe we can reach a compromise. All of us."

"Lendon?"

"They are difficult as ever, especially after the general's death. Philip is distrustful of us now. Thank goodness we do not need his help as badly as we did before."

Farron looked at her. Even after everything, she was as radiant and beautiful as ever. He was glad that his brother kept her around. Her level head was what Derenan needed, what the realm needed, what his brother needed. "How are you?"

She sighed, her shoulders falling slightly. She set her gloves on the table. "It is exhausting," she said. "All this new responsibility. Court politics are not much fun without the threat of my powers."

"Do you miss them?"

"Of course I do. If it were up to me I would have never restored magic to the land." She gave him a sympathetic look. "But I suppose it needed to be done. I do not enjoy feeling so powerless."

Farron laughed, the first time in ages. "You? Powerless? I highly doubt that will ever be."

Lianna grinned. "I can no longer bring down a mountain, summon the very elements."

"If you put your mind to it, I think you could do it even now. Somehow."

She hummed a laugh to herself. "You may be right. How are your newfound powers treating you? Does it feel strange?"

He nodded. "Very. Knowing I can bring down a mountain is a very heady feeling."

"Indeed."

"But it's more. It's like I can feel the world around me, the magic flowing in the earth, the water. How alive it all is. But still, everything is dull to me."

Lianna grew sober. She approached him and ran her hand down his cheek "It has been very hard on you, has it not?"

He looked up at her, at the sorrow in her eyes. The pity. He drew back from her, his mask slipping into place, the Ice Prince returning. He didn't want her pity. "Why are you here, Lianna?"

She let her hand drop back to her side. "There is something that I think you should see."

He raised an eyebrow, waiting for her to go on, but she didn't. "And what would that be?" His interest was slightly piqued, but not enough to go running off with her. He couldn't face the world just yet. He needed more time.

"Well, if I told you, it would ruin the surprise."

"Maybe I'm not in the mood for surprises."

"You will be for this one." She ran a hand through his short hair, down his cheek to his chin, where she gripped to tilt his face up to hers. "I promise."

The earnestness in her eyes almost swayed him. It had to be important for her to personally travel all the way to Isailo, into the mountains. No one ever came here unless they had to. There was a reason the school had been established here. But still, he couldn't bring himself to leave. Not yet.

Lianna let go of his chin and dropped onto the bench beside him. "Well then, I suppose I will have to stay until you agree to come with me. I will not leave without you." She looked around the room, her eyes silently critiquing. "I should have brought more clothes," she murmured to herself. "This place could sure use a feminine touch…"

Not looking forward to having Lianna take over the place, Farron sighed, relenting. "It's that important?"

"It is." She looked over at him, her eyes boring into his.

"And you won't tell me? Not even a hint?"

She shook her head. "And miss the look on your face? I think not." She rose from the bench and dusted off her backside in a dramatic way. "Besides, it will do you good to get out of this place. I am depressed already and I have only been here for an hour at most."

"It's not so bad," he said, though even he didn't believe that. There was more than one reason he'd never wanted to come back here, its austere accommodations being one of them.

Lianna placed her hand on his. "Come, Fare. Let me take you away from here. Just for a little bit. If you do not like what you see, you can always come back."

He was quiet for a moment. What did he have to lose? She wasn't going to leave without him, it seemed. So, with some reluctance, he said, "All right."

It didn't take him long to pack. What little possessions he had could fit into a single bag. Lianna had traveled in style, as befitting a king's mistress, the carriage embellished with elaborate carvings, red velvet seats, and silk curtains, pulled by the finest horses the realm had to offer. Nothing but the best for her.

Lianna noticed him taking it all in. "Well, since I have to take the long way these days, I may as well do it in comfort." She swept into the carriage without another word.

Though he was no stranger to the finer things in life, he felt out of place in the extravagant carriage after spending so long at his old school.

When they had both settled in, Lianna gave an elegant wave to the coachman outside and a moment later the carriage jerked forward.

"This will be worth it," she said, giving him a sly look. "You will see."

Farron crossed his arms and settled back into the plush seats. He hoped so.

Florin was the last place he thought Lianna would take him. He eyed the city through the small window. It looked different than the last time he'd laid eyes on it. Though, that had been years ago. Was his mother still here? He'd lost contact with her a while ago. Was she why Lianna had brought him here?

The journey had taken weeks. If he had known their destination, he could have flown here. He'd never done it before, but it couldn't be that hard. It wasn't that he hadn't enjoyed Lianna's company; it was just the longest he'd spent with her alone since they used to—well, that was in the past. Too many unpleasant memories surfaced in his mind, and too many good ones. His mind was in turmoil, not knowing where she was taking him, nor why.

"Don't worry," Lianna said when she noticed his apprehensive look. "Your mother hasn't resided here for a while now. She preferred to move to a warmer locale."

He raised an eyebrow in question. He had never been close with his mother, but he still cared for her in a way.

"She has been set up courtesy of the king in a nice estate in Cales, just south of Solaniki."

Farron nodded, though he was even more confused now. Why had she brought him here then?

Consumed

"Not yet," is all she had to say, a smile slipping into place. She was enjoying the torture a little too much.

Flowers were still in bloom throughout the city, even with autumn fast approaching. It was the most colorful, vibrant place he had ever seen, and the reason he'd wanted to bring her here. She would have loved it.

He swallowed hard. He couldn't go down that road now.

The carriage twisted through the narrow cobblestone streets for the better part of an hour before coming to a stop in front of a modest estate along the edge of the city. Though not a hovel by any means, the two-storied house wasn't lavish enough for Lianna's tastes. It had a sort of understated opulence that was pleasing to him. The gardens surrounding it were lush and manicured.

Then a thought dawned on him. "Is this mine?" he asked. "How kind of my brother." Though he didn't hate it—in fact, he liked what he saw—it was unusual for his brother to gift him with something so generous without expecting anything in return.

Lianna gave him a sly look as she got out of the carriage, not waiting for the coachman.

Exasperated, Farron followed her. He'd tried getting an answer from her the entire trip, but the woman was sharp. She hadn't fallen for his schemes. She had taught him half of his conversational tricks, after all. He left his things in the coach, not knowing how long he'd be staying.

Lianna dug a brass key from the purse at her waist and unlocked the front door, painted a bright red, contrasting to the white-washed exterior. "It could be yours, if you ask the owner nicely." She glanced back at him. "But you were never good at asking nicely."

She swept through the door and paused in the grand foyer. A small table stood in the middle, a vase atop it filled with red and purple flowers. She paused for a moment, tilting her head, listening. Farron did the same but didn't hear anything. What had she meant? He was getting more confused by the moment.

Lianna turned toward him. "Would you like a tour?"

Farron sighed. He supposed he didn't have much of a choice.

He followed Lianna through the house—the front room decorated with ornate furniture, the study and all of its books, the numerous opulent bedrooms, all expertly designed, all filled with fragrant flowers and plants from the gardens. It was impressive, but he couldn't see himself living here. It was too much for him.

He'd drowned out Lianna's words after the fifth room, following her blindly, wondering what was going on. It just didn't make sense, any of it.

They were walking down the second-floor gallery along the back of the house when his ears heard it. A familiar sound that made his stomach twist, his blood grow cold. Goosebumps shivered across his skin as he stopped abruptly. Lianna paused to look back at him, her voice trailing off.

He tried to swallow the lump growing in his throat. It couldn't be…

He looked at Lianna, his gaze intense. Was this all a trick? The sound had come from outside in the gardens below. He didn't dare look. The laugh that had haunted his dreams for the past six months bubbled up on the breeze again, this time fuller, louder. There was no mistaking it.

"Claire…" he whispered.

Lianna nodded toward the window, a smile tilting her lips. "The balcony was added at a later date, and as you can see, gives an excellent view of the estate's gardens."

Slowly, Farron turned his head to look, afraid of what he might find, or not find. If this was some sort of sick scheme…

But then he spotted her.

Consumed

His body was moving before he could think about it. Was it really her? He rushed through the glass doors, flinging them open so hard the panes rattled. He ran to the banister, his eyes never leaving the girl in the white dress playing with a puppy in the gardens. His hands dug into the wood as he leaned over to get a closer look. It looked like her. But how could it be?

Without a second thought, he leaped off the balcony to the soft grass below. Then he ran. The seconds seemed to stretch on forever, his feet leaden, his heart almost beating out of his chest. It couldn't be. How could this be? Was she real? Or just an illusion made of magic?

When he finally reached her, he stopped in front of her, his shoulders heaving, his eyes wide to take her in. "Claire," he said between breaths.

She spun and looked at him, gasping. Her eyes went wide and she said, "Who are you?"

His strength left him and he dropped to his knees. Claire. It was really her, as real as the plants and stone and earth surrounding them. The mark was gone from her arm, but the scars remained. It was her, but she didn't recognize him. How much did she remember? Had she forgotten all about him?

What cruel torture this was, but she was alive. And that was all that should matter. She was alive and safe. What did it matter then if she remembered him or not? He buried his face in his hands. Too many emotions passed through him to process them all. Tears slid down his cheeks. He was happy but devastated. And hopeful. She'd fallen for him before; surely he could do it again, get to know her all over.

A soft hand brushed through his hair. "You cut your hair," she said.

Farron looked up at her in astonishment and she smiled.

"I was finally able to scare you. All it took was for me to die. Who knew?"

Farron gripped her by the waist and pulled her down onto the grass, his heart overwhelmed. She remembered him. And she was alive. She remembered him and she was alive. He smothered her lips with his, memorizing her all over again. She was here, safe, alive, real. He had never been more grateful for anything in his entire life than this moment.

When they were both breathless, he drew back to look down at her. She looked unharmed, well rested, better than she had in months. The mark was no longer taking over her, it seemed. He traced a finger across her cheek, along her jaw, down to her neck.

"Is this a dream?" he asked. If it was, he didn't want to wake up.

"If it is, it's some dream," she said. She framed his face in her hands. "I've missed you."

He smiled. "It must be if you are freely telling me that."

She pinched his side and he jerked back. "Not a dream then."

"Good," he said as he kissed her again. And again. "Good."

Claire sat back on her hands as she reveled in the warm, late summer air, the fragrance of hundreds of flowers filling her nose. It was hard to believe that she'd finally found herself in the City of Flowers with Farron after all this time. It was everything and more than she'd imagined all those months ago when he'd first told her about it.

The elf in question sat next to her, staring, not taking his ice blue eyes off of her, as if terrified that if he blinked she'd float away with the wind. She grasped his hand in hers to reassure him that she wasn't going anywhere.

Consumed

"How?" he finally said. "What happened?"

Claire shrugged and gazed up at the vibrant blue sky. "I don't really know. I went to sleep. It was so warm and comfortable, and then I came to in a field. I didn't know where I was, who I was, how I got there. A sheep farmer found me wandering. He took me in for a while and that's when my memory started to come back. It was only small pieces at first—what my name was, where I came from." She looked at him. "I was in blissful ignorance for almost an entire month before it all came rushing back—the attacks, the mark, my journey, an exasperating silver-haired elf."

He laughed. "I told you I'm not that easy to get rid of, nor forget, it seems."

A smile tugged at her lips. It was nice to know he still had his confidence after everything he'd been through. "Once I remembered, I reached out to the palace. I didn't know what had happened to you, where you might have gone. That was the best place I could think of to contact. Lianna or the king might have known, or at least know how to find you. Without my magic, it took months for me to hear anything. And then a few months more for Lianna to finally find me. And then it took several weeks to locate you, and now you're here."

Farron took her hand and raised it to his lips, where he laid a light kiss on her palm. "I thought I had lost you for good."

Claire sat forward and touched his face with her free hand. "I can't imagine how hard that must have been."

"It was a nightmare," he said, his agony apparent. "A neverending one. I couldn't bear a world without you in it."

Claire sat on her knees and kissed him, starting with his forehead, down to the bridge of his nose, to his cheek, then across to the other one, his chin, then finally his lips, her kiss as light as a butterfly, then gradually deepening, all of her passion and love for him flowing into it.

"I'm sorry that I put you through all of that. This silly little barmaid has caused you enough trouble for a lifetime."

Farron smiled. "It keeps things exciting."

"You're free to stay here," she said. "Unless you would like to go back to—"

"I would love to," he said a little too quickly. "So, this is yours then?" He glanced back at the sprawling estate.

Claire nodded, though she still couldn't believe it. "A very generous gift from the king of Derenan for helping him save his kingdom from ruin."

"Is this all?" he said, standing and pulling her up beside him.

She pinched his side again. Any gift was greatly appreciated. She hadn't done it for the accolades, after all. Besides, as a barmaid, she had never thought she'd own a place as grand as this even in her dreams.

"I suppose it will do," he relented, frowning slightly. He looked at her again, something dawning on his face. "Your mother, does she know?"

Claire shook her head. She hadn't told her mother what had happened at all. "She's arriving soon," she said, dread setting in. "Once she hears she'll murder me for sure. So, don't get too attached to me."

Farron laughed, a rich, hearty sound, music to her ears. "Well then, I suppose I'd better enjoy my time with you while I still can." He pulled her close, tilting her face up to his. "You're not going anywhere this time?"

She shook her head. "No," she said. "I'm all yours. No centaurs, no Syndicate, no Council. For now. There's an upside to being dead for a while."

He drew her into a tight embrace, holding her as if she would disappear.

Consumed

She hugged him back, feeling safe and warm, tranquil.

"What will become of us now?" she asked, pulling back to look up at him. She looked forward to some quiet time for a little while, but what then?

Farron arched an eyebrow. "You've always dreamed of adventure. Who says we can't have any?"

Claire smiled, her mind starting to race with possibilities. "Adventure without the peril. Sounds like fun."

"Well, I wouldn't say no danger," he said with a grin. "Where would the fun in that be?"

Claire laughed. But with the world changed, who knew what life had in store? After what they'd been through, they could handle anything. For the first time in a while, the future seemed bright and full of possibilities and she looked forward to enjoying every moment of it. Even if it was with the Ice Prince.

Connect with Me Online:

My Website: www.CaseyOdellAuthor.com

Also check out my Story Inspiration board over at Pinterest:
http://pinterest.com/curlyq139/story-inspiration/

Made in the USA
Lexington, KY
24 July 2019